nipped and tasted

When Sabastiano opened his mouth, Julie didn't need any encouragement, and they plundered at will.

Then his mouth stilled against hers. She steadied herself against the vibrations tingling her whole body.

"Well, that was unexpected, but clearly enjoyable. Why did you stop?"

"There are rules. Morals," Sebastiano explained, though obviously with some difficulty on his part.

"What? Adversaries have morals in this day and age?"

He looked at her askance. "When it comes to taking advantage of damsels in distress, even adversaries in this day and age have rules."

Julie smiled. "Perhaps it's time to suspend the rules?"

Dear Reader,

Autumn has come to Grantham again, and it's time for school!

Julie has been chomping at the bit to have her story told. Let me tell you, it wasn't easy keeping the opinionated obstetrician at bay. But I think you'll agree that Julie has met her match in suave hospital administrator Sebastiano Fonterra. Was there any doubt that sparks would fly in a class in Italian conversation? They don't call Italian a romantic language for nothing.

On a separate note, you'll see that Julie loves to do needlepoint—a hobby I am addicted to, as well. There is nothing like handwork to clear the mind and relax the body. And in the end, you have something to show for your efforts—though I think my friends and relatives probably have enough pillows by now.

As always, I love to hear from my readers. Email me at tracyk@tracykelleher.com.

Tracy Kelleher

Invitation
to Italian
Tracy Kelleher

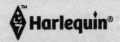

TORONTO NEW YORK LONDON
AMSTERDAM PARIS SYDNEY HAMBURG
STOCKHOLM ATHENS TOKYO MILAN MADRID
PRAGUE WARSAW BUDAPEST AUCKLAND

Recycling programs
for this product may
not exist in your area.

ISBN-13: 978-0-373-71721-7

INVITATION TO ITALIAN

Copyright © 2011 by Louise Handelman

This edition published by arrangement with Harlequin Books S.A.

For questions and comments about the quality of this book please contact us at Customer_eCare@Harlequin.ca.

® and TM are trademarks of the publisher. Trademarks indicated with ® are registered in the United States Patent and Trademark Office, the Canadian Trade Marks Office and in other countries.

www.Harlequin.com

Printed in U.S.A.

ABOUT THE AUTHOR

Tracy sold her first story to a children's magazine when she was ten years old. Writing was clearly in her blood, though fiction was put on hold while she received degrees from Yale and Cornell, traveled the world, worked in advertising, became a staff reporter and later a magazine editor. She also managed to raise a family. Is it any surprise she escapes to the world of fiction?

Books by Tracy Kelleher

HARLEQUIN SUPERROMANCE
1613—FALLING FOR THE TEACHER
1678—FAMILY BE MINE

Many thanks to Maria Engst for her expertise in Spanish and Dan Shapiro for sharing his knowledge about obstetrical care.

This book is dedicated to two people:
Bob Bogart, *the* man to have in a flood.
I owe you much more than a case of beer.
And to Anna Ruspa Fedele—
una professoressa straordinaria.
Mille grazie.

CHAPTER ONE

Sunday, 10:00 p.m.

"I'M HAVING SOME TROUBLE getting a heartbeat," Julie Antonelli said. Her tone was steady despite the bad news. She looked at the anxious mother in labor who shook her head and turned to her husband who hovered by her shoulder. Too nervous to muster his meager language skills he grimaced in confusion.

"Espere un minuto." Julie held up a finger before turning to Maria, one of the delivery nurses. By law, the hospital was required to have a translator, and Maria spoke Spanish fluently.

"Tell them what I just said and add that this happens sometimes," Julie said. Maria translated efficiently and without drama.

The husband nodded stiffly and gripped his wife's shoulder. She lay back and closed her eyes. The concern was etched in the lines on their faces, but they both breathed a little easier now.

Julie's breathing, by contrast, sped up. After six years as a practicing obstetrician, she recognized a potential crisis in the making, and she wasn't about to let that happen. She already carried around enough guilt.

Not that guilt was all bad, she liked to tell herself, or, more accurately, to fool herself. Either way it reminded her just how precious life was. She focused on the nurse at her side.

"Maria, could you explain to Mr. and Mrs. Sanchez that I'm ordering an ultrasound machine brought in? I want to get a better look at the baby." So far neither a fetal monitor nor a scalp probe on the baby's cranium had yielded evidence of a heartbeat.

Maria translated while eyeing the monitors. "Two hundred over one-fifty," she whispered in English.

Julie nodded. The patient's blood pressure was dangerously elevated. Julie leaned toward the patient. "Carlotta, are you a diabetic?"

"*¿Carlotta, es usted diabética?*" Maria translated.

Carlotta shook her head.

"Have you had regular prenatal checkups, Carlotta?" Julie continued with a kind smile.

"*¿Carlotta, Usted ha tenido chequeos prenatales regularmente?*"

Carlotta shook her head. A contraction gripped her. She reached to squeeze her husband's hand.

Julie leaned over and patted her shoulder, watching the monitors for signs of distress.

Carlotta breathed through her mouth as the pain passed. She wet her lips. "*Yo trabajo durante el dia cuando la clinica esta abierta,*" she said.

"I work during the day when the clinic is open," Maria translated quickly. Carlotta spoke some more. "She says that she couldn't leave work because she was afraid to lose her job."

Julie bit back an oath. "What kind of job does she have?"

"*¿En que trabaja?*"

"*Soy la ninera de una familia en Grantham.*"

"She says she's—" Maria started to translate.

Julie waved Maria off before the nurse could finish. "That's okay. Even I get that she's a nanny. You wanna make a bet that her employer never misses *her* doctor's appointments!" Julie could feel her anger mounting, but she needed to keep a lid on it for now. Concentrate on the situation at hand. But later all hell might just break loose.

The door bumped open as Tina, the other nurse, wheeled in the ultrasound machine. Julie wasted no time and moved to the side. "Tell her I need to raise her hospital gown to get a better picture of the baby."

Maria translated, explaining how the lubricating jelly made better contact with the transducer. Then she pointed to the monitor.

"Now, we'll get a look, all right?" Julie said calmly. She placed the ultrasound wand on Carlotta's raised belly.

Carlotta wearily lifted her head. Her husband peered into the monitor at the gray image. *"¿Ese es el bebé?"*

Julie nodded and flicked some dials. "Yes, that's the baby." She switched to another view, hoping to find what she had not been able to register so far. And then she caught it. The rapid, shallow flutter of the baby's beating heart.

Just then, another more severe contraction gripped Carlotta. She let out a piercing scream. Blood gushed out between her legs and onto the sheets.

The room erupted into emergency mode. Lights flashed, and an alarm sounded. "Call the O.R. for us," Julie ordered.

Maria got on the phone. Tina whipped open cabinet doors. She reached for some pads, and all three of the women packed them to staunch the blood flow, but it kept coming. "Let's get FFP going, stat." Julie didn't stop working on the patient as she ordered, calling for fresh frozen plasma containing clotting factors.

"I'm already on the way," Tina called as she rushed out of the room. She hastily pushed aside the ultrasound machine and banged the doors behind her.

"I need it yesterday," Julie urged.

She turned back to the expectant mother, whose face was streaked with tears as she hiccupped away her sobs. "Carlotta, the ultrasound shows that your baby is very weak. And we can't wait any longer for it to come out." Tina stormed in and hooked up the IV bag. She got the line going immediately. She read out the signs to Julie in a trained staccato.

Underneath the hubbub and rapid-fire activity, Maria translated Julie's instructions, looking from mother to father and back to Julie.

Carlotta blinked rapidly and shook her head. She reached blindly for her husband's hand. *"¿Qué, qué es lo que esta diciendo?"*

Julie knew they couldn't waste precious time. She needed Carlotta and her husband to understand what was going on—now, sooner than now. "You are experiencing eclampsia or pregnancy-induced hypertension. This is a very serious condition. Both you and the baby are in jeopardy, and I will need to perform an emergency cesarean section," she said quickly, urgently.

"¿Que le pasa al bebé? I don't understand?" Carlotta's husband looked from Julie to Maria. His face was contorted in fear. The tendons stood out in his neck.

Julie opened her mouth to spe—

There was no time to answer. Carlotta's limbs went

suddenly rigid. Her eyes rolled back. As if struck by lightning her body jolted, and foam immediately gurgled from the corner of her mouth.

"Magnesium sulfate. Now!" Julie yelled. She needed to control the convulsions. Tina readied the injection and handed it to Julie.

"Carlotta, Carlotta!" her husband screamed, his hands going to his face.

Julie administered the dose and checked Carlotta's vital signs. "Maria, explain to Mr. Sanchez that we are doing everything to ensure his wife's safety," she said, not bothering to stop, let alone look up. The antiseizure medicine was fast-acting, and Carlotta settled into unconsciousness, her breathing aided by an oxygen mask. Julie turned to the nurses. "Let's get a move on. I want this baby out of here and the mother out of danger. O.R. knows we're coming?"

"They're waiting for us," Maria said. "That was my first call."

"Then we're outta here," Julie ordered. Tina readied the IV poles. Julie put up the side guardrail and bent to push the bed. Maria, at the foot of the bed, pulled backward, banging the door open with her butt.

Julie put all her weight behind her efforts, keeping her eyes on her patient as the bed rolled swiftly forward. "Maria, explain to the husband that he'll have to stay in the waiting room, but we'll keep him informed."

Maria spoke rapidly.

Carlotta's husband brought up the rear, jockeying to get closer to his wife and reaching out his hand to touch the rolling bed. "You will save her and the baby, won't you?" he pleaded in Spanish with Maria translating.

Julie didn't need the English. She could sense what

he was asking from the tone of his voice. And she could feel him breathing hard as he rushed to catch up with her. *"Le prometo,"* she said as she continued to move forward. "I'll do every—" Hanging on to the bedrails, she swiveled to reassure him face-to-face...

And never saw the ultrasound machine.

The corner clipped her right in the side of her face. She momentarily saw stars.

"Doctor, are you all right?" Tina asked.

Carlotta's husband blanched. He held out a hand to help.

Julie blinked. "No, no, I'm fine, really. *Estoy bien.*" She tried not to wince. "It's my stupidity. Really. Let's just keep moving everybody." She pushed the bed and nodded to Tina to get going again. "And, *please,* somebody get a social worker who speaks Spanish to stay with Mr. Sanchez." *It's the least we could do,* she thought.

They reached the operating theater, and an orderly held Mr. Sanchez by the arm as they whisked through the doors. Julie didn't bother looking back. All she thought about was the delivery and that it was going to be difficult. She would need all her training and expertise to guarantee a happy ending.

Then—no matter what—somebody was going to pay.

And she knew just who.

CHAPTER TWO

Monday morning

DR. SEBASTIANO FONTERRA folded his arms and leaned on the blotter positioned precisely in the middle of his immaculate desk. A Venetian glass vase, black with orange swirls, was juxtaposed against the flat plane. It was a gift from the board of directors of Grantham hospital, and in Sebastiano's opinion, hideous. Naturally, he kept it prominently displayed.

Sebastiano offered a sincere nod to demonstrate his attentiveness to the stately woman sitting across from him who had been speaking to him—no, haranguing him—for more than half an hour.

He smiled politely, masking the subversive fantasy bubbling in his brain, the fantasy of jumping atop his desk and, with his arms outstretched and his face raised heavenward, shouting at the top of his lungs, *"Per me questo lavoro non vale la pena!"* Which somewhat loosely translated to, "They can't pay me enough to keep doing this job!"

Not that he would ever allow himself to act so... indecorously. So emotionally. Sebastiano didn't do emotional, let alone fantasy.

What he did do was perform his job as the CEO of the University Hospital of Grantham with admirable skill and considerable grace. He needed both qualities when dealing with the woman seated across from him, the woman who headed up the hospital's fundraising committee and who had, through personal donations, ensured that her late husband's name would be emblazoned on the oncology wing of the new hospital.

So with seeming equanimity, he shifted his posture and rubbed his chin thoughtfully. Since he didn't have the slightest idea what she'd been talking about—having tuned out somewhere between her description of her newest peony cultivar and her criticism of how the ink on the local newspaper, the *Grantham Courier,* came off on her cream-colored Chanel suit—he offered his tried-and-true conversational gambit. "You always bring a unique perspective, Mrs. Phox," he said warmly. Then he offered up a smile meant to convey sincerity and sensitivity. Not many could carry off the feat with such visible genuineness.

The society dame rotated her head slightly. If a weighty volume of *Emily Post's Etiquette* had been atop her immaculately coiffed gray hair, it wouldn't have shifted a millimeter. She eyed Sebastiano with arched brows. "I was merely inquiring if you were free for a working breakfast at the Grantham Club on Friday to meet with Rufus Treadway. We need to discuss the impact of the new hospital building on the neighborhood," she said. Rufus was the former mayor of Grantham and unspoken representative for the historical African-American neighborhood where the hospital was located.

"As I am sure you are well aware, the proposed expansion is not completely welcome in the immediate neighborhood, and I thought that Rufus could prove to be an effective mediator." She looked at him with a skeptical eye. "And, please, I insist. Call me Iris."

Sebastiano cleared his throat. "Of course. Iris. What I meant was your suggestion to meet over lunch at the club presents a less confrontational setting." He wondered if Iris Phox bought it.

She didn't blink.

Sebastiano sighed. "Listen, I have to apologize. I must confess my mind wondered a second there, not a reflection on your conversation but my own hectic schedule."

Iris nodded. "You do work hard. And don't think that we on the board don't appreciate it. Your efforts at ushering the building plans through the zoning and planning committees have been masterful. Your ability to attract corporate sponsors beyond compare. And needless to say, your embrace of the community hasn't gone unnoticed."

Sebastiano had long ago lost count of the number of rubber chicken dinners he'd attended to support various local causes, everything from the Grantham Open Space Committee to the Grantham After-school Program, with the Grantham Historical Society, the Grantham Chamber Music Society and the Grantham Public Library Fund somewhere in between.

"You're too generous," he said, still experiencing the indigestion from Saturday evening's Friends of the Grantham University Art Museum fundraiser. The meal had a Spanish theme in honor of a recent acquisition of a Goya painting. The chicken paella had left a lasting impression.

Iris sat ramrod straight. She placed her gloves beneath the stiff handles of her alligator bag, which was neatly positioned on the side of his desk. "Do you mind if I ask you a personal question?" She tilted her finely pointed chin a precise fifteen degrees.

Sebastiano winced. "Personal?"

"Yes, I don't mean to pry."

That seemed exactly what she was trying to do.

"I was wondering…are you happy here?" she asked.

Sebastiano frowned. "If you mean am I content with my job, you don't need to worry that I am considering other offers."

Iris pursed her lips. "That's not what I mean. And I know you've been offered positions at larger hospitals."

Sebastiano raised his eyebrows.

"However tantalizing some of these offers may be, I am a good enough judge of character to know that you wouldn't think of leaving until new ground is broken and all the funds are raised." She crossed her still trim legs at the ankles. "No, what I'm talking about has nothing to do with professional contentment. On the contrary, I'm talking about personal fulfillment." She eyed him closely. "Are you happy?"

Sebastiano ground his back teeth. His dentist had warned him at his last checkup that he was doing this. "What *is* 'happy'?" he asked.

"Please, I'm not discussing Schopenhauer here," Iris said, dismissing his question. "Though after taking a course on German philosophy at the Adult School, I wouldn't mind. Still, that is not the point of this discussion. What I'm getting at is that to me, you appear disconnected, which is not to say uninterested or lacking empathy. Nor am I referring to the fact that you seem overworked. What I mean to say, and, please, you must remember that I am not one to mince words."

Sebastiano bit back a grin. "How could I forget?"

"What I mean to say then, is that you appear quite alone, one might even say lonely. Is there anything I can do to help?"

Sebastiano couldn't think of anything he wanted less than company. "That's very kind of you, but I'm really quite all right. There's absolutely nothing wrong, and as a doctor, I make sure to stay atop my physical condition."

"I'm not talking about blood tests and annual check-ups," Iris clarified.

"I understand, but rest assured."

There was a knock. His office door swung open.

He narrowed his eyes, hesitated, then focused his attention again on Iris. "Trust me. Nothing's wrong."

A sarcastic laugh from across the room mocked his statement. "Well, you might not be able to think of anything wrong, but believe me, I can tell you more than a thing or two!" the irate female voice announced.

Sebastiano stood up. He buttoned the middle button of his charcoal-gray suit jacket. "Mrs. Phox...Iris... excuse this unexpected interruption. I'm not sure if you've met one of our obstetricians?"

Iris leaned around the side of the wing chair to get a view of the intruder. "Ah, Julie, my dear, so good to see you again. I was just speaking of you this morning."

CHAPTER THREE

"DR. ANTONELLI. I WAS unaware we had an appointment." Sebastiano stood stiffly. He shot the cuffs of his starched white shirt and straightened his sterling silver cuff links.

If he had wanted to appear more intimidating, it would have been difficult to say just how, Julie observed. *Well, he could grow four more inches,* she thought with a certain amount of self-satisfaction. She was six foot one in her stocking feet. Right now she had on clogs, her usual footwear for surgery, and she topped him by a good three inches.

It was a silly sense of superiority, but she'd take it. Because frankly, Dr. Sebastiano Fonterra scared her witless.

True, the old CEO of the hospital had never been her favorite person. He hadn't seemed to be the brightest bulb, but he *had* been approachable, always appearing open to suggestions even when he didn't have the least intention of following through on those suggestions. Still, he listened.

Sebastiano Fonterra was anything *but* approachable. He was aloof, often arrogant and, even more maddening, sexy as hell.

There was something about that voice of his—the faint Italian accent to an otherwise flawless command of English. The vowels were more distinct. The enunciation a little crisper. He simply didn't have the lazy lips of American speakers. Although her female colleagues didn't normally bring up the topic of enunciation when it came to discussing them.

Still, when she'd come storming in, dressed in her operating scrubs and minus a shower, enunciation had been the furthest thing from her mind. Not that her mind was functioning all that well after having been awake for more than twenty-four hours.

Julie slowly pulled off the blue cotton cap left over from surgery. Her short dark hair was matted to her forehead.

"Dr. Antonelli, I'm waiting," Sebastiano said again.

Sebastiano might look gorgeous and wield more than a fair share of authority at the hospital, but she refused to be intimidated.

Iris Phox was a completely different matter.

Nevertheless, this was too important for Julie to back down now. "I have something that couldn't wait." She took a step forward, positioning herself to the right of Iris, who was sitting in the high-backed chair and within easy spitting distance of Sebastiano. Julie leaned forward and braced her hands on his desk. Spitting from this distance would be a slam dunk.

"I've just come from an emergency cesarean on a patient who had seized out from eclampsia." Through her peripheral vision, she could see Iris's blinking stare of fascination, but Julie narrowed her eyes and focused on the man across the desk.

"The mother made it?" he asked, still standing. There was no emotion in his voice.

"Yes."

"And the baby?"

"Underweight and with a low Apgar score, but she'll pull through."

"I presume this came as an emergency room admit?" Sebastiano said.

Julie nodded.

"Then you are to be commended. They were lucky that you were on call."

"This is not about me. This is about the fact that she had never received any prenatal checkups simply because the clinic is not open long enough during the day," Julie decried in frustration. She threw up her hands... and bumped the glass vase. Before Julie could react, it skittered off the desk and seemed to hang suspended until it fell on the rug, thumped loudly, then bounced twice more. There was an ominous *clink* as it landed against the metal heater vent.

"Oh, my God, I'm so sorry." Julie rushed to retrieve the vase. She brought it back to the desk, wincing when she noticed a visible chip in the rim. "Please, I will gladly replace it."

"You can't. It's a one-of-a-kind piece." Sebastiano spoke so quietly it was clear he was seething internally.

Julie put her hand to her mouth. "Oh, no. I suppose it had sentimental value, too?" *What a total screwup,* she thought.

"It was a gift upon my acceptance of my position here at the hospital."

"Oh..." Julie's voice trailed off.

"Never mind the vase," Iris said behind her. Julie turned.

Sebastiano glanced at Iris. "As a board member, I'm sure you're well aware of its value."

"I never cared for it. If it had been left to me, I never would have chosen it. Black and orange may be the colors of Grantham University, but I always found the piece somewhat garish. I'll make sure we give you something more suitable to replace it—a simple Paul Revere-style silver bowl."

"You're too kind," he said. That didn't stop him from glaring at Julie. "But that still doesn't eclipse Dr. Antonelli's carelessness."

"Let's move on for now," Iris ordered, ignoring the obvious tension in the room. She turned to Julie. "I'm curious as to your comment about the clinic," she said. "I wasn't aware there was a problem."

"With all due respect to Dr. Antonelli, if I may?" He measured his words.

Julie crossed her arms. She tapped her fingers on her elbows. She didn't like being preempted.

Sebastiano forged ahead. "With all due respect, the clinic is open three days a week and one evening, more than the state mandates. Moreover, the hospital maintains these hours despite the cuts in government spending." He waited, looked at Iris, then back at Julie.

She wasn't ready to give up yet. She raised her hand.

"Which way are you aiming this time?" he asked, jutting his chin out.

Julie paused. She knew just where she'd aim. But she didn't. Instead, she clenched her jaw. "I realize the hospital is trying to do its part for the community—but it's simply not good enough. Here we live in one of the richest towns in the country, and we still find expectant mothers risking death due to inadequate medical care. Do we really want it written on our tombstones that we exceeded state mandates? Wouldn't we rather be known as the local hospital that did everything it possibly could?"

Sebastiano lowered his eyes to the blotter of his desk. He lined up his Montblanc pen exactly in the middle, parallel to the horizontal edges. "You know there are proper channels for lodging a complaint about hospital policies." He lifted his head and focused on Julie. "An unannounced visit to my office while I am discussing business with the head of the board is not one of them." He didn't threaten.

He didn't need to.

Julie wet her lips and realized that some of her fury was starting to seep away. Maybe it was all the hours with no sleep. Maybe it was the thought that she could lose her privileges at the hospital. And then maybe it was staring into Sebastiano Fonterra's disturbing deep-brown eyes that finally took the wind out of her sails.

She had felt she was right to barge in when she did. Maybe that was the problem. Too much emotion, not enough strategy. When would she ever learn?

Julie held up her hand. "You're right. I apologize. To you and to Mrs. Phox."

Iris nodded in acceptance. In fact, she seemed to have an amused look on her face. "No need to apologize, dear."

Julie swiveled on her clogs to leave but caught herself before she had fully turned away. "I still have to ask, though." She couldn't help herself.

He waited silently.

"How can you live with the thought that a baby could

have died knowing we could and should have done more?" She peered at him closely.

He remained standing like a man in charge, barricaded on the other side of his desk, but something about him—be it his normally entrenched aura or some indefinable spirit—appeared to contract within.

Until finally, after what Julie felt was one of the most awkward moments of her life, he responded, "I do what I do every morning. I get up and try to do what I think is best for the future of this hospital."

"And you can be sure that members of the Grantham community recognize that," Iris said in support.

Oh, hell, who was she kidding? Julie thought. Iris was right. Sebastiano had improved things at the hospital. He appeared to have an almost miraculous green thumb when it came to raising money, and he had spearheaded interim renovations on the chemotherapy infusion clinic besides increasing the number of social workers to help patients navigate the intricacies of insurance coverage for various levels of care. Charging full steam into his office, wanting to do the best for her patients, she'd made a mess of things. "As those of us on staff at the hospital realize what you've done, as well," she said belatedly.

Suddenly she ached, inside and out, and she wasn't sure what hurt more. She brought her hand to her cheek and rubbed it. She felt a bump. *That's right.* That stupid ultrasound machine. Well, she'd have a doozy of a bruise tomorrow. That was for sure. The sooner she got out of this predicament, the better. "So, if you'll excuse me…" she said, easing her way toward the door.

"Before you go, Julie." Iris caught her in midflight. "Just the other day, Sarah was showing me the baby pillow you made for little Natalie—my granddaughter," she said by way of explanation to Sebastiano, with a beaming smile. "And then she gave me the sampler pillow you made for me. It's beautiful, and it will definitely take pride of place in my library. And I just love the saying, 'If I had known how much fun grandchildren would be, I would have had them first.'" She mimicked writing the words with queenlike aplomb.

Then she turned abruptly toward Sebastiano. "You do know, of course, that Julie does absolutely magnificent needlepoint, extraordinary stitches."

He raised his eyebrows. "No, I learn something new every day about Dr. Antonelli."

"Yes...well...I have many facets, including my innate ability to run half-cocked into a situation. So, if you'll excuse me again..." She winced. The talking was really starting to take a toll on her composure, not to mention her sore cheek.

Sebastiano frowned. "Actually, you're not excused. If you ladies would stay here for a moment, there's something I need to do. I'll be right back." He circled the desk and left the room quickly.

Julie looked over at Iris. "Well, that was a little weird," she said, feeling embarrassed.

Iris looked at Julie, then glanced over her narrow shoulder at the open door before slowly turning back to Julie. She waited a second before commenting, her pearls shining with a yellow, old-monied hue in the morning light coming through the bank of windows. "I believe you've taken him out of his comfort zone."

"Is that a good thing or a bad thing?" Julie asked.

Iris smiled. "We'll have to see, won't we?"

CHAPTER FOUR

SEBASTIANO COOLED HIS heels beside his assistant's desk while she ran his errand. But he needed to do more than cool his heels. His temper had reached the boiling point, as well. And all because of Julie Antonelli.

He had always found her an annoying presence—constantly emailing him with suggestions, or, rather, demands, on how to run the hospital.

Even more infuriating was the fact that she was undeniably attractive. She had a kind of insouciant sexiness. Too tall, of course, but one couldn't deny the appeal of her coltish figure and the way her legs seemed to go on for miles. Normally, he wasn't fond of women with short hair, but somehow her boyish cut worked with her larger-than-life brown eyes, her classically straight Roman nose and her sharply delineated cheekbones. One of which he couldn't help noticing during the course of their conversation—no, confrontation was more accurate—was rapidly suffering from edema and a contusion.

"Thank you," he said to his assistant when she came hurrying back. He didn't bother to offer any explanations. Then he marched back into his office. "Sorry for my brief absence." He thrust his arm at Julie. "Here. Take this."

Julie looked down, confused. "A towel? I mean I know my hair is all sweaty and I need a shower...."

"It's not your hair that concerns me," he said gruffly. He forced the bundle on her before circling back to the safety of his side of the desk. "That's an ice pack. Your bruise is swelling quite nicely. Now, please tell me you didn't infuriate someone else on these premises, thus necessitating another ice pack and a call to our legal counsel?"

Julie unwrapped the towel and saw the plastic Ziploc bag filled with ice cubes. She shook her head. "No, I didn't irritate anyone else. It was entirely my own clumsiness. But thanks anyway...for this."

"Don't thank me, thank my assistant. She was the one who ran to get it. I can just imagine the rumors circulating through the halls already given the noise of the vase crashing." He looked sternly at Julie.

She grimaced.

Sebastiano should have felt triumphant, only he didn't. Another source of irritation.

"Yes, one can just imagine," Iris said with a chuckle.

Julie pushed the towel-wrapped ice pack up against the side of her face, causing her short hair to stick out the side. He had an incredible urge to lean across his desk and gently pat it in place....

Don't be ridiculous, he chastised himself. He gulped purposefully. "Dr. Antonelli, I can appreciate that in the heat of the moment and after an arduous night you are tired and upset. Still, the hospital has proper protocol for handling complaints."

"I know, and I am sorry," Julie said. "And once more, I apologize, Mrs. Phox. I know how much you've done for the hospital and the people of this community."

"Don't even mention it, my dear. And next time you see your father, please give him my best. I always tell everyone that I would never let anyone else touch my Mercedes." She looked over at Sebastiano. "You've been to Antonelli Auto Mechanics, haven't you?"

Sebastiano fought the urge to roll his eyes. "I can't say I have."

"You must. It's immaculate. You could eat off the floor."

He saw Julie suppress a smile.

"And they have very good espresso," Iris added.

"I'll remember that the next time I need to take my car to the shop—or need a coffee."

Julie held out the towel, carefully folding it over to catch where the bag of ice cubes had started to leak. "Here. Thanks."

"Don't be ridiculous. You need it more than I. It's the least we can do as a proper hospital."

"You sure you don't need my insurance card first?" she asked.

"Don't press your luck," he warned.

"Dr. Fonterra, Mrs. Phox." Julie nodded and left.

"An interesting woman," Iris commented.

Her words brought his attention back into the room. "Dr. Antonelli certainly is…ah…unique."

"If you mean she has chutzpah—"

Sebastiano frowned. "Chutzpah?"

"Yes, such a lovely Yiddish word. It just rolls off your tongue. I find Yiddish so useful when dealing with people. I can see that I must give you a Yiddish dictionary."

Sebastiano had this uneasy feeling they were about to go down the rabbit hole again. "I take it that it means rude?" he asked.

Iris pursed her lips thoughtfully. "Rude, yes, I suppose so. But at the same time passionate." She paused. "I'm no expert of course."

By which Sebastiano took it to mean that Iris thought she was indeed an expert.

"But," Iris continued, "I would think that in her line of work that kind of passion—or should I say compassion—often goes missing after the first year or so on the job."

Sebastiano picked up his pen. "There's merit in what you say. But I would also argue that sometimes one's strength is also one's weakness."

Iris touched her chin and laughed softly. "You put a lot of stock in logic and order, don't you?" she asked.

"For someone in my position, they are traits to be expected, I suppose."

Iris studied him closely. Then she picked up the leather-bound folder resting on the corner of the desk and flipped it open. She slipped on a pair of reading glasses. "You have the agenda that I sent over?"

Sebastiano slid his copy out from under the blotter. Whatever he might think about Iris Phox—and unfortunately, there seemed to be way too much spare time in his evenings to ponder such questions—she was impeccably organized.

"Now," she said, "as you will note, there are several items for discussion." She paused, lifted her head and blinked in his direction. "However, I'd like to deviate from the usual protocol, take a moment to digress. That won't prove inconvenient for you, I trust?"

Only several other pressing appointments and meetings, not to mention the rest of my life, Sebastiano thought.

But since he really had no choice in the matter, he smiled graciously. "For you, Iris, I have all the time in the world."

CHAPTER FIVE

Monday, noon

"I DON'T KNOW WHO was the bigger ass—him or me," Julie confessed. She rested her head in her hands and rubbed her tired eyes. It was lunchtime, and even though she'd showered and changed, and downed several cups of black coffee, she still felt like crap. Whatever. She would just have to deal with it. Besides, it was her day off, and here she was with her best friend, Katarina. The two of them were sitting at the kitchen table at Katarina's grandmother's house. She should count her blessings.

Which was hard when she'd just been relating what a fool she'd been.

Katarina settled in against the pillows in the window seat. "Hey, watch your language. *Babička* may be upstairs checking on the baby, but, trust me, she has ears more sensitive than the latest CIA listening device." *Babička* was Slovak for "Grandmother" and harked back to Lena Zemanova's Eastern European origins.

"Sorry," Julie said, nodding. "Anyway, what can I say? As usual I flew off the handle—not that it wasn't a matter of urgency. But he got all officious, with that 'I'm in charge' attitude." She gingerly felt her bruised cheek. She'd applied massive amounts of concealer, hoping to cover the worst.

"Just please tell me that bruise isn't his fault. I can put up with temper in a man—God knows I'm living with a teenage son. But violence is completely unacceptable."

Julie waved off her concerns. "Not to worry. *Il Dottore* had nothing to do with my shiner. I have my own klutziness to thank for that. Then, there was the glass vase I also chipped today." She left out the part about it belonging to Sebastiano Fonterra in her own defense.

"I don't understand how you can be so coordinated at sports, and the next minute trip over your own feet. My God, I remember during the summers as kids how you were the star of the swimming and softball teams. Didn't they even recruit you to play in the men's basketball summer league when you were in high school and college?"

"No, by college I'd called it quits. Anyway, I might be coordinated when it comes to sports, but in real life—forget it."

Katarina studied her childhood friend.

Did she know? The reason I'd quit? Julie wondered. She had never talked about it with Katarina, and she still couldn't now. Only her family knew why she'd given up a full basketball scholarship to the University of Connecticut, and even they'd never discussed it with her. Ever.

Not that Katarina was the type of person to dwell on the past. After all, she had her own issues growing up with a single mother, who was always moving. From what Julie had gleaned, the only source of stability in Katarina's life had been her grandmother Lena.

Maybe that's what drew them together: a refusal to dwell on the past. Or maybe it was because they both loved red wine and sappy movies, and that despite the unspoken vagaries of childhood and young adulthood, they were still there for each other.

From upstairs in the small clapboard house, a fierce cry could be heard. Katarina immediately tuned in. "Ah, it sounds like my son and heir is awake. I knew it was too good to last. Thank goodness *Babička* was able to watch him while I met with Rufus." She slanted her head to listen to her grandmother's sturdy footsteps descending the stairs. Then she leaned toward Julie. "I was there to help him evaluate his financial situation if he decides to sell the bar—"

"He's going to sell the Nighttime Bar? It's a Grantham institution. He can't just sell it!" Julie protested. The Nighttime Bar might have been a hole in the wall off Route 206, but it was a hole in the wall that had attracted some of the top names in jazz over the years, musicians who sought an intimate, knowledgeable crowd and Rufus's easy bonhomie.

"We'll see. But let me finish, would you!"

Julie sat back against the cushions and crossed her arms. "I'm waiting."

"Okay. While Rufus and I were talking, somehow the conversation got sidetracked onto the hospital expansion."

Katarina looked up when her grandmother came into the kitchen holding her son. "Ah, my favorite little boy," she cooed and clapped her hands. "Hello, Rad. Did you miss your mommy?"

The three-month-old baby boy was named for Lena's late husband, Radko, who had died before Katarina was born. His still sleepy eyes were red from crying, but they lit up as soon as he saw Katarina. She held out her arms, and he immediately cuddled close, his mouth rooting around her breasts.

"Men, they're all alike," Katarina complained as she unbuttoned the front of her loose blouse and undid the snaps on her nursing bra.

Lena looked on, smiling. "He slept the whole time you were gone, I'll have you know, so he deserves a reward. And it's a gift to nurse your child."

The baby latched on and started to suck with a steady determination.

"Oh, my goodness, your cheek, Julie!" Lena exclaimed. "What happened? Do you need something? Calamine lotion? I have a bag of frozen peas in the freezer."

"It's nothing, really," Julie assured her. "Just a little bump." She needed more concealer, clearly.

Rad's voracious eating produced a smacking noise.

Julie laughed and leaned across the table to stroke his tiny fingers. Julie's touch made him quiver, and he shifted to grip the skin above Katarina's nipple and feather it with his tiny fingers.

"What little starfish hands," she marveled. "I'm always amazed the way they come out with all the little wrinkles at the knuckles and tiny little nails."

Katarina glanced her way. "All the better to scratch me with."

"And you wouldn't give it up for a moment," Julie replied. She heard Lena clattering pots and pans behind her and swiveled around. "Can I help you with anything there, Mrs. Zemanova?"

"How sweet of you to offer." Lena turned on a stove burner and placed a frying pan on it. She cut a generous hunk of butter and dropped it into the pan to melt. "I'm just frying up some onions to go with the *pirohy*," she said, referring to the Slovakian stuffed dumplings. "Just a little something light, you know."

A little something light? Julie mouthed to Katarina behind Lena's back.

"But if you really want to do something, you can get the container of sour cream out of the fridge and put it in a bowl." Lena nodded toward an overhead cabinet to indicate where the bowls were kept.

Julie slid across the window seat, got up and headed for the refrigerator.

"If you think we need more to eat, there's mushroom soup that I made in a Rubbermaid container on the left," Lena said in a raised voice as she fried the chopped onion.

Julie chewed her lower lip. "It's tempting. What do you think, Katarina?" She turned to her friend.

Katarina moaned as she shifted Rad from one breast to the other. "Please, I'm trying to lose weight after the baby. Not all of us can eat anything and everything and still look like a long toothpick."

"I guess no soup then." Julie finished dishing the sour cream into a blue-and-white pottery bowl. "I'll put this on the table, okay?" she said on her way to the dining room.

"Yes, that's good," Lena called out. "Put it next to the silver serving spoon. Meanwhile I'll start to put up the *pirohy* because it looks like our little man is just about finished." She removed a clean dishcloth covering a cookie sheet and exposed a neat array of crescent-shaped dumplings. She carefully dropped them into the pot of boiling water, and when they floated to the top, she ladled them out and placed them on a large china platter. She had already dished the sautéed onions into a matching bowl. "Who wants to take these in?" she asked.

"Julie, why don't you take the baby, and I'll help with the food," Katarina said, passing him over and doing up her bra. "He still needs to be burped so take the receiving blanket. Otherwise he'll upchuck all over your sweater." She smoothed her long red hair off her shoulder.

"That's what dry cleaning is for is what I say." Julie mugged at Rad as she held him up. She confidently maneuvered the baby to her shoulder and patted him repeatedly on his back.

"Okay, *Babička,* now I'm all yours. Give it here." Katarina nudged Lena aside and lifted the platter. "My God, you've got enough to feed an army."

Lena picked up the onions and marched on her Easy Spirit walking shoes to the dining room. She might be in her early seventies, but she was fit as a fiddle from tennis three days a week and tai chi classes at the Adult School.

"I know, I know," she said, "but I wasn't sure if Wanda was going to join us with little Natalie. They have music-and-little-tikes class today." Wanda was a retired high school math teacher who now lived with Lena and took care of the one-year-old daughter of Julie's other friend, Sarah. Sarah was a physiotherapist and her husband, Hunt, Iris Phox's son, was in med school.

"You have enough here to invite the whole class," Katarina joked. She rested the platter on the corner of the dining room table. For the occasion, Lena had set the table with a white damask tablecloth. The silver shone and the Bohemian crystal sparkled. A round glass bowl in the center held an informal arrangement of purple lobelia and feathery pink asters from her small garden.

Lena took her place at the head of the table. "Here, Julie, you can sit on this side while Katarina can sit next to the bouncy baby chair."

"No way I'm giving up this cutie," Julie said as she followed everyone else in. She continued to pat the baby on his back until he emitted a loud burp. "Good one, Rad." She let him snuggle into her shoulder and breathed in deeply. "Don't you just love the smell of babies?"

"Julie, you're so good with babies. I'm still terrified I'm going to drop him." Katarina pulled out her chair and sat.

"Just be the oldest daughter in a large Italian family and you'd be good with babies, too. Trust me, it doesn't take any special gifts, just a lot—and I mean—a lot of practice. Anyway, my brother Dom hit the floor a few times, and he seems to have survived intact." She deftly switched Rad to her other shoulder and raised her plate to *Babička* so she could dish up her dumplings.

"You should have children of your own. It's much more fun than minding little brothers," Lena said as she passed Julie back her plate. A succulent aroma filled the room.

"Have you been talking to my mother, Mrs. Zemanova? Or maybe my grandmother? Sometimes I think I see her staring at me, visualizing the size of my ovaries. She tells me she has powers, you know? Supposedly even the evil eye," Julie said with a laugh. "Hey, come to think of it, maybe that's what's been keeping all those eligible bachelors away."

"She would never do that!" Lena looked aghast, as if she had taken Julie seriously. "Here, have some sour cream. It will make you feel better."

Julie took the bowl. "It can't hurt." She plopped a generous amount on her plate, then passed the dish to Katarina.

Katarina studied it and frowned. "Oh, all right. But that means an extra thirty minutes on the stationary bike tonight." She added a modest dollop of sour cream to her dumplings, paused and added a speck more. "You know, let me just throw this thought out, knowing full well that you'll probably shoot it down immediately. Maybe, just maybe, the problem isn't your grandmother, but you. I mean, you never get out at all." She took a bite of dumpling with sour cream and onion and smiled. "Oh, bliss!"

Julie stopped patting Rad's diaper-covered bottom. "I do so get out. I'm here today, aren't I? I see my folks. And what about the girls' nights out with you and Sarah?" Actually, since Katarina and Sarah had gotten married and had children, the sad truth was the three of them rarely had time to get together. If they did find the time, they were usually so tired that they tended to lie around Julie's condo, watch DVDs and eat too many chips and salsa.

"Somehow I don't hear the mention of any men, outside of family members, in that scenario," Katarina said. The baby started to fuss on Julie's shoulder. "Here, let me take the squirt. You haven't even touched your food."

"I'm fine," Julie protested.

"No, you're not." Katarina stood up and walked around.

"Here you go, lover boy." Julie reluctantly let Katarina take the baby. "I think you might find he needs his diaper changed."

Katarina sniffed the baby's bottom. "Oooh! You are stinky. It never fails after I feed him. I'll just go change him and be right down."

Lena winked at her great-grandson and made kissy noises. Then she addressed Julie with perfect sincerity. "Maybe what is necessary is for you to go some place where you can find single men?"

"Listen, I am not about to start hanging out at bars, looking for a pickup," Julie said circumspectly.

Lena rested her fork on her plate. "I would never suggest that!"

Katarina stopped at the doorway to the hall. "How about at the hospital? Didn't you just tell me you ran into an eligible doctor this morning?" She laughed and headed up to the bedrooms.

Lena pressed her hand on the table. "You don't mean you bumped into Sebastiano Fonterra? Now I understand the cause of the bruise."

Julie shook her head. "No, Katarina got it all wrong. I just had a run-*in*, a disagreement. What makes you say it was Sebastiano Fonterra? Don't tell me you have special powers, too?"

Lena shook her head. "No, no. I met him a while back at a hospital fundraiser, and since then at my regular physical therapy session with Sarah—my tennis elbow, you know. She talks all about the new hospital administrator." Lena leaned more closely. "So tell me. Do you think he's as sexy as Sarah says he is?"

"Well, it depends on what you mean by sexy," Julie hedged.

"Tall, dark and handsome?"

"Well, he's tall, but not as tall as me. And I suppose he's got brown hair, but I wouldn't call it dark-dark. And I'm pretty sure there're even a few wisps of gray starting to show."

"You noticed that, did you?"

"Yeah, but it wasn't like I noticed-noticed. I mean, between you and me—and probably the whole hospital by now—Sebastiano Fonterra and I don't exactly see eye-to-eye."

Lena picked up her fork again. She had a sly smile on her lips, which with her short gray bob and dazzling blue eyes, made her look like some Eastern European pixie up to no good. "So you are taller, but only a bit."

Julie could see which way this was headed. "It's not so much a height thing. It's more that we are diametrically opposed to each other," she clarified.

Lena shook off her remark, fork in hand. "Good! Forceful opinions are good! That shows passion!"

There was a loud knock at the front door.

Lena and Julie looked up.

"Maybe Wanda made it after all?" Julie asked.

"No, she has a key." Lena shook her head. "I'm not expecting anyone that I know of."

"Let me get it," Julie said. It was a good excuse to change the topic of conversation. She started to get up.

Lena put a wrinkled but firm hand on hers. "No, I'll get it. You are a guest, and you haven't even had a chance to have one bite. Please, I insist."

The knock repeated.

"Don't bother, *Babička,*" Katarina called out, coming down the stairs. "I'm already on my way."

Lena smiled. "She's a wonderful granddaughter. I am so lucky. Just like your grandmother is lucky to have you," she added to Julie.

From the dining room, they heard the wooden front door being opened. There was a sound of muffled voices. Julie tried not to eavesdrop and dug into her food. "Oh, my God, this is like heaven! I can't tell you the last time I ate, and that was probably a candy bar."

Lena looked horrified.

The footsteps grew louder as they made their way down the central hallway to the dining room. Lena raised her chin and looked over the centerpiece. Her mouth dropped open.

Julie saw Lena's startled expression, turned and saw Katarina standing awkwardly in the doorway. She held the baby tightly in her arms as if protecting it from gale-force winds.

Next to her stood a middle-aged woman. Her thick braid was dark blond with streaks of gray. Her face was tanned and lined from the sun. She wore a fleece vest, jeans and work boots.

"Lena," the woman said, offering a tentative smile.

Julie stared at the woman's cornflower-blue eyes. She was sure she'd seen ones just like it before. She glanced over at Katarina's grandmother.

"Julie," Katarina said.

She turned.

"I don't know if you remember. It's been many years. But this is my mother, Zora."

CHAPTER SIX

"FOR AN OLD MAN, you can still pound the ball." Sebastiano mopped his forehead as he walked to the bench beside the tennis court.

"I may be fifty-three, but I'm not old. I just feel old most of the time." Paul Bedecker stopped to gulp down half a bottle of Gatorade. Still breathing hard, he wiped his mouth. Despite the years, he had a wiry build. Dark red stubble covered his gaunt cheekbones. If the man had an ounce of fat on him, he was hiding it well.

He waggled his racket menacingly in Sebastiano's direction. "Just don't get the idea that I'm about to start playing like an old man. Those little dink shots. The underhanded serves." He demonstrated some ditsy hand motions. "Don't you just hate them?" He pulled the beak of his baseball cap down over his shaved head. It bore the logo of a reality TV show from a bunch of years back, a remnant of his time in Hollywood.

Sebastiano deliberately folded his towel into thirds and draped it over the end post of the net. "So you played and lost to an old man recently I take it?"

Paul shrugged. "Monday, which was…was it just yesterday? I'm starting to lose all track of time these days."

Monday had been one to forget for Sebastiano, as well, thanks to Dr. Julie Antonelli. Why that woman insisted on periodically getting to him was beyond him. He did his utmost to maintain control over his emotions and his life, and she seemed somehow...somehow...to upset the applecart. Sebastiano smiled. He liked that image. Metaphors in English frequently seemed mysterious to him, but this time he could easily picture Julie lying sprawled on the ground as a mound of tempting red apples spilled over her long, lanky torso. Her *tempting* torso... Sebastiano's smile became more thoughtful.

He shook his head and looked at Paul. Their relationship was the closest thing Sebastiano had to a friendship in town—a friendship basically consisting of a standing tennis game once a week. They played at eight in the morning, before Sebastiano went to the office and Paul helped out at the family garden center or nominally worked on his novel. The two had met a few months ago, right after Paul had returned to Grantham. Talk about the prodigal son. Paul had been a whiz kid who seemed to have it all—top of his class at Grantham High School, Ivy League education and hotshot job in Hollywood. But the air had gone out of his dream bubble—due to his own fault, Paul would have been the first to admit. And now he was back living with his father and helping out with the family business.

Sebastiano wasn't a snob. He didn't need to hobnob exclusively with members of the upper tax bracket, let alone the glitterati. In fact, he was more comfortable with Paul the way he was now—for many reasons. He liked Paul's humor, his sardonic take on the world. He even found his edginess interesting. But that didn't mean Sebastiano was blind to Paul's faults.

"Paul, are you okay? Something bothering you?" He paused. "Have you started drinking or using again?"

Paul breathed in deeply. "Thanks for asking. And, no, I'm not using. And I haven't touched a drop."

"I'm glad to hear it because I haven't seen you at the A.A. meetings lately."

"Hey, I know you're my sponsor, but you don't need to keep tabs on me. I was busy with my father. I had to take him to his eye doctor for a checkup. His eyes were dilated, so he couldn't drive. Then there was my niece's birthday. Other stuff, too." He idly watched a doubles match a few courts away.

Sebastiano waited.

Paul sighed. "Okay, it's just that being back in Grantham has a way of dredging up old memories, not all of which are good. But, I can deal with it. Really. I know not to sit around and let them get to me. Anyway, sometimes you just miss meetings, you know? Everyone's done it, even you."

Sebastiano hadn't. Ever. Not for six years anyway. Not since he decided to get control of his life, stop drowning his guilt in vodka and join Alcoholics Anonymous. It hadn't solved all his problems, but it allowed him to wake each morning and face each new day and do the best he could. In fact, hadn't he just explained yesterday in his office to Julie Antonelli that he worked daily to do what was right by the hospital? Sebastian blinked, startled at where his line of thinking had unintentionally wandered. Julie Antonelli? Suddenly insinuating herself into his very thoughts?

THAT SAME MORNING, Julie headed to Fine Threads, Grantham's premier knitting and needlepoint shop. After poking around the piles of needlepoint canvases spilling over the table in the center of the store, she approached the cash register with one she'd chosen. "I saw you had a trunk show, so I decided to come in."

Caroline, the owner, held up the printed canvas. "It so looks like something you would do, Julie. I can see all your different stitches on the flowers and along the geometric border."

Julie rested an elbow on the gray granite bench surface and admired the pattern on the canvas. "I really liked the Hungarian peasantry feel to it. And after getting the twenty-percent-off coupon, I couldn't resist."

Caroline, a thin middle-aged woman with short gray curly hair and the placid demeanor of a seasoned kindergarten teacher, beamed. "You got the coupon? That means it's your birthday this month! Congratulations! When is it?"

"Oh, I have days to go." Julie waved off her enthusiasm. "Besides, I'm at the stage where I try to ignore birthdays." Actually, Julie had made a point of ignoring her birthday since she was twenty.

Caroline shook her head. "You've got a long way to go before you get to that stage. Anyhow, do you want to pick up the needlepoint thread, too? It's twenty percent off the entire purchase, you know."

"I'm not sure what I need, but maybe I'll just take another peek at the pile?"

"Take your time. And you know what? I was going to call you. I just put together your latest pillow, and I've got it downstairs. I'll just go look." Caroline headed down to the storage area.

Julie wandered over to the display. Neat rows of needlepoint threads in silks and wool, some shot with glittery strands, covered the walls. Jars of buttons, knitting needles and books rounded out a cozy seating area, where knitters of all ages gathered together.

Julie liked the shop and Caroline immensely. In fact, she sometimes thought of Fine Threads as her little club. When she wasn't working or thinking about work, she was most likely curled up in an armchair in her apartment with the television tuned to some sports channel, while she compulsively needlepointed.

The bell over the front door chimed, signaling a new customer. Julie glanced around. Her heart sank. Not again.

"Julie, my dear, fancy meeting you here. And to think I was just about to get in touch." Iris Phox entered the small shop, preceded by a well-loved L.L. Bean canvas carryall and her oversize confidence.

"Mrs. Phox. How nice to see you, too," Julie said. Maybe she'd just forego collecting her pillow.

"Here you are, Julie," Caroline announced, mounting the stairs to the checkout counter. She carried a blue Fine Threads bag with a sausage-shaped pillow peeking out from one side. "It looks fabulous."

"Oh, I must see." Iris undid the belt and buttons of her Burberry raincoat.

Caroline removed the pillow from the bag and unwrapped the plastic covering. "Isn't it magnificent. I love the way you mixed in beads and buttons with the needlepoint. And the idea to roll the canvas into a bolster pillow was brilliant."

Julie looked over Iris's formidable shoulder. The large patchwork of scrolls and hibiscus flowers in a mixture of warm yellows, oranges and brick-reds, coupled with the light greens and beige and pale yellow background, had come out nicely, even she had to admit it.

"Yes, the shape is quite clever." Iris squinted. "Whatever made you think of doing that?"

"My grandmother has been complaining that her lower back hurts, and I thought it would provide some support when she's sitting down."

Iris ran a boney index finger over the loopy stitches with beads attached that formed the anther tips of the flowers' stamen stalks. "Yes, very clever. Indeed, you're just the person to help me." Iris marched back to her carryall that she'd left on the high worktable in the center of the shop.

"I am?" Julie asked, looking warily at Caroline before turning to Iris.

"Yes, indeed." Iris pulled a giant canvas from her bag. "I'm making a Christmas stocking for my granddaughter Natalie—the start of a family tradition—and I am having trouble with Santa's beard. According to the instructions, it's supposed to be something called Turkey Work, but I am completely baffled. Clearly, the instructions were not written by an educated person."

There was much to be learned from a person like Iris, Julie realized. Here was someone who felt no compunction about blaming others for her own failings. She, on the other hand, assumed she was responsible for any and all failures.

And she would have liked to tell her so, but she decided instead to be nice—as hard as that was. She had already messed things up yesterday, and Iris was too powerful a figure in Grantham to risk further alienation. "I don't know if I can help very much, but let me try," she said with the correct amount of humility. "Turkey Work is one of those stitches that I seem to have to reteach myself every time I do it, using the big black stitch guide that Caroline carries here in the shop."

Iris raised an eyebrow at Caroline, who immediately grabbed a copy from the store bookshelf.

The doorbell jingled again and a group of women came in. They carried bulging bags and were laughing. Then two more women came in. Julie smiled as they all walked by and headed downstairs to the lower level where the classes met.

"That's my afghan knitting group," Caroline announced. "If you and Mrs. Phox are all right up here, I'll leave you?"

"No problem." Julie flipped open the book and found the right page. She placed it on the center island and looked at Iris.

"Just a moment, please." Iris reached into her leather purse and extracted a pair of tortoiseshell reading glasses. The necessity of pleasing a granddaughter apparently won out over vanity. Then she passed over the canvas printed with a Victorian illustration of Father Christmas.

"What I tell myself when I do Turkey Work is two forward front, one back behind." Julie demonstrated as she spoke. "Then you just need to remember to alternate the loop with the flat stitch on the front." She glanced at Iris. "Why don't you try?"

Iris peered closely and held up her hands. "Yes, I think I understand." She asked Julie to repeat the mnemonic once more and pursed her mouth in concentration.

After a few more minutes of practice while Julie offered encouragement, Iris stopped, resting her work on the table. She took off her reading glasses and placed them on the needlepoint. "You're very good at this type of thing. A good teacher. No wonder your patients speak very highly of your communication skills in addition to your expertise."

"Thank you, that's very generous," Julie said. Was it possible that Iris was a nice woman after all?

"Yes, it is."

Well, maybe not completely.

"And it's the same generosity that spurred me to convince Dr. Fonterra that you might be allowed to make amends for your…shall we say…physical outburst yesterday?"

"I don't know what to say." Julie really didn't.

"A written note of apology addressed to my home address on fine stationery is always appropriate, much preferable to email. Dr. Fonterra strikes me as someone who only reads email though. Still…" Iris let the single syllable hang in the air.

"Still?" Julie asked.

Iris smiled serenely.

Julie spotted trouble immediately.

"Still, even the most finely penned apologies don't totally address the problem."

"The problem? Oh, you mean my breaking the vase. I'm happy to reimburse the board, if that would help."

"Yes, there is that. Might I suggest, shall we say, a nice contribution to the new hospital fund?" Iris named a figure that easily equaled the monthly mortgage payment on Julie's condo.

Julie worked hard to keep her jaw from scraping the floor.

Iris slipped the needle through the webbing in her canvas and folded the piece deliberately. "But I think we're talking about more than money."

"We are?"

"Dr. Fonterra pointed out to me—and very wisely, indeed—sometimes one's strength is also one's weakness."

"And did he mention what mine was?"

"Your passion," Iris answered.

Julie felt a wholly uncalled-for flutter in her stomach. "He used that exact word?"

"Actually, that was my word. His was perhaps better left unsaid."

The flutter turned to a knot.

"Nonetheless, it was clear that the best way to establish a better working relationship and to demonstrate remorse for the destruction of a valuable gift, accidental as it might have been, would be to demonstrate your appreciation of his way of thinking."

Why did Julie get the feeling she was being painted into a corner by a master, a master whose clout at the hospital was second to none, who just happened to be the mother-in-law of a close friend and who could easily drop a negative word here and there about her father's garage, thus causing his business to dry up faster than a day-old prune?

"And what exactly did you have in mind?" Julie asked, trying to tamp down her anger.

Iris paused dramatically, placing her hand to her throat. "Let me see. The issue becomes what type of activity would harness that passion of yours in a social context yet still foster your wonderful interactive skills."

Julie didn't buy Iris's putting on her thinking cap one whit. Then she saw the older woman dig into her sewing bag and pull out a pamphlet.

"As I said, we need to focus that keen mind of yours onto something other than medicine, thereby allowing you to take pleasure in the world around you and mitigate outbursts due to a singular focus on work, which transforms it into a strain rather than a calling." She said all of that in one magisterial breath before slapping the pamphlet on the white work surface.

Julie furrowed her brow. "Grantham Adult Education School? I'm not sure how that is going to mitigate or curtail or…to do whatever it is I'm supposed to be addressing."

Iris sat up extra straight. "Never doubt the power of learning." She flipped open the cover and read out loud from the introduction. "'Above all, we at the Adult School believe that education does not end with a diploma. Hence, our motto—Education: the Wellspring of Life.'"

"That's very commendable," Julie agreed. *And totally predictable,* she realized in one of those ah-ha moments. Twice before, Iris had manipulated her friends Katarina and Sarah into participating in her pet project.

Iris gazed over the words. "Commendable, indeed. I know. I wrote them." She flicked the pages to where a sheet of paper was inserted. "Do you speak Italian with your parents?" She turned her head.

"Why, yes."

"I recommend the advanced Italian conversation class then."

Julie leaned forward and read the description. "And you really think this is the best way to say I'm sorry to Dr. Fonterra?" She glanced at Iris and saw the woman raise a condescending brow. Julie looked at the booklet again. "Okay," she agreed. Then she noticed a critical bit of information. "But it says here that the class meets every Wednesday at seven-thirty for an hour and a half? What if I'm in the middle of a delivery?"

"Then you'll deal with that when it happens, won't you? Besides, I doubt all babies are born on Wednesday evenings. And before you offer any more excuses, may I just point out to you how adept you were at explaining to me about Turkey Work. Clearly, you are someone who shines in a classroom scenario, whether as teacher or pupil." Iris tucked her glasses into the side of her bag and gathered up her work.

Julie scrambled to stand up, too. "But I'm not registered."

"Don't worry. I've already registered you and paid the fee. You may write a check to me and include it in the note that you will be sending me. Oh, in case you were wondering, the Adult School has a strict policy of taking attendance. And needless to say, in my capacity as head of the Adult School board, I'm always there for the first week of the semester." Iris slipped on a pair of gloves and carefully smoothed the kidskin leather down each finger. "By the way, I recommend a generous application of powder to cover that bruise on your cheek."

It would have been simpler just to wear a paper bag over her head. *And I hope the good doctor realizes how much I am sacrificing,* Julie couldn't help thinking.

Unfortunately, when it came to Sebastiano Fonterra, that wasn't the only thing that Julie couldn't help thinking.

CHAPTER SEVEN

KATARINA LOOKED UP from washing the pots and pans from dinner. Only the day before yesterday her mother—Zora—had dropped back into her life after one of her periodic absences. One of those absences had included not coming back from Antarctica after Katarina had been shot in a robbery at an ATM in Oakland. In fairness, Katarina had insisted she was fine, but still…? And while Zora had made it to Katarina's wedding, she *had* scheduled her departing flight in the middle of the reception. They'd barely had time to exchange pleasantries.

Needless to say, when Radko was born Katarina hadn't even bothered to invite her mother back to Grantham to celebrate the event. Instead, she'd sent an email with all the relevant information. Her mother had mailed a little hooded sweater she'd knitted from genuine yak's wool from a trek she'd made in Mongolia on some sponsored research grant. Unfortunately, the oils in the yarn seemed to irritate the baby's tender skin.

Nevertheless, Katarina still harbored a sentimental notion of family. That's why she had made dinner and invited her mother to meet her husband, Ben, her stepson, Matt, and, of course, to get better acquainted with Zora's new grandson Rad. She should have known it was a mistake.

Rad had a slight fever and was cranky. She'd kept him up until her mother had arrived late—something about having to check the tire pressure on the pickup truck she'd rented and not being able to find a gas station with a free air pump. *Who rented a pickup truck anyway?* Katarina had wondered. In the end, then, her mother barely managed a pat on the baby's bald head before Katarina put him to bed.

Perhaps Matt should have gone to bed early, too. He'd been a monosyllabic teenager over the dinner of lamb stew while Zora grilled him about a physics course. What could you expect of a teenager, overstressed from waiting to hear about college acceptances? Katarina asked herself.

But thank God for Ben. For a man who professed not to be a people person, he'd had the inspired idea to ask Zora about her work—something she had no trouble discussing, especially since Ben made sure the wineglasses were full.

Katarina wiped down the tile countertop and put away the dishcloth. She had tried to create a "normal" family with Ben and Matt and Rad, and of course, *Babička,* and her life really was good. She had nothing to complain about, she told herself regularly. But still, that hadn't prevented her from feeling an emotional hole in her being.

Julie sometimes complained about her mother and father—and her scary grandmother—micromanaging her life. Katarina often wished she could voice the same complaint. She had never even known her father, nor had anyone else. Sometimes, she wasn't even sure if her mother knew, having led what she referred to as "a liberated existence." And except for the summers in Grantham with *Babička,* she had never called any place home. They had moved incessantly, as her mother pursued college, then graduate school in geology, then field studies, post-docs, and appointments at a government lab here, a university there. When Katarina had broken her elbow horsing around on the high dive board at Grantham Community Swimming Pool, *Babička* was the one she had called. When she'd broken up with her boyfriend in college, she'd known not to bother her mother but to call *Babička,* who had consoled her, telling her there were bigger fish to broil—she never could get her American sayings straight.

But tonight when she needed her most, where was her grandmother?

"Wanda and I are catching a quick bite at the Chinese restaurant around the corner before we go to our tai chi class at the Adult School," she had said, begging off. "We can't possibly be late to the first class. Besides, you two have a lot of catching up to do. You don't need me."

Katarina was thirty-three years old, and she wasn't too proud to say she needed her grandmother, especially when it came to dealing with the mother she never really knew and certainly didn't understand.

She heard footsteps coming down the hallway.

"Oh, there you are," her mother said blithely as she entered the room. "I didn't expect to find you here—the little woman in the kitchen."

Katarina tried not to be riled by her mother's barb. She affixed a smile. "You're going so soon, Mom?" She saw her mother scowl. "Sorry, I mean, Zora. You're leaving already?" Zora had on a windbreaker. A small knapsack was slung over one shoulder.

"Yes, well, the dinner was lovely."

"I'm sorry the potatoes were a little undercooked."

"Don't be ridiculous. I've never even mastered making scrambled eggs. You can imagine my mother's dismay." Zora paused. "Anyway, I decided as long as I was back in Grantham for a while that I'd keep myself busy. I saw a pamphlet on the sideboard from the Adult School and noticed an entry for an Italian conversation class. It's been years since I did field work at Vesuvius, and it's time for a language refresher, especially since I'll be giving a lecture at the University of Naples later this fall. I think I may have mentioned my plans to you?"

Katarina picked up the dishrag again and began wiping down the counter tiles that were perfectly clean already. "I can't say that I remember you doing that."

Zora awkwardly patted her daughter's upper arm. "We'll have other evenings, and the first class meets tonight. Luckily when I called, they still had a spot." She fished her keys out of a side pocket of her backpack. The toggle from the rental agency hung from her hand. "I don't want to be late then."

Katarina realized her mother had small, almost childlike hands. But then, she was small in stature, a good three or four inches shorter than she. Strange. She had this memory of her mother being taller.

Katarina sighed. "Yes, it wouldn't be good to be late to class. I'll let Ben know you had to leave." He had left earlier to take Matt back to school to work on editing the school newspaper.

"Thank you. He's a lovely man. You've done quite well for yourself. Ben, Matt, the baby. This house. I'm glad to see you're settled so nicely." She squeezed out a smile.

"Settled so nicely. That's a funny expression coming from you," Katarina said. Then because she didn't want to pick a fight, she leaned in and gave her mother a quick hug. For a moment, she felt the other woman melt into her embrace. The moment passed. Katarina stepped back.

So much for trying to create the happy "normal" family. Maybe she'd give Julie a call and find out just who in her family was bugging her now?

ZORA DROVE THE DARK winding road from Katarina's house back to town. She gripped the wheel tightly. She'd driven a pickup before, but this rental model was far larger than she was used to, and she hadn't been able to resist the appeal of its outdoorsy, independent image. She sank her teeth into her upper lip and squinted.

Oh, who was she kidding? It wasn't the driving that had her on edge. She was anxious about coming back to Grantham, to her mother. To her daughter.

So why had she come home?

Guilt for one. How long had it been? About a year? Not that bad, really. No, it was a different kind of guilt that gnawed at her. Despite all her university appointments, prestigious research grants, the accolades from her colleagues, Zora felt restless, unsettled. She found herself searching for a sense of inner peace in her life that she had never really needed before.

Okay, so she was having a midlife crisis. Somehow, she had hoped coming back to Grantham would provide a certain ease that came with the familiar. Yet despite the outpouring of love from her mother, Zora couldn't help noticing the ever-present vertical crease that bisected her brow. Then there was Katarina, her daughter.

She never said a critical word, but Zora could feel the resentment bubbling beneath the surface. And she could also see the strong bond between Katarina and Lena. If anything, they seemed to share what would be a classic mother-daughter relationship, which of course, meant Zora was the odd man—or woman in this case—left out of the equation. That hurt. Not that she'd ever admit it. Or should she?

But then she could imagine their retort.

"What do you expect if you spend more time with rocks than with your own daughter, not that I am not proud of you," her mother would say, damning her with faint praise.

"It's not personal," Katarina, ever the pragmatic survivor would reply. "It's just that she was there and you weren't."

They needed to have a heart-to-heart even if Zora didn't do heart-to-hearts. Too much emphasis on past decisions that couldn't be changed anyway. Too many recriminations for old offences that were best forgotten. Still, she should talk to her mom. Her daughter. And she would. She really would. Just…just…not right now.

Now she just wanted to take it easy. Find pleasure in just being. Regain that sense of confidence that had always come so naturally, but now seemed to have given way to doubts and unnamed desires.

Zora parked the truck on the street near the high school and grabbed her knapsack. She hiked the short distance to the school, passing along the familiar tree-lined sidewalk, the football field and tennis courts. The building had changed since her day. Heck, a lot had changed. Her daughter was married and had a son. And a stepson. God, that made her a grandmother twice

over. No wonder she was depressed. Then her mother
had gone and gotten a roommate—her old high school
math teacher Wanda Garrity, no less. When she came
down late to breakfast in the morning, Zora had almost
expected to find a detention notice.

She headed toward the main entrance of the original
brick building with its Gothic tower. The course listing
gave a second-floor room number, and Zora honed in on
a stairway down the hall and to the left. The hallways
were teeming with adults, some chatting, some seemingly lost. A few officials from the program and what
looked to be students from the high school were there
to give directions. She spotted the familiar face of an
imperious older woman at the central crossroads. It had
to be Iris Phox. *Great!* Another person from her past
she'd just as soon forget. She had always felt the woman
looked at Grantham as her personal fiefdom.

"I can't stand her. She's such an elitist snob," Zora had
announced one day when she'd stopped by her mother's
hardware store after high school. She had just witnessed
Iris Phox lecturing Lena on the inferior quality of the
hot water bottles she was now carrying.

Zora would have gladly told the woman where she
could put her water bottle, if Lena hadn't shot her a
warning glance. She waited until Iris had glided out
the door like the Queen Mother—she even carried a
pocketbook over her wrist the same way—before turning to her mother. "I can't stand her. The way she treats
you like a peasant."

"That's just her way. Besides, we should all be grateful to her," Lena had argued. "Most rich people keep
all their money to themselves. Iris gives away to people
who need. And that makes her feel needed, too."

Zora, with the black-and-white perception of the world that only an eighteen-year-old could bring, had shaken her head defiantly. "And if she gives away money, it's because she likes to control people."

"Sometimes that's the same as being needed," Lena had said with a shrug of her shoulder before turning to serve the next customer.

And now Iris Phox was approaching her. Zora tried to pretend she didn't see her making a beeline in her direction and tucked her chin down into her coat. She swerved to the right toward the stairway.

"Zora! Zora Zemanova!" Iris called out. Her highbrow tones carried above the anxious din of the crowd.

Zora stopped. There was no point in pretending she hadn't heard. She turned around and only marginally masked her irritation. "Mrs. Phox, a voice out of my past, a voice that one might say carries an unmistakable quality."

Iris pursed her lips. "Yes, my son Hunt once said I sounded like a Boston Brahman foghorn, which I always took as a mixed compliment."

Zora smirked. She never really knew Iris's son, but she had a newly found regard for him.

"I see you're taking advanced Italian conversation," Iris went on.

Zora raised her eyebrows. "You memorized all the class lists?" She saw the sheaf of papers stacked neatly atop the folder in Iris's arms.

"I *am* the president of the Adult School, you know."

"No, I didn't, but why would I have thought otherwise," Zora said.

If Iris had felt the criticism in Zora's words, she didn't show it. "I wanted to welcome you back to Grantham and commend you on your choice. It's been one of the more popular offerings over the years, one we're quite proud of. In fact, I personally recommended that Julie Antonelli enroll in it. You know Dr. Antonelli, of course? I believe that besides your dear mother, her family practically raised your daughter, Katarina, over the years?"

She had felt the criticism, Zora realized, feeling the sharp blade of Iris's words. "I'm forever grateful to them," Zora responded, knowing when she had been bested.

"Yes, well, it's always good to see one of our own return. Here in Grantham, we like to think our little town has much to offer in the way of scholarly stimulation as well as personal guidance."

"A little bastion of academic exclusivity to nurture the soul?"

"I prefer to think of it as intellectual chicken soup for the heart."

Zora wasn't sure if Iris had just made a joke. She wasn't really sure if Iris Phox even had a sense of humor.

"But don't let me keep you from your class," Iris said before Zora had a chance to make up her mind. "Do you need my help to find where you're going?"

Zora shook her head. "No thank you. I'm sure there're others who need more guidance."

Iris studied her. "You'd be surprised." Then she dismissed Zora with a serene nod and honed in on a lost-looking man.

Talk about judgmental! Zora fumed. But she pushed thoughts of Iris to the back of her mind as she headed up the stairs to the second floor of the school. She checked out the numbers above the doors, until she found the right one. She pushed open the door and entered a world in which she felt entirely comfortable.

During the day it must have served as a Spanish classroom because there were posters of Machu Picchu and a map of Spain.

Zora maneuvered her way down the first aisle, nodding at her fellow students in the front-row seats. They seemed to be mostly women over fifty, casually but well dressed in cashmere turtleneck sweaters. Zora clutched at the open neck of her green anorak. Underneath she wore an oversize men's button-down Oxford cloth shirt, its sleeves rolled up. It was still wrinkled from her duffel bag, and ironing was something she avoided at all costs.

Everyone seemed to be talking loudly, mostly in American-accented Italian, though she thought she detected some other native inflections like Spanish and French.

Then she saw a face that she recognized. Julie Antonelli, Katarina's old childhood friend whom she'd seen only the day before yesterday at *Babička*'s. She was slouched down in a seat toward the back of the room and seemed intent on texting or checking email on her phone. Iris may have recommended the class to her, but it didn't appear that she had embraced the learning experience with much enthusiasm.

Maybe she was worried about her language skills? *Good,* thought Zora, ever the competitor. Julie—and the entire Antonelli family, for that matter—might know more about her daughter's secrets, but Zora was sure she could surpass her in the classroom. Zora's Italian might be a little rusty, but she doubted the good doctor had spent a sabbatical stay in Italy like she had. And she marched to the back of the room, no need of anyone's guidance at all, thank you very much.

JULIE SLUMPED IN the seat at the back of the class. Rubbing her forehead with her index finger, she glanced without much interest around the room. A dusty-looking piñata hung from the ceiling in one corner.

Her phone vibrated in the pocket of her jacket and she instantly liberated it, hoping against hope that some emergency needed her attention desperately. She glanced at the message. It was from Katarina, wondering who in her family was bugging her now.

Julie texted back.

The family's at bay, but I'm at an Adult School class. Iris Phox's idea. Could you have guessed?

She grinned and wished she'd felt happy instead of irritated at being railroaded into being there—all because of some stupid vase, and…all right…her impetuous behavior. Still, if Sebastiano Fonterra had been a more reasonable person instead of…instead of…frustratingly…ooh! She wanted to scream. How could someone be so pigheaded and so attractive at the same time?

It wasn't fair. Life wasn't fair. Why else had she been forced to go back to Grantham High School of all places? Unless you're the prom queen, who really wanted to go back to high school. She growled, and this time didn't bother to keep it inside.

"I'm sorry. Is this seat taken?" a woman asked.

Julie looked up. Speak of the devil. No, not Sebastiano Fonterra, but Katarina's mother, of all people. Julie straightened. "Zora, right?" She held her hand out to the empty seat, trying to be friendly, or at least her best imitation of friendliness.

"That's right. We saw each other at my mother's house." Zora took a stack of three-by-five cards and a pen out of little pockets in her knapsack. She looked ready to attack any and all subjects.

"Well, it's nice to recognize a face," Julie said. "Everyone else seems to know each other, not to mention belong to another world. Take the woman over there." She nodded toward an older woman dressed in pressed designer jeans. Her frosted hair was set off by mega-carat diamond stud earrings. "She's been going on about how sad she was to find out that George Clooney sold the villa next to hers on Lake Como. Apparently, I quote, 'He's so down-to-earth.'"

Zora laughed. "I can believe it. Only in Grantham." She held out a note card. "Can I lend you something to write on?"

"That's okay. I'm here under duress. If I really need to make any notes, I'll enter them into my phone." She waggled her iPhone in its black case, in keeping with her black crinkly jacket, black tank top and black pants.

The class door started to open, then stopped.

"At last, our teacher," Julie whispered without much enthusiasm. "I gather from all the conversation that they all lo-ove her. Gabriella this. Gabriella that. They even know that she went back to see her family in Modena over the summer."

The door opened wide.

"Unless our teacher's had a sex change operation, I don't think that's Gabriella," Julie observed. "On the other hand, if it is, it could really liven up the discussion."

She looked over at Zora, who seemed for all the world like she'd just seen a ghost.

The "regulars" started chattering away again, and Julie figured it was a false alarm. Just a late student. He looked vaguely familiar, like someone she'd seen at the dry cleaners or the supermarket—not that she had the chance to frequent the supermarket all that much.

So she stared at him, not quite placing the face and certainly not knowing the name. He was middle-aged, thin, like someone who kept himself in shape. His head was shaved, and an outline of stubble showed his red hair was starting to recede. His face was lined, not so much from laughter as from too much time in the sun, too many worries or too dissolute a lifestyle. Still, he looked pretty good for a middle-aged guy, and in his expensive leather bomber jacket—Julie pegged it for Façonnable—and faded designer jeans, he clearly had more than a passing acquaintance with high-end boutiques.

She turned to say something under her breath to Zora, but Katarina's mother continued to appear as if she'd gone into anaphylactic shock. "Zora?" she asked, concerned.

"Zora?" Mr. Bomber Jacket asked a beat later. He stopped in the aisle and stared at Zora.

"Paul?" Zora shook her head. "I never expected to see you here."

"I could say the same," he said, still standing.

For an awkward moment the two just studied each other. The only movement was a whole lot of rapid blinking. Finally, Julie spoke up. "There's a free seat over there if you want it." She pointed to the empty desk next to Zora.

"Oh, yeah, thanks." He swallowed and slipped into the vacant seat.

Julie stared at Zora, and when she finally looked up from straightening out her index cards and uncapping her pen, Zora acknowledged Julie's wide-eyed inquiring expression.

"Oh, sorry. I didn't realize you didn't know each other. Julie Antonelli, Paul Bedecker. Paul and I went to Grantham High School together." She held up a hand in his direction.

Paul waved a discreet hello. "That's right. Zora and I also went to Cornell together for a while."

"Before I transferred to Rutgers after my freshman year," she said, setting the record straight.

Another tense beat of silence followed.

"If you're Paul Bedecker, is that like Bedecker's Garden Center?" Julie asked, narrowing her eyes as she dredged up distant memories. "My dad always bought his tomato plants there, and I think you used to help out at the nursery a long time ago."

"That's right. I remember you now. Tall, skinny kid. Your father used to call you Giuli—"

The door opened with a start, catching Paul mid-word.

"*Buona sera, tutti. Scusatemi per essere in ritardo. Sono il vostro supplente.*"

There was a barely stifled collective groan from the in-crowd at the news. A substitute teacher!

Julie slumped as low as possible in her chair and covered her face with her hand.

It was Sebastiano Fonterra.

CHAPTER EIGHT

At the sound of the muffled groans, Sebastiano doubted yet again the wisdom of his agreeing to teach the class. Perhaps *agreeing* was not really the appropriate word. Railroaded. Yes, railroaded. He liked the sound of that. The image was almost—not quite—as painful as what he was experiencing now.

One thing was for sure. Iris Phox owed him big-time.

"Hello, everyone," he started again and reintroduced himself, this time in English, hoping against hope that this language would bring him a better response. "I'm Sebastiano Fonterra, and I will be substituting for Gabriella. I know you all were expecting to have her as your teacher, but unfortunately at the last minute she had to return to Italy because her father needed to have emergency heart surgery."

Immediately there were gasps.

"Is he all right?" "Do you have an address?" "Will she be checking her email?" "When will she be able to return?" "Soon?"

Not soon enough, Sebastiano thought. He forced a smile. "I don't have all the details, and I don't personally know Gabriella except through email. I'm just jumping in at the last minute as a favor to the Adult School, and

I presume she will be able to come back in a matter of weeks."

This last remark elicited an audible sigh.

"In the meantime, she explained the scope of the class, and how she normally emails around an article from the *Corriere della Sera* or another Italian newspaper, and then uses that as a starting point for discussion. She was kind enough to suggest an article for the first class, which I photocopied and brought with me." He slid his briefcase on top of the teacher's desk and unbuckled it.

He'd come directly from the office, having eaten half a plastic-wrapped turkey sandwich from the cafeteria at his desk. He couldn't make it through the second half. He still wore a suit and tie, which he now realized was much too formal. The few men seated in the front seemed to favor khaki pants and sweaters. In the back? He couldn't be sure but he thought he caught sight of Paul or at least his leather jacket.

He lifted the lid of his briefcase and fished out the material. "So, my thought was that I would pass around a pad and pen. You can sign your names and give me your email addresses." He leaned forward and passed them to the woman in the front row. "I also have the handouts, and I thought we could pass those around at the same time." Sebastiano circled the desk and gave the sheets to another woman.

"Grazie," she said, thanking him, with a confident American accent. She had a gravelly voice.

"And lastly, I have here a class list that I'll read off, so I can see who's here and also put some names to faces. But since you all are so busy writing, why don't I first tell you a little about myself? *In italiano adesso?*" he asked, switching to Italian.

He undid the button of his gray suit jacket and swung one leg over the desk, propping himself up on the corner. *"Mi chiamo Sebastiano Fonterra. Sono medico ed amministratore dell'ospedale."* Sebastiano explained he was a doctor and hospital administrator.

There were a few murmured remarks of recognition in response, and he soldiered on in Italian. "I was born in Milano and spent most of my childhood there, but also a number of years in the States when my father was transferred by the pharmaceutical company he worked for. I got my degree in medicine, but I became increasingly interested in how to provide medical care to a community, and switched to hospital management. I've been in Grantham a little less than a year, but I am very excited about the community and the future of the hospital. So that's all about me, and certainly enough of me talking."

He reached back and picked the class list off his desk. He began with the first name listed in alphabetical order. "Antonelli? Giulietta?" He raised his head and looked around.

"Giulietta?" he asked again, thinking the name was remarkably familiar even if he couldn't quite place it. He saw a hand tentatively rise from the back of the class.

"Mi chiama Giulietta." A woman's voice belonging to the hand identified itself softly in an excellent Italian accent.

Sebastiano stood up and peered over the carefully coiffed heads in the front row to get a better look. Which he did.

And nearly gagged.

And learned one very important lesson: never have even half a turkey sandwich before fulfilling a promise to Iris Phox.

JULIE WAITED UNTIL most of the students had filed out of the classroom to get up from her seat. She watched Zora fanatically pack each of her items into specific compartments of her knapsack. Paul, in the meantime, waited. He looked like he had every intention of leaving with Zora—something that seemed to have escaped her. Instead, Zora glanced at Julie. "I was wondering if you'd like to get a cup of coffee?"

Julie shook her head. "Sorry. I just need to talk to the teacher a moment. Maybe another time?"

"I'm free," Paul volunteered.

Zora barely acknowledged his offer. "Well, I guess we could always get something to go," she suggested without too much enthusiasm.

Julie could empathize with her lack of interest. The last thing in the world she wanted to do was confront Sebastiano, but that's just what she knew she had to do to clear things up. She gathered the sides of her loose-fitting jacket tightly about her body and trudged to the front of the room.

She waited while Sebastiano talked with Paul, their joking ending abruptly when Zora began making noises about having to leave. Paul signaled goodbye, and Sebastiano looked up to see who was next. His relaxed expression vanished.

Julie hesitantly sidled up. "Look, it's not like I really want to hang around after class, but I think we need to talk."

Sebastiano slipped the pads and handouts into his

briefcase and snapped it shut. He tilted his head and waited.

Julie didn't get the impression that he was overjoyed to have this little student-teacher conference. On the other hand, she couldn't help noticing that after his enthusiastic teaching for an hour and a half—including all the requisite arm motions one associates with Italians—his normally buttoned-up attire was now rumpled in an all-too appealing way. His tie was loosened and yanked to the side. The top two buttons of his dress shirt were undone. A lock of his ruthlessly barbered hair flopped roguishly over his forehead.

If he weren't he, and she weren't she, Julie couldn't help feeling…

"There was something that you wanted to say?" he prompted her.

Julie covered her mouth as she cleared her throat. "Listen, it's just that I didn't want you to get the impression I had anything to do with this…you…,me…the class." She pointed rapidly between the two of them. "Because, in point of fact, all the blame rests with Iris Phox."

"Yes, I'm beginning to realize that woman works in strange and mysterious ways."

"You're *only* beginning to think that?"

Sebastiano shrugged a laugh.

A very nice laugh, she couldn't help noting.

"When Iris lectured me on the wisdom of having you take a course at the Adult School as a way of saying you were sorry, I was imagining something more along the lines of…ah…" Sebastiano paused in thought.

"Anger management?" Julie suggested.

"I was trying to be more diplomatic. Perhaps, conflict resolution," he said with a smile.

She noticed how he wet his lips. "I guess advanced Italian conversation was the closest thing Iris could find," she said, enjoying the teasing undercurrents of the conversation.

"And you speak it very well," he complimented her. "You studied in school?"

"No, at home. We always spoke Italian. And my grandmother—*Nonna*—never really mastered English. I guess Iris Phox, being Iris Phox, realized all this before she enrolled me." Julie frowned. "Wait a minute. Don't tell me that your last-minute substitute teacher gig came about because—"

"Because Iris Phox recruited me? How else? She said they were desperate, and it wasn't as if I could say no."

Julie nodded. "So if I understand this right—she got me to take this class. Then she got you to teach it. So—"

"So she devised her own version of conflict resolution, all to the benefit of the Adult School," he said, finishing her sentence.

"Naturally, I would have said it all far more caustically, but then you are you, and—"

"You are you," he ended for her.

All very synergistic, one might even say simpatico, Julie thought. Which should have made her feel relaxed but somehow just heightened her discomfort. Or was it something else?

She rubbed her nose. "Whatever the ulterior motivations involved—" let alone the internal jitters she was feeling "—I just want to let you know that you did a really good job in class tonight."

Sebastiano lifted his briefcase off the desk and started to walk to the door. "Mostly it's just keeping out of the way to let people talk."

"No, it was more than that. You were very encouraging and made everybody feel comfortable." *Except me,* she could have added but didn't.

He stopped with his hand on the door. "To tell you the truth, I wasn't sure how much people wanted me to correct them. I didn't want to make them self-conscious about their speaking." He seemed genuinely concerned.

She joined him to leave. "I think you could correct people more. They all want to improve. And I think people liked that you encouraged them to contact you with suggestions for discussion topics."

A smile crossed Sebastiano lips. "Yes, I gathered quite quickly that politics is probably a no-no. Too many strong opinions." He turned toward the light switch. "By the way, your bruise is looking better."

Luckily, Julie wasn't prone to blushing. Not that she would have, but…

He switched off the lights. And the two stood in the darkness of the classroom, shadowy figures, as light filtered in from the hallway fluorescents. Without the harsh overhead light, Julie's other senses were instantly more alert—to the sound of his breathing, the light, citrusy smell of his cologne.

"So, I guess next week then?" he said.

She concentrated on forming one word at a time. "You bet. Iris already warned me that attendance would be taken regularly. So I guess if I want to stay out of the doghouse, I'd better show."

"Her doghouse or mine?" he asked.

She tasted her shallow breaths. "I'm not sure. They're both pretty scary."

CHAPTER NINE

"I'M GLAD YOU MADE IT to the meeting tonight," Sebastiano said to Paul. It was Thursday, A.A. night.

The two men sat at an impossibly small table at Bean World, the local coffee shop that was beyond cool. And even though it was nine-thirty at night, the café was still packed—students and graduate students from the university taking study breaks and young singles discreetly trying to hit on each other over their iPhones and laptops. The moms-with-strollers demographic was safely tucked in bed or watching some PBS documentary on the plight of the rain forest. Or so they liked to think. Sebastiano was sure that astutely fed the right questions, they'd confess to being addicts of *Dancing with the Stars*.

"Yeah, the writing's suddenly going well, more than well. So I thought I'd take a break and come to the meeting," Paul replied. He nursed his cup of decaf.

Sebastiano finished his double-shot espresso in one gulp, yet another in a long line of coffees he'd drunk all day. He didn't do decaf. He also didn't do sleep.

"Something inspired you?" he asked, crossing his legs to the side. The tip of his brown suede shoe touched the messenger bag of a young woman. Her dyed black hair was cut to brush her shoulders and a severe layer of bangs followed the line of her eyebrows. The black tresses matched her tight sleeveless top and hip-hugging skirt, its hem stopping just short of a pair of laced-up boots.

She looked at the foot, annoyed, then glanced at its owner. Her frown turned to a welcoming smile.

Sebastiano shifted his foot and looked away. He was usually attracted to women with long hair. Yet somehow in the past week, that had changed. Now short, spiky hair captured his fancy. He had even awakened from one of his typically light sleeps after dreaming of watching a woman retreat from his car, only to be enveloped by a thick low-lying mist so that only the top of her head was visible, her short dark hair getting smaller and smaller as she retreated into the distance. He didn't have the faintest idea what the dream meant, but he had a pretty good idea whose hair it had been. And yes, if memory served him correctly, he'd also woken with something else besides an image.

"It wasn't so much a something as a someone who inspired me," Paul said in answer to Sebastiano's question. He nervously tapped his fingertips on the rim of his coffee cup. "You know how I told you that coming home raised some issues for me that I needed to address? That I thought they'd be the key to this book I'm writing?"

Sebastiano nodded. "So tell me, who is this someone who has proved so inspiring?"

"Zora Zemanova."

"The woman in the class who sat in the back?" Across from Julie, he could have added, but didn't.

"That's right." There was a long pause. "We used to be an item."

Sebastiano lowered his chin. "When was that?"

Paul waved his hand. His nails were bitten to the

quick. He wore a braided leather-and-aluminum bracelet on his wrist, all very high-tech, Japanese-looking. "We were classmates here in high school, and then we went away to college. That's when things started to happen. The God's honest truth? She was my first. And you know what they say? You always remember your first."

"Do they now?" Sebastiano recalled his first. Raffaela. How she had smiled nervously as they lay together in the long grass in a valley near her parents' rustic country retreat. Another lifetime ago.

"So you're thinking of seeing her again?" Sebastiano asked.

"Kind of. I tried to have coffee with her after class yesterday, but she begged off. She said she needed time to think about it. It's complicated. Our breakup wasn't exactly amicable. Needless to say, I was the one who screwed up. Typical idiot male."

Sebastiano could identify. "So what are you going to do about it?"

"I'm not sure. I mean, after all this time to suddenly see her in class. It was like…pow!…a sudden jolt to the old solar plexus. And the weird thing is, over the weekend, while I'm sitting with my dad drinking a cup of warm milk and honey—his version of chicken soup for the soul, which to tell you the truth, I'm kind of growing fond of—my dad starts telling me about her kid, a daughter, Zora's daughter, coming into the nursery to buy some holly bushes for their yard. I don't know why, but it takes me a while to realize that this 'daughter' is a woman, a young woman…say thirty, early thirties."

Paul hurriedly drank the rest of his by now tepid coffee. "So, that got me wondering. Have you met her?"

"Who? The daughter?" Sebastiano asked.

"Yeah, her name is Katarina."

Sebastiano narrowed his eyes and ran through the extensive list of names he kept mentally ever at the ready. "Oh, of course. Katarina Zemanova and her husband, Ben Brown, a former investment guru who now runs his own charity. And I believe she's a financial advisor of some sort to senior citizens. I've talked with them several times. Very nice couple." What he didn't say was that he'd been courting them for a large donation for the new hospital. He just needed to find the right project to excite them.

"Anything else about Katarina?"

That he'd seen her having coffee with Julie Antonelli at the hospital on occasion? He shook his head. This conversation was *not* about his own current fixation. Instead he attempted to focus on Paul's question. "Not that I can think of. Is there something in particular you want to know? I thought it was the mother you were interested in?"

"It's about Zora *and* Katarina."

"Now I'm confused."

"When we were in college? Zora and me? As far as I know, I was her only lover. I could be wrong, but I'm ninety-nine percent sure."

Sebastiano didn't speak. He didn't need to. The direction the conversation had suddenly taken was about as far from his own preoccupation as imaginably possible. Besides, he could already guess where Paul was going—that in all likelihood, Paul was Katarina's father.

Paul gripped the edges of the table with both hands. "I can't believe what I've missed out on. What was taken from me! Only now, instead of getting drunk and running away from the truth, I've got to pull myself together and deal with it. I need to confront Zora."

Sebastiano schooled his features to remain impassive. Because he knew exactly what Paul was talking about. And in the old days, he would have also run away and grabbed the vodka.

Only now what he wanted to do was run to Julie, confide to her about Paul and eventually pour out his own problems. Not that he ever would. But he could think it.

CHAPTER TEN

"I DON'T UNDERSTAND WHY you'd want to avoid seeing him," Julie's friend Sarah said. Sarah was a physical therapist whose practice was affiliated with the hospital. The two had met each other through work, then found out they had a mutual friend in Katarina. Sarah had even ended up marrying an old high school acquaintance of Julie's, Iris Phox's son, Hunt. The whole thing was *so* Grantham. There were no degrees of separation when it came to life in a small town.

It was midmorning on Friday, and Julie had just finished rounds before heading to her office for her day's appointments. Sarah was about to start her sessions with the hospital patients who needed therapy. When things weren't too crazy, the two had a standing date for coffee every week at this time in the hospital lounge.

Coffee for Julie was a double-shot espresso. Sarah had an herbal tea, a habit she had developed after giving up caffeine while pregnant and later nursing baby Natalie—the same Natalie who would be the recipient of the famed needlepoint Christmas stocking.

"I don't know what you're talking about," Julie replied. She swirled the last bit of coffee around her tiny paper cup and downed it in one swallow. She had decided to play dumb.

"Don't play dumb," Sarah said. She switched the tag

of the tea bag to the other side of her cup. "Sebastiano Fonterra is the most exciting thing to happen to this hospital since computerized record-keeping, and, frankly, a whole lot better to look at at the end of a long day."

Sarah raised both eyebrows. "Excuse me, but I thought you were a happily married woman."

"I *am* a happily married woman, but that doesn't make me blind. Besides, from what I can see, he's doing a damn good job, between managing this place and then getting this new building done. I mean, if he can make my mother-in-law *and* me happy, he must have something magical about him. In addition to those dreamy brown eyes, of course."

"Hazel. Hazel eyes," Julie corrected.

"Are they now?" Sarah lifted her cup and blew on it to cool the tea. "So is it true you and the hazel-eyed doctor came to blows?"

"Absolutely not!" Julie tossed her cup into the corner wastebasket. Nothing but net. "Who told you that anyway? Katarina?"

"No, one of the receptionists at the main desk saw you leave with an ice pack on your cheek. And you don't usually wear foundation, so you must be trying to cover up something."

Sarah lightly touched her cheek. "It's not really foundation. It's tinted moisturizer. Anyway, we only came to verbal blows. And the ice pack was merely a way of him ministering to my needs."

"His words had that much sting?"

Julie laughed. "No, the bruise was a stupid accident. Anyway, I think our little tiff—"

"Tiff? Is that how you describe it? The high school volunteer, who was pushing a mail cart outside the office, said he could hear you two arguing from the other end of the hallway." Sarah took a fortifying sip of tea. "Then I heard from my mother-in-law when she came over for dinner that you smashed a vase."

"It was only a chip, a tiny one."

"She also said that you and he had 'deep, though reconcilable, philosophical differences.' That's a direct quote, by the way."

"Well, Iris appears to have worked her diplomatic charms because she has managed to corral both of us into an Italian class at the Adult School—me as a student and him as a substitute teacher," Julie elaborated.

"That sounds like my mother-in-law. When in doubt, solve the world's problems via the Grantham Adult School." She leaned on one elbow. "So, tell me. How is he?"

"How is he?" She left the question floating in the air as she found herself fantasizing about Sebastiano, standing in the rain, wearing his customary dress shirt. Only it was unbuttoned far too low to be respectable, and the material was plastered to his body, outlining every muscle, and, being a doctor, she could name every one....

"That good, huh?" Sarah asked with a laugh.

"Oh, this is ridiculous." Julie gathered herself. "Anyway, why all these questions about Sebastiano Fonterra when the real topic of conversation is what you think of my latest hair iteration?" She shook her head and blinked her eyes dramatically. In her frenzy to forget the unfortunate events of the week, she'd put several magenta streaks in her dark brunette bangs. That was in between cleaning out her medicine cabinet, refrigerator and bedroom closet.

Sarah gulped the rest of her tea and gathered up her clipboard with her empty cup. "It was only years of friendship and tact that kept me from commenting." She stood. "I gotta go. But before I do, just tell me. He was that good?"

Julie knew immediately why Sarah's physiotherapy patients responded to her programs. Beneath that Midwestern wholesomeness laid the indefatigable soul of a drill sergeant.

"All right. As much as it pains me to say, he was that good. No, he was great. He was a natural teacher—clear, funny, interesting, a good listener. He had all those middle-aged Granthamites who vacation on the Amalfi Coast eating out of his hand."

"The question is, whose hand were you eating out of?" Sarah laughed. She looked back as she stepped off the raised platform of the lounge area into the main lobby, turned abruptly...and barely sidestepped an older African-American man coming into the lobby.

"Oh, my gosh, Rufus, I'm so sorry," she apologized. "That's all we need. Accidents in the hospital. With a former patient no less."

"Not to worry, Sarah. Thanks to your ministrations, my hip replacement is better than ever. Here, watch." Rufus walked confidently ahead, then swiveled on one heel to turn. He held up his hands triumphantly before heading back. "See, a regular Fred Astaire. I've even taken Estelle out dancing," he said with a laugh, referring to his wife of fifty-seven years. "And you'll be pleased to know that I signed up for the light water aerobics course at the Adult School."

"I'm glad to hear it. And needless to say, I can personally vouch for the effectiveness of that course." Sarah had met Hunt in the same course almost a year ago. She smiled at the memory, tilting her chin up to make eye contact.

Rufus might have been in his late seventies, but his back was ramrod-straight. "Well, I've got to keep fit if I'm going to keep teaching the Adult School's dog obedience course. I've got a full class this semester, including one very active Husky."

Sarah laughed. "Why don't you trade Adult School stories with Julie?" She pointed her out at the table in the lounge. Then she patted Rufus's arm. His old brown barn coat was meticulously washed and ironed, but the patches on the elbows and the leather trim around the edge of the sleeves were testament to its long and well-loved life. "Listen, I'd like nothing better than to stay and talk, but duty calls." She squeezed his arm and headed for the elevator bank.

Rufus turned to Julie and waved. "Got a few minutes?"

Julie looked at her watch. It was the same gold-tone Citizen watch that *Nonna* had given her when Julie had graduated from Grantham High School. God knows how many overtime hours her grandmother must have worked to pay for it. Katarina still remembered her grandmother's words.

"I do not know about all this basketball business," *Nonna* had said in Italian, her customary pessimism seeping into every word.

"It's a full athletic scholarship to U Conn—a powerhouse for women's basketball. And Coach Auriemmo is a legend," Julie remembered snapping back.

Nonna had shaken her head. "At least he's Italian. Just remember—someday you won't play this basketball anymore, and out in the real world, you'll always need to know the time. Some things I know. Now give your *Nonna* a kiss."

Julie smiled at the memory and waved to Rufus. "So, I gather we're supposed to trade Adult School stories? You've got a feisty husky in your obedience class?"

"Not as feisty as I heard you were in Dr. Fonterra's office last week. Is it true you threw a paperweight at him?" Rufus asked. He slipped into the chair next to Julie.

Julie cringed. "Does the whole world know about that meeting? And it was a vase, not a paperweight, that I happened to knock over by accident, not anywhere near him, I swear." She held up her right hand. "And in my defense, I was functioning on very little sleep and high doses of stress after a difficult delivery."

"So Iris told me."

Julie leaned her elbow on the table and rested her mouth in her hand. Then she let her hand drop to the table. "I should have known. Did she also tell you that she made me take an Italian class at the Adult School that Sebastiano just happens to be teaching?"

"And would you believe that I can also tell you what article you talked about in the first class?"

Julie looked taken aback. "Iris is powerful, but I never knew she was clairvoyant."

Rufus chuckled. He rubbed the tip of an index finger on the laminate surface of the table. It was a speckled gray-green, the au courant color palette of hospitals these days, it seemed. A thin gold wedding band hung loosely from the dark, wrinkled skin of his third finger. "Iris has many qualities, but as far as I know, only your grandmother has a sixth sense. No, the reason I know is simple. Lena Zemanova takes tai chi with my wife Estelle, and she told Estelle that her daughter, Zora, had told her all about the class and a Dr. Fonterra. She also mentioned a student, an old friend of her daughter's named Giulietta, who sat in the back and spoke Italian very well."

Julie shook her head. "You call that simple?"

"And something else you might find amusing," Rufus added. "Lena said she thought Zora was mighty teed off that your Italian was so fluent. Seems she expected to be top dog."

"Please, an Adult School class is hardly the place to get competitive. Besides, anyone who grew up in my house *had* to speak Italian. It was a matter of survival."

"I know what you mean. Way back, it was the same thing around this neighborhood." He pointed outside the picture windows. "There used to be a large Italian community right around the hospital. I remember your grandfather's candy shop on Whalen Avenue. Your grandmother used to give my son Billy an extra free licorice every time he came by."

"*Nonna* gave away something for free?" Julie was amazed.

Rufus chuckled. "You just need to know how to sweet-talk her."

Julie nodded. "Well, sweet-talking was never one of my strong points."

Rufus burst into louder laughter. "Which is why I like you so much, Julie. You call it like it is." He switched his expression to one of seriousness. "I was just coming from a meeting with Sebastiano at the Grantham Club before starting my volunteer shift at the front desk.

You know, the neighborhood is a bit nervous about the planned hospital expansion—the whole larger structure instead of houses and lawns."

"I know."

"Anyway, in the course of the discussion, your name came up."

Julie rolled her eyes. "I bet it did."

"You'd be surprised. Sebastiano said he was impressed with your conviction about the importance of the community clinic and its availability to the residents of the neighborhood."

Julie sat up straight. "He did?"

Rufus nodded. "He told me that he followed up with the woman whose baby you delivered to understand her circumstances better."

"You're kidding me?"

"Not at all. As an immigrant himself, Sebastiano understands your concern." Rufus held up his hand when Julie started to say something. "Hold your horses there, girl. Not all of us can talk as quickly as you."

"Rufus, of course. Please, go ahead," Julie apologized. "Besides, I understand your concerns about any changes to the neighborhood. My family, like most of the Italians who came to Grantham, first lived in this area, too. Even today, it has a special place in their hearts."

"As well it should. It represents their first step on building a better life in America. Italians came here when the university hired them as stonemasons. They saw a chance to build a better life—literally. And look how many saw their dreams come true. I bet your grandmother is proud as punch to have a granddaughter who's a doctor."

Julie shrugged philosophically. "She's delighted that I'm a doctor, for sure, but totally dismayed that I'm still single. But tell me, Rufus, other than providing a little history lesson about the town, what are you really driving at?"

"Maybe after my meeting I just needed to think out loud. In the past we created safety nets to help new immigrants in town—Clara's House was founded to help new Italian immigrants adjust to their new homes, learn English, learn their legal rights and integrate themselves into the community. In the sixties, the Y helped with the influx of Vietnamese immigrants and the prejudices that followed due to the war."

"But those issues don't exist anymore," Julie protested.

"Yes, and no. Grantham may seem like an all-inclusive bastion, but just remember, until about sixty years ago, the public schools here were still segregated. Problems of inequality have existed and will always exist." Rufus stood. "I'm just asking you to think about what I've said in terms of the neighborhood here around the hospital, the neighborhood where your family first came when it sought to make a better life, the neighborhood where my family has lived for more than two hundred years, and where folks from Guatemala and Mexico now want to make a home for their families."

"But I'm a doctor, not a politician," Julie replied.

"Think of it this way. Sometimes in order to treat the patient you have to deal with the whole community. I brought up the same issue with Sebastiano and now I bring it up with you. Just food for thought, mind you." Rufus peered at her closely. "You know, you can hardly see where he hit you, by the way." He fastened the buttons of his jacket.

Julie rolled her eyes in exasperation. Did no one listen? "Nobody hit me—nobody meaning Sebastiano or anyone else. I don't know why everybody and his little brother, cousin or aunt perpetuate these rumors."

"Ah, if only you had the right pipeline into the community." He let his words hang in the air before stepping down to the lobby.

Julie watched him greet a few more people as he headed along the main hallway of the hospital toward the information desk. Then she rose.

Great. All she needed was another responsibility. On top of working nonstop, she was now supposed to solve the problems of the neighborhood? Because the really infuriating thing? She was already hooked. With her deep sense of guilt, she was bound to try.

Guilt. It hung around her neck like an albatross. She'd like to blame her Italian Catholic heritage, but the truth was she had only herself to blame. That one fateful night the fall of her freshman year—her birthday, to be exact—when one of her teammates was killed in the car Julie was driving. The truck had come out of nowhere, broadsiding the vehicle and driving the passenger door halfway into the driver's side. The same accident had injured another teammate's legs, making walking difficult and playing basketball impossible.

Julie had quit the team. She didn't care that that meant she'd lose her athletic scholarship. She got a job after classes instead. She didn't mind hard work. In fact, she craved it. Only when she was working hard did her mind switch off from the horrors of that night.

She didn't need counselors to tell her that there was

nothing she could do to change the past. But she *did* know that she could do something about protecting people in the future. With the same intensity she'd used to play basketball, Julie concentrated on her studies, taking an overload of premed courses. Her grades skyrocketed. Professors asked if she wanted to work in their labs. She worked in two. She'd applied for and won an academic scholarship. Determined to reach her goal of becoming an obstetrician and gynecologist, she graduated in three years, living on no sleep and Diet Coke.

Her mother protested. *Nonna* had muttered fateful words. Julie had ignored them. "It will be good practice for med school," she'd responded.

She didn't mention anything about not being able to sleep. That if she did manage to sleep, she invariably woke bathed in sweat, her heart racing.

No, she didn't tell anyone. Just kept her head down, dedicating herself to her studies. She'd been pleased though not overly surprised when she had her choice of med schools. She'd even been accepted to Yale Medical School, but knew she couldn't stay in Connecticut any longer. She needed distance.

In the end, she chose the University of Pennsylvania to be near her family, for good and bad. Opening up a practice in Grantham had been almost serendipitous. The obstetrician who had delivered her had looked her up, letting her know that he was retiring and interested in selling his practice. She jumped at the prospect.

She worked hard to gain her patients' confidence and attend to their needs, and she was proud that she'd never lost one. But the possibility always loomed in her mind, and it made her more obsessed than ever—with work, and when she wasn't working, needlepoint. A lot of needlepoint. In fact, if she had ever had the inclination to plot her productivity—and, okay, her manic impulses—on some sort of graph, she wouldn't have been surprised to find that it peaked every year around this time. Her birthday. Duh…

She glanced at her watch. She had a patient in about an hour and fifteen minutes.

Julie got up and headed toward the revolving door. She waited while an aid pushed a patient in a wheelchair. The middle-aged woman was dressed in a loosely fitting top and pants, and had a windbreaker draped over her shoulders to ward off the early fall chill. A bunch of gaily-colored balloons was tied to the arm of the chair. Whatever she'd been in for clearly had a happy ending. Julie could hear her tell the hospital volunteer that she'd spotted her husband in their Subaru station wagon pulling up to the curb.

Julie smiled. That's what she wanted in the world— happy endings.

The sound of electronic marimbas erupted from the pocket of her jacket, a knitted asymmetrical cardigan that she'd bought just last weekend. It was wildly expensive, but she hadn't been able to resist. *And it's not a birthday present to myself,* she'd told herself at the table. She never celebrated that occasion, not after what happened with the car crash.

Julie didn't have any patients in labor right now, but that didn't mean problems couldn't arise anyway. She looked at the caller ID—her parents' home phone. Normally, her father and mother would be at the garage during the day, and her grandmother never called. She answered immediately, not knowing what to make of it.

"Giulietta," her father spoke rapidly. "I'm sorry to bother you at work."

"No problem, Dad. I don't see any patients for about another hour. What is it? Is something wrong?"

"It's *Nonna*. She's complaining about pains in her chest."

Julie stepped away from the door. "Get her to the E.R. right away."

"Impossible. You know *Nonna*. She refuses to budge from her chair in the living room."

Julie nodded along with his narrative. Her heartbeat raced. "Okay, okay, just give me a few minutes because I biked to worked today. On top of which, I'm at the hospital now, so I'll need to pop across the road and grab my bag from the office before I head over." Most of the doctors had their offices in a building that faced the entrance to the hospital on the other side of the circular drive.

"*Grazie, Giulietta*. I knew I could count on you," he said anxiously before hanging up.

Julie sprinted to the revolving door, ready to barge ahead of the elderly and infirm if necessary.

"Dr. Antonelli," a voice came from directly behind her.

Julie pretended not to hear and slipped into the first segment of the revolving door that opened up before her. She stared straight ahead and shuffled impatiently as the automatic turning mechanism advanced at a glacial pace.

"Excuse me." The words accompanied the sound of light, audible breathing next to her shoulder. Someone else was in the door along with her.

CHAPTER ELEVEN

WITHOUT TURNING SHE knew who it was.

Sebastiano leaned his head toward her as they shuffled forward onto the sidewalk. "If I didn't know better, I'd think you were purposely avoiding me," he said. "Hold on…I do know better. You *were* trying to avoid me."

Julie frowned. "Listen, I don't have time to argue one way or the other."

"Wait a minute." Sebastiano held up his hand. "I need to mark this down on my calendar." He pulled out his BlackBerry. "On September twenty-second, Julie Antonelli did not argue a point." He tapped in quickly and expertly.

Julie gave him a withering stare. "If you stopped me to tell me about your meeting with Rufus, he already talked to me about doing something more for the neighborhood, so you don't need to go into that."

"Actually, I'm glad he talked to you about that, but that's not why I stopped you." He appeared annoyingly upbeat.

Julie crossed her arms. "Can it wait? I'm really in a rush here."

"Actually, it can't really. I can walk with you if that works?"

"It doesn't. Unless you think you can fit on my bicycle handlebars!"

SEBASTIANO HAD HAD strange offers before, but this was a first. "How big is your bike?" he asked.

Julie made a sour face and charged across the pavement to her office building. She put her hand on the entrance door. "Look, my father called, saying that my grandmother seemed to be in some kind of distress, her heart possibly."

Sebastiano pulled up next to her. "She's coming to the hospital?"

"No, *Nonna* has a mind of her own."

"Is she far?"

"Not far. Over by the shopping center. She lives with my parents. It should take me ten, fifteen minutes to bike."

"My car's quicker. It's in the hospital garage and my bag's right in it."

Julie shook her head. "Really, there's no need."

"I'm a doctor."

"I am, too."

"My field is cardiology."

"True, but…"

Sebastiano held up his hand. "Do you really want to waste more time arguing?"

"No," Julie admitted.

Sebastiano led the way. As CEO, he had a plum parking spot right up front.

Julie stood by the front passenger door of his BMW 3 Series sedan, her lips pursed as he used his key fob to unlock the doors.

"What?" Sebastiano opened his door and gazed at her over the roof of the car.

She shook her head. "Never mind, nothing." She got in and fastened her seat belt.

Sebastiano slipped into his seat and started up the engine. He glanced across and saw Julie still frowning. "What now?"

"Your seat belt?"

"I'm going to do it. I just wanted to get the car started."

"Sorry. I'm just a little touchy when it comes to automobile safety," Julie said. She rubbed her fingers together nervously.

He studied her before backing out of the space, then asked, "So where exactly does your family live?"

Julie rattled off the name of the street. "It's between North Henderson and Southerland."

"I think I know it. It's a cut-through below the shopping center, right?"

"That's the one."

Sebastiano looked for oncoming traffic before taking a left into the road. They zipped soundlessly past the high school where a few students were hanging around outside. Then it was a right at the light before turning left into her parents' street.

Julie held her hand up. "It's four houses down on the left. The white split level with the red shutters."

Sebastiano pulled into the double driveway behind a Ford Explorer. A maroon Honda Accord was parked to the right. He turned off the engine and nodded toward the house. There was a middle-aged man standing at the front door. The familial resemblance was unmistakable, Sebastiano thought, minus red highlights, of course.

Julie didn't wait. She unsnapped her seat belt and reached for the door handle.

Sebastiano touched her arm, holding her up.

"What? You and I both know that quick action might be necessary," she snapped impatiently.

"Yes, but sometimes it doesn't hurt to take a deep breath."

"I don't understand?" She reached for the door handle again.

"At the moment, my concern is for the doctor."

JULIE DIDN'T BOTHER TO analyze his words let alone grace them with a response. She hurried up the concrete path that her father and second brother, Frank, had redone a few years ago. "Dad, where's *Nonna?* Is she all right?" She planted a quick peck on his cheek.

"She's fine. Sitting in the living room, probably watching out the window as we speak." Luigi "Lou" Antonelli arched his neck to the side to see around Julie. In his mid-fifties, he still had a powerful, fireplug build. But at barely five foot six, his only daughter towered over him. Not that his shorter height diminished in any way the capable authority that his body seemed to radiate. He could be quite intimidating to all—except his immediate family, who knew he was just a pussycat.

Lou nodded toward Sebastiano, who stood down from the front stoop. "You decided to bring in reinforcements?"

"No...yes..." Julie shook her head. "Dad, this is Dr. Fonterra, the head of the hospital. He offered to help out."

"Not the same one you...ah...had little *disputa* with?"

Julie rolled her eyes. "I don't believe it! Everyone seems to know everything in this town! Can we just forget about that and let me see *Nonna?*"

Julie's father stepped back and let her pass through the door.

Sebastiano stepped up to the stoop and nodded. *"Signore, con piace,"* he said, acknowledging him politely.

"Dottore Fonterra," Lou said formally.

"Sebastiano, please. My field was cardiology and I thought perhaps…" He held up his doctor's bag.

Lou held out his hand toward the living room, which was separated from the entryway by a half wall.

"Nonna, ecco il dottore Fonterra, il primario dell' ospedale e un cardiologo," Luigi repeated Sebastiano's professional pedigree to his mother.

Carmella Antonelli was seated stiffly in a high-backed chair upholstered in gold velvet. Her hands clutched the arms. Her small slippers barely reached the floor. She wore an immaculate dark-gray skirt and white short-sleeved blouse.

Carmella lifted her discerning chin. The bifocal lenses of her glasses with their plastic pale pink frames covered her face from eyebrows to cheekbones. Her short salt-and-pepper hair was combed in the same bob she'd worn since the fifties. *"Un esperto nelle malattia del cuore?"* An expert in illnesses of the heart? she asked.

Julie knelt down and took her grandmother's wrist. She felt for a pulse. "So, *dimmi, Nonna. Ch'è succeso?* Tell me, Grandma, what happened?"

Carmella shrugged with weariness and reluctance. "Just some pains… In my chest… But they have passed now," she explained in the Abruzzese dialect of her home in Italy. She turned to Sebastiano, who walked in his socks across the cream-colored wall-to-wall carpet.

He had left his shoes by the front entryway. Then she
eyed Julie critically. "He not only had time to see me,
but he had the good manners to take off his shoes."

"See, I bring you only the best, *Nonna,*" Julie said
in a good-humored tone.

Sebastiano rested his medical bag on the coffee table.
Its flared legs and rounded corners had gilded detailing
worked into the wooden carving. "*Signora,* if we could
examine you, with all discretion, of course," Sebastiano
said in Italian. "We could go to your bedroom, if that
would make you feel more comfortable?"

Carmella held up her hand. "No, here is fine."

Just then, Julie's mother walked into the room from
the dining room. She wiped her hands on a dishcloth.
"Oh, my gosh, I didn't hear you come in. I was in the
kitchen. *Nonna* insisted it was nothing, but naturally we
were worried. So of course we called you, Giulietta."
She stopped. "I'm sorry. I didn't know we had company.
I could put some coffee on, if you think that would be
good? I even have some *pignoli* biscuits from the Tren-
ton Farmer's Market. They're not as good as the ones I
make, but they will do."

Julie looked up. "That's all right, Mom. Don't worry
about the coffee and stuff. This is Dr. Fonterra from the
hospital. He's here for *Nonna,* too."

Sebastiano glanced over long enough to smile.
"How do you do, Mrs. Antonelli. You know, if you
get a chance, coffee would be wonderful, thank you."
He turned to Julie and whispered, "One fewer worried
family member, don't you think?"

She nodded when she realized he was actually trying
to help.

Sebastiano smiled at *Nonna* and spoke Italian in a

calming voice. "Now tell me, what type of pain was it?" He discreetly unbuttoned *Nonna*'s top shirt button and applied the stethoscope. He and Julie asked questions and worked together.

"I guess I'll get the coffee then?" Julie's mother scrunched the tea towel between her hands. "Espresso for everyone?"

Lou shrugged. "Why not?"

"None for *Nonna*, Mom," Julie insisted. "I don't want her eating or drinking anything until we know what's going on." Her mother nodded and marched back to the kitchen, still working the hand towel as she went.

"Only for you would I give up coffee," *Nonna* complained, speaking in heavily accented English, a language she rarely admitted to knowing.

"You will have many opportunities for coffee," Sebastiano said, placating her. "Just this once, humor us— especially Julie." He winked at the older woman.

"I don't need humoring," Julie retorted. "Just cooperation from everybody." She shot Sebastiano a lethal glare, then reached in his bag for the blood pressure cuff.

Sebastiano appeared not to hear. He stood up and asked *Nonna* to lean forward so he could listen to her heart from behind.

"*Voi siete Bastion contrari,*" chuckled *Nonna*.

Lou laughed.

Sebastiano pressed his finger to his ears.

"*Mi scusi*—excuse me," *Nonna* said, now being quiet.

"What was that you said, *Nonna?* Something about us being opposing *Bastion?* I don't know that expression." Julie noted the blood pressure readings. Then she took the flashlight from his bag and checked her grandmother's eyes. "Okay, look this way," she ordered, pointing to the side.

"It means you're always arguing. Bastion, Sebastiano—they're the same. A good play on words, don't you think?" Lou said from across the room. He didn't bother to hide his amusement.

"Terrific. Two doctors make a house call and you can make jokes?" Julie exclaimed. She pointed in the opposite direction, and *Nonna* alertly followed with her eyes. "I don't know what that says about the medical profession."

"Maybe I am not talking about the medical profession?" *Nonna* said under her breath. Her eyes flicked toward Sebastiano.

Julie narrowed her vision. "I think *Nonna* is just fine." She leaned close to her grandmother and whispered, "You planned this somehow, didn't you?"

Her grandmother looked away, leaving Julie wondering.

Sebastiano knelt in front of her and spoke in Italian. "Your vital signs all appear normal now, and you say it's been more than an hour since you experienced chest pains. I don't think there is any reason for immediate concern, but I want to be on the safe side. I'd like you to come in for some tests as soon as possible, this afternoon, in fact. When was the last time you had a physical?"

Nonna shook her head. "My doctor, he doesn't know anything. I want you," she said emphatically.

"I'm not currently practicing because I now spend all my time as an administrator," he said.

"I can give you the name of the best cardiologist in town," Julie said.

Sebastiano pulled out his cell phone. "I know the one. I'll call him right now."

Nonna nodded wisely to Julie. "*Tu vedi.* A man of action."

"I was happy to call, too, you know."

Sebastian waited for the connection. "You don't always have to do everything."

"Excuse me. Was I asking for help?" Julie snapped back.

Sebastiano held up his hand and turned away to talk in the phone.

His lack of confrontation galled her even more. "Why did I let him talk me into driving me here?" she grumbled.

Lou laughed. "*Hai ragione, Nonna*—you're right, *Nonna*. They're always arguing."

"SO, YOU'RE COMING FOR dinner on Wednesday, right?" Julie's mother, Angela, asked her. This was after Julie had called to push back her first appointment by a half hour and her mother had managed to ply everyone with strong espresso and cookies. Her mother had used the painted Deruta demitasse cups and matching tray that was usually reserved for holidays and special occasions, a fact that Lou had mentioned out loud, much to Julie's embarrassment.

That had been after *Nonna* had eaten the cookie that Sebastiano had not-so-discreetly slipped to her.

Julie shook her head. "I'm not sure I can make it, Mom." Wednesday was the day after her birthday. Even though she figured the invitation was for nothing more than a simple family meal—if there was such a thing as a *simple* family meal as far as her mother was concerned—she didn't want to take any chances that it might be a surprise party. She didn't want to go there. Couldn't. Time did not heal all wounds. Not for her at least.

"Thanks, Mom, but I don't think I can. You see…you see…I have Italian at the Adult School." Never would she have thought of a standing appointment with Sebastiano Fonterra as a gift from heaven. "That's right. And Dr. Fonterra here is the teacher. So, I couldn't possibly skip out."

"We eat late anyway. Surely you could come after class? And Sebastiano, of course, too," her mother persisted. After the first espresso they had switched to a first-name basis, and Julie had noticed that she repeatedly patted her hair.

In truth, Julie had always thought her parents were still a very handsome couple, and her mother looked much better since she'd started buying her clothes at Tyrell's, the fancy women's clothing shop in town—on sale, of course.

"If you don't mind having simple Italian food, that is," Angela added shyly.

"*E le mie polpettine in brodo*—and my little meatballs in broth," *Nonna* announced in a voice that brooked no compromise.

Julie moaned inwardly. You'd have thought the Pope had come for a visit the way everyone was carrying on.

"I'd be delighted, Angela," Sebastiano said, "as long as I'm not putting you out."

"Don't be ridiculous," Lou said, putting his cup on

the tray. "It's not like my wife isn't used to cooking for men. Julie has three brothers, you know."

Julie closed her eyes. "Tell me that Dom, Frank, Joey and *their* families are not coming, as well?"

Angela clapped her hands. "What a good idea! I hadn't thought of that."

If only she were eating a *pignoli* nut cookie. She could have had an excuse to gag.

Julie felt a pat on her knee. She stole a glance over at Sebastiano. He was busy responding to a question by her father about his BMW. She peeked down and recognized the veined hand immediately.

Nonna. She should have known. She squared her shoulders and smiled at her grandmother.

Carmella patted again, then leaned back in stately fashion against her golden upholstered throne. "*Senti il mio canarino?*—do you hear my canary?" She cupped her hand to her ear. "*Ti parla, dicendoti di ascoltare*—it's speaking to you, telling you to listen."

True enough, *Nonna*'s pet bird, Caruso, could be heard warbling away from his cage upstairs in her bedroom. Her grandmother had always ascribed special powers to Caruso. The superstitions of Italian women always seemed to include birds.

Julie patted her grandmother's hand. "Whatever you say, *Nonna*." Julie wasn't born yesterday. She knew not to disagree. "But to tell you the truth, I have a hard enough time keeping up with the rest of the family, let alone a bird."

WHAT WAS LEFT TO DO? Accept the invitation and leave quickly, saying she had patients waiting. It was true!

And they made it, held up only by a few minutes when her mother raced off to get Sebastiano a container filled with the remaining cookies. "Men, they don't think of having things like this," Angela had insisted, pressing the container into his hands.

Julie slipped into the passenger seat and snapped her seat belt. She dipped her hands in her jacket pockets, searching for something more than her phone. "I would kill for a Three Musketeers bar right now."

He started the engine and turned around to back out the car. "You can have some of my *pignoli* biscuits if you're hungry."

"They're not junky enough, and right now I need real junk food. It's a girl thing." Julie glanced out the side window of the car. "Wave goodbye before leaving. They're all standing at the window." It was true. Like the three bears they stood in the bowed picture window. A scrupulously trimmed hedge reached the lower edge. In the corner, her father had already wrapped his prize fig tree for the winter.

They drove in silence, with Julie replaying the morning's events over in her mind. When they were a few blocks from the hospital, she looked down at her watch. Good. She'd make her first appointment without too much fuss.

"I want to thank you for…you know…helping with my grandmother."

"There's nothing to thank me for. Surely, you knew I would help—you."

Julie tried hard not to read too much into his words.

Sebastiano put on his turn signal, and pulled into the parking garage. On one side of the street were the older buildings of the hospital that now served as administrative offices and auxiliary services. On the other were one-story public housing buildings, their white-painted brick separated by patches of grass and individual gardens.

He reached for his parking card. "Actually, there is something you can do for me. It's why I was trying to stop you earlier at work."

"Oh, my God, that's right. I completely forgot about that. So what is it?" Despite all logic, all rational thought, Julie felt herself getting a little excited that he actually was asking her to—

"It has nothing to do with work," he went on, slipping the card under his visor as the gate raised.

Her heart skipped a beat. *You are so lame. You don't even like him. You argue all the time,* she told herself. Another beat went missing.

He pulled into his space and cut the engine. He slipped off his seat belt and turned to face her. An eternity of silence followed until finally he spoke. "It was about the Italian class. I wanted to ask you about a few suggestions for articles that I read online. Get your opinion, since I've never done this before, you know."

And like that, Julie knew that despite *Nonna*'s prognostications, her grandmother's bird wasn't playing her tune. "Oh" was all she could say.

He frowned. "You were expecting something else?"

If only he knew, she thought.

CHAPTER TWELVE

AT THE END of the first appointment on Friday morning, Julie accompanied her patient—one of her regulars—out to the hallway and watched the young woman toddle down the carpeted hallway in her Laboutin heels. She was a buyer for Saks Fifth Avenue—hence the shoes at "a *very* good price" Julie had learned. More than the amazing shoes though, the woman was positively glowing in her fourteenth week of pregnancy, her concerns less about water weight than finding an appropriate nanny, preferably French-speaking.

"It's never too late to get a leg-up on getting into college," she had said in all seriousness.

Julie had smiled. Grantham was a town of notorious overachievers and status-conscious residents. "Knowing any foreign language is enriching," she had replied, even though she had never thought of growing up and speaking Italian at home as "enriching."

Although—come to think of it—Sebastiano's class was turning out to be *very* interesting. *But was it the subject matter or the teacher?* She'd like to say both, but, now, as she thought about her question, she knew she'd be kidding herself.

Whatever. She turned back to her office, where she compulsively straightened the pillow in one of the armchairs—another one of her needlepoint creations, this one a rabbit leaping in a blueberry patch. The mechanical actions didn't prevent her thoughts lingering on the discussion, but even more so—Sebastiano. What had brought him to America? Employment? Money? A love interest?

She really didn't know. True, in this age of the internet, Skype and cell phones, it wasn't as if coming to America were akin to trekking through remote Outer Mongolia. But still, to come alone? And the thing of it was, Sebastiano really did seem alone. She couldn't picture him in the context of a family, let alone children. Or could she? He had seemed more relaxed with her parents and grandmother than she usually felt, but then who didn't get along better with someone else's parents than your own?

The phone buzzed on her desk. She walked back and lifted the receiver. It was Lakshmi, the receptionist, originally from Bangalore.

"Kelley has already done the preliminaries on your next patient, and she's waiting in room number two," Lakshmi said. Kelley was Julie's nurse.

"Thanks." Julie hung up. She squared her shoulders and walked across the hallway, first removing the patient folder from the pocket on the door and peering briefly at the information. A red Post-it signaled that the patient was new. She was middle-aged with slightly elevated blood pressure.

"Hello, I'm Dr. Antonelli," she announced after knocking. She held out her hand and stopped.

"*Ciao, Dottoressa.* Remember me? Katarina's mom?"

"Mrs. Zemanova," Julie said, the surprise evident in her voice. "Somehow I didn't put two and two together when I glanced at the folder." She flipped to the front page.

"Please, call me Zora. Mrs. Zemanova sounds like my mother, God forbid." Even though she sat on the examining table dressed in nothing but a blue paper gown and a pair of gray Smartwool socks, she exuded confidence.

Unlike most patients, Julie couldn't help noticing that Zora hadn't bothered to use the skinny plastic cord to tie the gown together, nor did she seem at all inclined to clutch the sides together. No, Zora Zemanova proudly sat with her shoulders back and her gown gaping, her slightly overweight middle-aged body with all its bumps proudly on display. Her dark hair was sprinkled gray and pulled back in a thick braid that hung down her back. Other than a coating of Chapstick on her lips, her face was free of makeup. There was no question that Zora was unique for her natural, healthy look. Of course, given her Eastern European genes, her natural looks had a lot going for it, especially her clear skin. Forget microdermabrasion.

Julie snagged her rolling stool with the toe of her Ferragamos and sat down. "Gee, this makes three times in less than a week that we've seen each other. That must be a record for us," Julie said as she rested the folder on her lap and unclipped the pen from the top.

"About as many times as Katarina has seen me in the last five years," Zora joked. Within the confines of the small examining room and its four white walls, the joke fell flat. Zora winced.

"Well, many of us wish we could limit our exposure to our mothers for even less time," Julie admitted, trying to lessen the tension.

"Katarina might not agree, but I like to think I've instilled in her a sense of adventure and self-worth, even if I wasn't there for many of the day-to-day things—going to school plays, teaching her to swim, helping her with college applications."

Julie rolled the chair closer. "Seeing as Katarina got into Stanford, I think she did just fine anyway. And watching her go through the anxieties of Matt applying to college, I'm becoming more and more convinced that being far, far away from the process might be better for all concerned. Funny, I was just talking about the same thing to another patient."

"Well, whatever our choices, it's not as if we can change our past, can we?" Zora remarked.

"I guess not," Julie said, her voice trailing off. She cleared her throat. "But enough of that. What brings you here today?" She cocked her head in anticipation.

"It's time for my gynecological checkup. I haven't had one for a while, so I probably need all the usual bells and whistles. As a scientist, I fully appreciate the benefits of preventive medicine and having a proper baseline from which to evaluate further data," Zora said as if she were clinically evaluating some geological substrata. She paused. And swallowed.

Julie smiled. "Anything else?"

"Oh, yes, there is something. Since I no longer get my periods, birth control is not an issue. And while I haven't been sexually active for a number of years, I'd like to get checked out for the possibility of any infections that I may have become exposed to."

"Are you showing any symptoms of STDs? Any reason to think you may have contracted the HIV virus?" Julie asked, her voice professional.

"No, nothing like that. It's just that I've met someone…." Zora glanced down and flattened the paper material of her gown against her thigh. Then she looked up, leading with her chin. "The long and short of it is, I plan to become sexually active. Soon. In fact, I had next Wednesday—class night—in mind."

CHAPTER THIRTEEN

JULIE WAS STILL standing in the examination room, trying to digest Zora's loaded statement while one flight up, in the same medical office building, Paul was doing his best to control his temper.

"Listen, Dad, I said I was happy to come with you to the doctor, so don't keep asking me if I'd rather be some place else," Paul said, the irritation evident in his voice.

Clearly, dealing with old people was not his strength. He'd nearly lost it when his father had had problems finding his Medicare card in his wallet when they'd first checked in at the cardiologist. And did he have to go on and on about the wonderful free pen the receptionist gave him to sign for his co-pay?

"I have the best collection from all my doctors," Carl Bedecker had told her with a twinkle in his eye. "But I have to tell you, the urologist has the best. Those Viagra pens are nice and big, easy to grip."

The receptionist had smiled politely, even chuckled. But there was no way she really wanted to hear all the details, especially when she had someone on hold on the telephone the whole time.

Paul steered his father toward the chairs in the reception area. Two rows of upholstered armchairs faced each other across the beige carpet. In the center was a coffee table with pamphlets about blood thinners and plaque buildup and back issues of *Popular Mechanics*. "You want a magazine, Dad?" Paul asked, trying to make amends.

"No, I'm fine. You never have to wait here long anyway," Carl said. He unzipped his golf jacket and placed his cap on his lap. "You know, I could have come by myself."

"We all agreed that two sets of ears are better than one," Paul said. Carl had suffered a heart attack over a year ago, and while the bypass surgery had been a success and Carl was watching his diet and exercising regularly, he still needed regular checkups to monitor his condition.

"In which case, Norm could have come. He never objects."

"Norm's busy running the garden center. He's the one earning the money that pays the bills and supports his family—and me, at the moment, I might add. Norm's the responsible son, Dad. We all know that. I'm the screwup."

"No, you're not. You just went down the wrong path for a while. But you're home now. You've got your priorities straight," Carl said, his baldpate gleaming under the overhead lights. For some reason, Carl insisted on combing over a few strands of gray hair. He'd done that as far back as Paul could remember. Once, it had been a source of embarrassment. Now? Now it was just something his dad did.

"Let me tell you, son. Your mother would be proud of how you've pulled yourself together," Carl went on.

Then he coughed and reached for the white handkerchief in his pants pocket.

Paul looked away. The door next to the receptionist opened. He expected a nurse to emerge, calling his father back to the examination rooms. But it wasn't a nurse. It was a middle-aged woman, chubby. Her hair was short, brown. She wore khaki pants and a boiled wool jacket. She looked vaguely familiar. She was holding on to the arm of an older woman dressed in a gray skirt and black cardigan sweater buttoned primly over a white shirt. With her Roman nose, black-and-white clothing and curved back, she looked like something out of central casting for a post-war Italian film.

"Paul? Paul Bedecker?" The middle-aged woman dragged the older woman along with her. "It's good to see you. It's Angela, Angela Marcesano. Actually, now it's Angela Antonelli. I married Lou Antonelli. We all went to Grantham High together?"

"Oh, yeah, Angela. You look great," Paul said even though the words didn't carry any real weight. He and Angela had never run in the same crowd. He was more the AP Calculus type. She played on the softball team. Truth was, he had probably thought he was too good for her. Now he complained about the snobs in Grantham to Sebastiano, but when he had been young, he'd been one of the biggest intellectual snobs of all. He'd been embarrassed that his father owned a garden center. What was worse, his father probably knew it.

"Well, you look great. Still nice and trim. I wish I could say the same thing about me." Angela patted her round tummy beneath her jacket. She briefly chatted with Carl, an old acquaintance, made the introductions of *Nonna* to Paul.

"I hope everything's okay," Carl spoke to *Nonna*. He knew the woman's English was limited.

"Oh, she's fine, aren't you, *Nonna*?" Angela said.

"*Si, si,* yes." *Nonna* nodded. "Just…just—" she pressed her stomach "—*lo stomaco.*"

"A bad case of indigestion," Angela clarified. "She had us worried this morning though. Luckily Julie, that's my daughter—"

"Yes, I've met her. In Italian class at the Adult School," Paul interrupted.

"Oh, good, then you know she's a doctor. Anyway she and Dr. Fonterra rushed over to help out, and while they said it didn't appear to be anything serious, they got her an appointment this afternoon, just to make sure. The good news is, the EKG and the stress test were normal, and even though we still have to wait for the results from the blood tests, the cardiologist is pretty sure that my attempt to make this dish I'd seen on the Food Network was to blame. You were right, *Nonna*. Cream sauces are never a good idea for pasta." Angela laughed.

"In the old days, I loved cream with anything—pasta included. Now they won't let me touch the stuff," Carl said. "It's miserable. We're supposed to watch our diet, how much we drink, not smoke. I tell you, what kind of fun is left for an old man anymore?"

Paul smiled nervously. "Who said life was supposed to be fun?"

"You know, I heard you were back in town," Angela said, changing the subject, for which Paul was eternally grateful.

On the other hand, he could only guess what she had heard.

"Actually, I was hoping you could help out," Angela said.

"Help out? I'm not quite sure I know what you mean?"

"It's our thirty-fifth reunion from high school, and seeing as you were always such a leader in school— gee, I remember you as editor-in-chief of the newspaper, right?"

Paul nodded.

"And then you went to Hollywood and all. Well, we'd be so honored if you'd consider being a speaker, talk about your career, things you've done."

"I don't know if I'd be such a good person for that. As I'm sure you know, my career peaked a long time ago, followed by a long downhill spiral," Paul said, trying to back out nicely.

"But I hear you're writing a book. That's so exciting. We don't have any other authors in the class. You could talk about where you get your inspiration," Angela suggested.

Paul figured that Angela Antonelli would be shocked if he told her his latest chapter sprang from an incident where he'd woken up after an all-night bender with two hookers in his bed and a loaded revolver under his pillow. "Someone told you I was writing a book?" he asked instead. He looked over his eyebrows at his father.

"I might have mentioned something to Lou when he came in to get fertilizer for his grass," Carl admitted. "And why shouldn't I? I'm a proud father. I got a right to brag."

That was his dad, Paul thought. Supportive to a fault, when he could have easily given up on his son. Not that he had been blind to Paul's addiction. The one time his late mother and father had flown out to see him in Hollywood, he'd had them stay at his Brentwood mansion. Paul had thought he'd been discreet about his drug and alcohol use, but his father had approached him one afternoon while his mother was lying down.

"Son," he'd said, "I'm speaking as a father, as someone who loves you. You've got to clean up your act before it gets you. I know you can do it."

Paul had thought to deny the accusation, but realized it would have been futile. "Yeah, you're right," he had said, not really believing it. "I suppose it would kill mom if she knew about it."

Carl had shaken his head. "It will kill you. Don't do it for your mother. Do it for yourself."

In the end, Paul had heeded his advice. And he'd come home. Each day was a battle. But at least he had the unqualified support of his father, despite all his past behavior. He might have gotten sober for himself, but that didn't mean he wasn't still trying to make it up to his father.

So Paul stretched a tight smile on his lips and replied to Angela's request. "You know, I'd like to help out, but I can't make any guarantees where I'll be then. Could you just pencil me in for now?" he asked.

"You're planning on leaving?" Carl asked.

Paul could see the hurt in his eyes. "No, no plans for the moment," he tried to reassure him. "It's just I've learned that for now, I don't make plans too far ahead."

The only plans Paul had for the future? To clear up certain matters with Zora Zemanova—sooner rather than later.

CHAPTER FOURTEEN

IT WAS ONLY the Monday after the first Italian class—with just two more days to go until the next, not to mention dinner at Julie's parents' house. But Sebastiano was desperate. Julie's home number and address weren't in the phone book. No doctor's were. But that didn't stop Sebastiano from finding out where she lived. He had access to the hospital data bank after all, and he dipped into it knowing that the motivation for his search was far from professional. At least he could satisfy his conscience by saying that he'd held off using the information all of Friday, and what seemed a long and torturous weekend. Granted, he'd halfway dialed her number several times before stopping. He didn't want her thinking…wait a minute—maybe he did want her thinking. But about what?

Finally, Monday rolled around and as Sebastiano sat through a dinner with a prospective donor that had dragged on for hours, he decided that he'd had enough of being discreet, low-key, even properly reserved—when it came to Julie, that is. He could barely contain his impatience as the hedge-fund manager went on and on about his new ski lodge in Utah, all the while indulging in multiple after-dinner brandies. That was the thing about a lot of rich people Sebastiano had come to realize. They knew how to linger—and to make other people pay. On top of which, Sebastiano still had his A.A. meeting to go.

But at last, he'd fulfilled his obligations. Now he was in the car on his way to Easton. That's where she lived, a tiny town just outside of Grantham, a hop, skip and a throw past Lake Vanderbilt. It had its share of quaint clapboard storefronts, a café, a tasteful tack shop and rival Methodist and Presbyterian churches.

Yet, despite its picture-postcard quality, and the usual claim that Washington had slept there, Easton had never achieved the cachet of Grantham. It lacked the Ivy League university for one. It was closer to New Brunswick with its working class neighborhoods for another.

Still, any town that boasted Lou Antonelli's garage, which Sebastiano drove past as he entered Easton, had a lot going for it—considering Iris Phox's recommendation.

He glanced at the GPS and took a right through a small development of 60s ranch houses and split-levels until the road ended at a pair of impressive gates marking the entrance to Haversham Farm. Now that the land had been sold off, the Colonial revival stone mansion was all that what was left of what was once an extensive holding. Even the mansion itself had been divided up into condos.

Sebastiano buzzed the intercom but didn't get any response. He should have phoned ahead of time. She could be asleep. She could be out. She could be at the hospital delivering a baby who didn't know to be cooperative and come at lunchtime. Or still, she could have a visitor.

He decided to ignore that possibility and pressed the

buzzer once more. What the heck? The worst that could happen was for her to yell at him for waking her up. No, that wasn't the worst that could happen.

The worst was that a male voice, known or un-known—better unknown, he decided rapidly—would yell at him for disturbing them.

He had already wrestled his keys out of his jacket pocket when he heard a muffled voice through the inter-com.

"Hello? Is someone there?" It was Julie. She sounded as if she had a bad head cold.

He bent down and pressed the speaker button. "It's Sebastiano. I hope I'm not disturbing you." He lifted his finger.

"The timing couldn't be worse, but how come I'm not surprised," she responded in a less-than-enthusiastic voice.

Ironically, her caustic tone immediately warmed his heart. "Does that mean I can come up?"

There was a moment of silence. "Why not? Up the stairs and to the right."

Sebastiano heard a loud buzz and pressed down on the brass handle. The door opened. He stepped inside to what must have been the grand entryway to the origi-nal mansion. The central lobby furniture was tastefully upholstered in fading chintz. A resplendent chandelier hung from a high ceiling open to the second floor. A spiral staircase ascended, splitting in two directions, allowing the full glory of a stained-glass window to rise from the intermediary landing. Off this central public space, heavy wooden doors with numbers and knockers closed off the wings of the house, forming two condos on each floor.

Sebastiano let his hand glide along the gleaming mahogany banister as he walked silently up the carpeted stairway. He could imagine sinking into it in his bare feet. At the top of the staircase he hesitated.

A door opened on his right. A familiar head of black shiny hair stuck out. "Come in," she said, holding open the door.

He followed her in and made a quick survey as she closed the door behind him. The room, which must have one time been the parlor, still had its original moldings. Tasteful, simple furnishings à la Pottery Barn were grouped around an oriental rug and a large coffee table. There were pillows everywhere, and a needlepointed footstool was positioned in front of a bentwood rocking chair. A fire was blazing in the fireplace, and on the couch a photo album lay open.

"I was worried you might be asleep when I buzzed, but I see that you were up." He looked over his shoulder to address her.

Her back was to him. She closed the door and turned. Her head was down as she ran her hand nervously through her short hair. She was casually dressed in sweatpants and an oversize T-shirt. Her feet were bare. Her burgundy-colored nail polish stood out against the gleaming hardwood floors.

Sebastiano felt the corner of his mouth twitch. He breathed in slowly. He wasn't some inexperienced adolescent who couldn't control himself. But he was also man enough to know it was time to stop pretending. He took a step toward her.

She raised her face.

And he saw that her eyes were swollen and red and

her cheeks blotchy where tracks from tears had formed down her face.

He rushed to her side. "What's wrong? It's not your grandmother? Nothing has happened since her episode this morning?"

Julie avoided his embrace and walked across the room, stopping in front of the coffee table. She hugged her sides and smiled too brightly. "No, she's fine. Everyone's fine. I'm the only one who's messed up at the moment. But that, too, shall pass. This is so embarrassing. I can't tell you." She made a wavy motion to dismiss her worries.

Sebastiano wasn't going to be put off. He wrapped his arm around her shoulders. For someone who normally towered over most of the world, she seemed suddenly small and vulnerable. "What's wrong?" he asked again.

She attempted to separate herself.

He only held on tighter. "It's okay," he said, even softer. "You can tell me. I won't bite."

Julie looked up. Her eyes welled with tears, but she sniffed them back. "And here I went and got a rabies shot for nothing."

He squeezed her upper arm. "You see, already I must be helping. You've managed to insult me within minutes of my arrival."

She glanced sideways and wet her lips. "It's complicated."

"What isn't?"

She looked down, but she didn't pull away from his embrace. "It's something that happened a long time ago, around this time of year. So, stupid me, I get upset when the date rolls around."

Sebastiano cupped her chin in his hand and raised her face so that they stood eye-to-eye. "No one would ever call you stupid, least of all me."

She pressed her lips together.

"Tell me, tell me, Julie. Does it have something to do with the photos that are spread all over the sofa?" He glanced over at the couch.

She nodded reluctantly. "Yeah, kind of."

Still holding on, he guided her over to the couch. He pushed the scrapbook to the side and sat her next to him in the middle. He reached over and spread the photo album on their laps. "So tell me about the pictures," he said, his voice coaxing. He flipped a page over and back. "They look a bit old. Wait a minute, is that you?" He pointed to a formal photo of Julie's college basketball team. He peered closely, raised his head and narrowed his eyes to study Julie, then went back to viewing the photo again. "Did you have blond hair at one point?"

Julie shrugged. "Just streaks. It was a phase I was going through."

He glanced at her pixie cut and red highlights. "You seem to go through many phases."

Julie studied the photo, too. "Well, that was probably not one of my better ones. I can't tell you how much the peroxide wrecked my hair—for months."

Sebastiano waited, waited for her to say what she really meant.

She fingered the faces in the team photo lightly. "Betsy, Chris, Mollie, Ann—though we called her 'Push.' Don't ask me why. I don't remember. That one at the end, that's Winn."

"They seem like a nice group. You played a sport together?"

"Yup. The women's basketball team—at the University of Connecticut."

"I see," he said, examining the picture closely. "Going by the size of your team members I assumed you weren't the gymnastics squad."

She angled her chin toward him. "Do you always think you're so witty?"

"Almost always." He smiled apologetically.

She still had the deer-caught-in-the-headlights look to her eyes, but some of the hollowness had diminished. *Thank God.* He guided her attention back gently toward the photos. "And this was taken when?" he asked.

Julie glanced at the page. "Sixteen years ago." She turned and gazed into the fire. "A lifetime ago. For the two on the right, especially. Ann, the second one from the end, is dead. And the one in the end? Winn?" She pointed. "She will always walk with a limp."

"The death, the limp? They're related?"

"They happened sixteen years ago on September twenty-sixth."

A date that fell tomorrow, on Tuesday, Sebastiano realized. "And you remember this so well because…?"

She screwed her mouth up. "Because it's my birthday. And it was my birthday. The three of us went out to celebrate. I was driving."

Sebastiano felt an immense pain in his chest.

"I came to a traffic intersection. There was a light. It was green. I didn't even think to look. I didn't even see the truck coming on the right—the truck that hadn't bothered to stop."

"You'd been drinking?" he asked.

"No, we were still underage. We were trying to be

good. We didn't want any hassles from the coach," she said, her eyes on the photo.

"So you had the right of way. The truck was at fault."

"What difference does it make? One of my best friends died because she was in my car that night. If I hadn't wanted to celebrate my stupid birthday so badly..." She gave him a steely-eyed glare. "It was my fault that Ann died and that Winn was permanently injured. No one can tell me otherwise."

"Well, I hope they at least tried."

"Oh, please, let's not talk about the college counselors and their touchy-feely approach to life. You would have thought Mr. Rogers had entered the room!"

"I don't know this Mr. Rogers, but what about your family? Surely they helped you?"

"An Italian-American family talk about something like that? That's the last place they would have wanted to go. Better to talk to the parish priest and sweep the shame under the rug."

"I don't care where your family comes from or what they believe, it's ridiculous that you're still feeling this guilt—guilt that you lived and your friend died. Besides, how old were you when this all happened? Nineteen? Twenty?" His frustration came out in his raised voice.

"Twenty," Julie concurred, looking into the fire again.

He placed his thumb and forefinger on her chin and gently guided it to look her straight in the eye. "And what did you do after the accident? Did you drop out of school? Run away from your memories like some people would?"

"Of course not. I gave up basketball, switched majors to premed and studied my ass off. I wanted to do something for women. So I could help them bring life into the world instead of snuffing it out."

"Then you're better than most. Better than me. But somehow, that's what I would have expected," he said, his voice a bit melancholy. It was his turn to gaze at the fire now. Then he snapped out of it. This was about her, not him.

"So now I understand why you charge into battle the way you do. As someone who's seen you in action, may I say you make a formidable opponent?"

"It wasn't you so much," Julie protested. She stopped. "All right, it was you, or rather what you represented. Or what I thought you represented. Sometimes…sometimes—" she shook her head "—it's just so hard, and I get so frustrated trying to help all those women who are not able to help themselves."

Before she could protest, he pulled her close and whispered against the side of her head, the wisps of her hair tickling his lips. "I think you're incredible."

"Don't be ridiculous." She started to pull away.

He held her tight, refusing to back down. "For once, don't argue with me, all right?" He squeezed her harder, only relaxing his grip as she stopped trying to squirm away. "This is what I have to say," he said, his voice gentle again. "I think you are incredibly brave. I think the world needs more people like you. But I also think you don't need to go it alone. You can't control fate or some careless truck driver all those years ago. Sometimes things happen and you can't do anything about them—that, indeed, you weren't meant to do anything about them. Then you have to forgive yourself, and overcome the guilt and the pain."

She listened, then brought her head up again. "And you know all this because?"

"Because that's what they teach you in A.A. That's right, Alcoholics Anonymous. I'm an alcoholic. I haven't touched a drop of alcohol in six years, but I'm still an alcoholic."

She blinked. "I had no idea." She paused. "Is that why you hold yourself in, act so disciplined and cautious?"

"It's nice to know you think I'm totally uptight."

"That's not what I think. Well…maybe I did think it, but I didn't know…"

"That's all right. You don't need to apologize. We are who we are. You charge unannounced into people's offices. I take extra starch in my shirt collars. But in any case, this is not about me. Tonight we deal with your problems." He lightly touched her cheek. "Will you try forgiving yourself—if not for yourself, for me?" He cocked his head and tried to look adorable.

As the only son of doting Italian parents, he'd had much practice in his youth making himself look adorable. But then it hadn't taken much to get his way. *Maybe it would have been better all around if it had been harder?* he reflected, but pushed the thought to the back of his mind. *Not tonight. Not with her.*

Julie sputtered a laugh. "You're incorrigible, do you know that? What am I saying? Of course you know that." She paused. "All right, I'll try. My worthy adversary."

"I like that you consider me worthy." He leaned forward. His idea was to kiss her playfully on the nose.

Only, at that moment she chose to tip her head up. Instead of brushing her nose, his lips grazed her parted lips. And then they did more than graze.

CHAPTER FIFTEEN

JULIE RESPONDED IMMEDIATELY. Her lips sought his and nipped and tasted. When he opened his mouth, she didn't need any encouragement, and they mutually plundered at will. He leaned back and took her with him. She straddled his hips and plunged her hands in his hair. His moved up her sides, first molding her sweatshirt then sliding to the bottom ribbing and sneaking underneath. His fingers spanned her rib cage, heat against heat. His thumbs moved upward, teasing her breasts through her bra.

And then he stopped. His mouth stilled against hers, and it took a fraction of a beat for Julie to realize that the action had come to an abrupt stop. She disentangled her body from his and sat upright, one hand on the back of the couch. She steadied herself against the vibrations tingling her whole body.

She coughed. "Well, that was unexpected—but clearly enjoyable. Why did you stop?"

Sebastiano maneuvered her body from beneath her weight. She accommodated by lifting up from her knees and letting him slide to the side. He sat up, cleared his throat and smoothed back the side of his hair, not realizing the top was still mussed.

"There are rules. Morals," he explained, though obviously with some difficulty on his part.

"What? Adversaries have morals in this day and age?"

He looked at her askance. "When it comes to taking advantage of damsels in distress, even adversaries in this day and age have rules."

Julie leaned back on her haunches and studied him. "So noble."

"Better than uptight," he said.

She played over the past few minutes. "No, you're definitely not uptight." She grabbed one of the many needlepoint pillows—this one a gaily patterned Provençal square—and squeezed it tight. "So if we're both going to be noble—something I'm not sure I totally want to go along with, by the way, but at least I'll play along for now—let's switch to a less...ah...charged topic." She could see he was still breathing hard. "You never told me why you came over tonight?"

"The truth? I came over after my A.A. meeting because I was thinking of you."

"You associate me with deprivation?"

"Quite the contrary. I've been thinking of you for quite some time, in fact. I want you to know just how hard it was for me to act so nobly."

Julie smiled "I'll take that as a compliment." She studied his face. His pupils might still be dilated, but lines of stress and fatigue carved deep furrows in his cheeks and forehead. She shook her head. "What was I thinking? Check that. I knew exactly what I was thinking when I responded like that. But what I mean is, it doesn't take a dummy to see how tired you must be, and since we've called off further...ah...action, maybe you want to go home and get some sleep?" She checked her watch, the watch from *Nonna*. "It's after ten."

"No, that's all right. I'm tired, but that doesn't mean

I'm sleepy. I'm one of those people who don't sleep much."

She dropped the pillow on her lap. "Me neither. Something we have in common. Don't tell me this is the start of a trend. I mean, if we find out we have other things in common, it would ruin all my preconceptions of just how incompatible we are."

"Well, if it makes you feel any better, I don't play basketball."

"I'm sure you can make a few baskets."

He shook his head. "No, I'm hopeless. I'm just not that coordinated. You would kill me on the court."

She nodded. "I think I like that idea."

He frowned. "Strange, but I think I might, too."

His response pleased her.

Sebastiano rose from the couch. "But maybe you're right. Perhaps, as you say, I should go then?"

She unfolded her legs and got up, too. "Don't be ridiculous. Surely we can act like civilized adults, even if that is *extremely* boring, in my opinion." She shot him a teasing stare.

He wet his lips but didn't bite.

"Okay, then," she continued, "civilized it is. In which case, why don't I play the good hostess? Tea? I have herbal? Caffeinated?"

"*Si, grazie.* Tea sounds very respectable, and respectable is my aim at the moment."

Julie crossed the living room and dining area to the galley kitchen. She opened an overhead cabinet. She moved a box of sweetened cereal to the side and pushed aside a bag of potato chips to peer in the back. "You know, just because you are aiming for respectability doesn't mean you need to suffer. And, don't worry, I'm not suggesting anything even remotely R-rated. How about hot chocolate? I have some cocoa mix?" She shook the box. The individual packets rattled.

"Ah, *ciocolatta calda*. My downfall. I shouldn't, but I can't resist."

"Please! You've sworn off alcohol. You say sex is out of the picture for the evening. I think you can indulge in a little hot chocolate." She put the kettle up to boil and rummaged in another cupboard for two mugs. Then she slid open a silverware drawer and retrieved two spoons.

Two of everything matching, she couldn't help noticing. Almost as if they were a couple. She shook her head. Sometimes two mugs and two spoons were just two mugs and two spoons, thank you, Sigmund Freud.

She strummed her fingertips on the counter and waited for the water to boil. She felt the need to fill in the silence. "So, if you weren't into sports, what did you do for fun as a child? Or were you totally serious, bent over schoolbooks all the time?"

"It's true I was a good student, but I had outside interests," he said, watching her pour the powdery contents into the mugs. "I loved the outdoors—camping, hiking, chopping wood."

"How very rustic." The kettle whistled, and Julie poured the water into the cups. She stirred them and passed him one. Then she stirred her chocolate a bit more, removed the spoon and licked it suggestively.

Sebastiano stared, his mouth slightly open. He cleared his throat. "I thought we were going to be civilized."

"Excuse me, I'm just drinking hot chocolate here," she protested and turned to put her spoon in the sink. She was enjoying this. But she should quit it, really.

Otherwise he'd leave, and she didn't want that. "So you were telling me how outdoorsy you were? All very natural and earthy."

He held his spoon out to her. It wasn't quite steady. She reached for it. Their fingers brushed. He coughed. She turned and placed the utensil in the sink.

"Not totally natural," he said, taking a sip. "Like most young men, and not-so-young men, I had a thing for power tools, things like chain saws."

"I see the potential for many hospital visits."

"No, I was very careful, as you've noted." He smiled knowingly.

She smiled back.

"Of course, there were a few visits to the emergency room from cycling accidents," he added. He leaned back on the island that separated the kitchen from the dining room.

Most people would have used it as a convenient work surface. Julie used it to pile her mail. She liked to think the flyers and junk mail livened up the pure-white Corian countertop and the high-gloss snow-white cabinets—the builder's idea of luxury, not hers. Kitchens for her were more than adequate if they had a microwave and a place to keep a box of Frosted Flakes.

"You had a few dustups?" she asked, searching for details.

"I used to compete in road races, and minor injuries are to be expected—a collarbone here, an elbow there."

"I wouldn't call those minor." She motioned toward the living room. "Why don't we go back and sit down?" she suggested. She swayed her hips to push past him in the narrow confines. She felt her sweatpants slip slightly, exposing the smooth skin below the hem of her T-shirt. She decided to live dangerously and not pull them back up.

She reclaimed her place on the couch, tucking one leg underneath as she sat. He seemed to find the movement fascinating.

"I bet you were very good on the hill climbs, am I right?" she asked.

He sat awkwardly and took a sip.

She did, too. It was hot and sweet. Like his mouth had been.

"You're right about the hill climbs." He paused, and the corner of his mouth twitched as he mused, "But I was also a bit of a daredevil on the descents."

She stared at him, trying to imagine him throwing caution to the wind, finding it difficult to do so. Her eyes wandered to his legs. "That explains it, the cycling, I mean," she announced.

"I don't quite follow." He looked over the rim of his mug.

"Why you have well-developed quads."

"You're speaking as a medical professional, of course?"

She could tell he was quite pleased that she had noticed his body. But then, he was a man. "Not necessarily," she answered truthfully.

"Please, you're not supposed to be leading me astray," he complained.

"In that case, what else should we talk about? Religion? Politics?"

"We agreed in class that they leave too much possibility for arguments."

"Not that we need any more possibilities."

"Exactly." Sebastiano glanced around. "So, tell me

about these pillows." He slipped one out from behind him. It was a brightly colored floral pattern, part Matisse painting, part Caribbean wicker basket. "This is nice. I like it. Did someone make it? Your mother?"

Julie scoffed. "As if. My mother is a great cook, don't get me wrong. But I would never trust her with a needle in her hand unless it was to truss a turkey. No, I did. I do needlepoint. I find it helps to relieve stress."

He surveyed the room again. "Then you must have a lot of stress."

She grabbed a pillow that sat between them and chucked it at him. He caught it with his free hand.

"You're not as uncoordinated as you claim," she announced.

He studied the pillow she'd sent his way. "I like this one, too. It looks like a Persian carpet. So, tell me. How you do it? All the stitches?"

"You really want to know?"

He nodded. "Yes, I really want to know."

She leaned over and placed her half-empty mug on a coaster that, naturally, was needlepointed in a Bokhara rug pattern. She scooted over more closely to him. "Okay. Let me tell you all about needlepoint." And she didn't even try to hide the enthusiasm.

CHAPTER SIXTEEN

JULIE'S CELL PHONE woke her with a start. Disoriented, she blindly fumbled for the phone's usual place on the nightstand next to her bed.

Only a body was where the nightstand was supposed to be.

She shot up. Sebastiano was slumped next to her on the couch. His head was slanted to the side, pressed up against a needlepoint pillow. He had one arm slung over the arm of the couch. A five o'clock shadow made the sharp contours of his cheeks and jaw stand out even more. A stray curl of hair sprung loosely forward. A mother would have immediately finger-combed it back.

Not just a mother, Julie thought.

She looked down. She was still dressed in her sweatpants and top. He still wore a dress shirt and gray slacks.

Her phone skittered on the table. The marimba tune sounded again. Whoever it was wasn't content to let the message go to voice mail. She gingerly freed her arm that was enmeshed behind his back and reached forward. She wiped the sleep from her eyes and glanced at the caller ID.

It was the maternity ward. It was two in the morning. "Antonelli," Julie answered. "What's up?" She kept her voice soft, not wanting to wake him. She nodded as information was relayed.

"How many centimeters dilated?" she asked before checking on other vital signs. "Okay, I'll be there in about an hour. Looks like we have a while to go, especially since it's a first delivery."

She ended the call and looked at her sleeping companion. She poked him lightly on the shoulder. "Sebastiano," she called quietly.

He sniffed.

She jostled a little harder. "Sebastiano? *Svegliati.* You need to wake up."

He breathed in loudly and raised his eyebrows before venturing to open his eyes. *"Que?"* What? He squeezed his eyes shut, then opened them abruptly and very wide. He pulled the pillow away from his cheek. He held it for a minute and studied it. It was a sampler that read Welcome to the Make Your Own B & B. He blinked slowly and looked at her. "Tell me I don't have the words printed backward on my face."

She craned her neck to check. "No, I think you're unblemished." She glanced around. "We must have fallen asleep. For two confirmed night owls it appears that we went out like a light."

"It must have been all that discussion of French knots and Hungarian ground and long-legged cross stitch."

"Hey," she protested, "some things are sacred."

"Pardon me. I should have known better. Please note, however, that I listened closely to your *very* detailed explanations."

She patted his thigh. "I always knew you were special, not always right, of course, but special." Then the phone call came to mind. She shifted away prudently. "Listen, I got a call. I've got a patient in labor."

"I thought I heard something."

"I have to leave soon before the real action begins."

"Tell me, did you ever consider getting a partner for your practice? Spread the load?"

"Only every other day. But somehow I can't seem to go through with it. I'm not sure I would trust someone else. It's a matter of control."

"Why do I get the feeling that we are treading on familiar territory?"

She inhaled through her mouth. "You're right. I know. But do I really look like the type of person who plays well with others?" She pressed her hand to her T-shirt. And saw Sebastiano's eyes linger there, as well.

"Listen, I want to thank you for earlier this evening." She started to smile, but quickly looked away. "I'm feeling better. Surprisingly. Thanks to you."

"What time is it?" he asked. Dark circles ringed his eyes. When had that ever seemed so sexy?

"Just after two a.m."

"That means it's already Tuesday. Happy birthday. I'm sorry I didn't bring you anything."

"That's all right. Just having you here has been nice, really nice, actually. But if you tell anyone that, I'll deny it completely." She got up off the couch, stretching her arms over her head.

He rose also. "For professional reasons, you mean? Not wanting to compromise your position at the hospital?"

Julie watched him bend over to straighten and arrange the pillows. "What good manners you have. You must have been a very good boy at home." She waited till he turned to face her before answering his question. "I suppose there's that. But, frankly, it's more that I don't want the word to go around that the two of us have mellowed about each other. I mean, can you imagine how that would get in the way of all the gossip around town?"

He laughed and collected his blazer from the back of the rocking chair. He fumbled in a pocket for his keys.

But she wasn't quite ready to let him go. "Listen," she said, "I just have to take a quick shower. If you want to wait a few minutes, we can leave together?"

"Sure, no problem." He didn't appear to need a lot of convincing.

"The fridge has an automatic water dispenser if you want something to drink. I think there might be some orange juice there, as well. Beyond that, I'm not sure. Cooking is not my forte."

"Don't worry. I'm still living off your mother's cookies," he quipped. He slipped on the jacket.

She had the urge to straighten his shirt collar. Truthfully, she wanted to remove his collar along with the rest of his shirt. Hell. He looked absolutely scrumptious. If only she didn't have to get to the hospital.

Julie wasn't into casual affairs for all the obvious reasons. And most nights she was too exhausted to get out and mingle and make things happen. But she could not deny the strong attraction she felt for Sebastiano, an attraction that had materialized out of the blue. Or had it?

Okay, they had initially been at odds, but seeing the way he taught and interacted with students during their first class, and the way he had consoled her last night, there was something more, something special. He had an empathy that seemed so rare in this age of speed dating and online relationships. Clearly, he wasn't perfect—witness his admission about his alcoholism. But it was his imperfections that made him all the more attractive, that much more approachable.

"Go ahead and shower," he urged her. "I don't want to hold you up. Besides, I think I can manage a glass of water on my own." He pointed to the kitchen.

She felt rooted to her spot, and only with great effort did she turn to go down the hall. "Okay, good then."

With her mind only half on what she was doing, Julie walked to her bedroom. Out of habit more than conscious behavior, she stripped off her clothes and dropped them on the floor, then went to the connecting bathroom via her bedroom rather than the hallway entrance. As she slipped her bath towel off the railing, she could hear him opening and closing the cupboards in the kitchen and the sound of water filling a glass. She gripped the towel and hesitated. Then she knew she couldn't wait any longer. She dashed down the hallway and skittered to a stop by the kitchen.

He turned around, visibly startled.

"I know this is bad timing, so nothing can happen right away, but I wanted to tell you—needed to tell you—that I don't want it to end here," she blurted out.

He opened his mouth and appeared to want to say something.

But she waved him off. "No, wait. Let me get this out before I lose my courage. What I mean…what I want to say…is that despite the fact you get on my nerves, probably as much as I get on yours—" she synchronized a side-to-side head bob along with that admission "—I think we have something special, the potential for some-thing even more special. That…that if we get together in some fashion it'll mean something…it'll be important. That it won't just be a way of scratching some itch or some short-term solution to the fact that my sex life is virtually nonexistent."

She saw his eyebrows arch up, but she continued to let the words spill out.

"Please, all I'm asking you is to think about what I'm saying and consider if it all jives with what you have in mind or maybe imagine. I realize you're the deliberative type and maybe you're not ready to commit—not that I'm asking for a commitment, mind you." The words rushed out. The she frowned and searched his face. "So, at the risk of putting you on the spot, do you have any reaction to what I'm saying? Like now? Thumbs up, thumbs down?" She mimicked her question with her hand.

He trained his eyes on her face. "I appreciate your candor." Then he swallowed.

"I try to say what I feel." She bit down on her lower lip.

"You know, ah, before I say anything, may I just ask one question?"

She nodded. "Of course. More than one if you want."

"Your decision to speak frankly? It just suddenly came to you?"

She nodded again.

"It just came to you? Just as you were about to take your shower, perhaps?" For the first time he dropped his chin and let his eyes follow.

Julie looked down, too. And suddenly realized—"Oh,

my"—that she was naked. She frantically covered her breasts, then her lower body with her arm. Totally ineffectually, of course.

"The other hand? The towel?" he coaxed her.

"Oh, right." She hurriedly wrapped the bath towel around herself. "I don't know what I was thinking. I wasn't thinking, that's what." She tried to tuck a corner of the towel into the top edge to try to make it stay put. "You know me. I just acted on impulse…. I mean, I can't explain why I didn't feel the air on my body, except to say that I was just so…so…"

"So you?" he supplied. "That impetuous way you have about you? Did I ever tell you it's infuriating but also highly attractive?"

"No, no, you didn't." She held onto the towel for dear life, fully conscious of the fact that it barely skimmed the top of her thighs.

He put his water glass down on the counter and seemed to want to take a step toward her. Then he caught himself. "You know, for my part, let me confess—no, admit is the better word—that I didn't come over just to see you naked—" he paused "—or even half-naked. As delightful as that is."

Julie saw the corner of his mouth twitch. Her stomach contracted.

He took a deep breath. "I, too, came here looking for something that might last more than just a night."

"You did?" That contraction in her stomach just got bigger.

"And I want to talk about it, I really do. But under the circumstances, I think now is perhaps not the best moment. Because just seeing you like this—" once more, his eyes drifted downward "—I am concerned that I, myself, might be doing something impetuous—which as we both know is highly out of character, but being a typical male is a real possibility." Then he took that step—closer. And he gently rubbed the back of his index finger along her cheek, an affectionate caress rather than a prologue to something carnal.

She felt her skin glow. "Never typical," she joked.

Sebastiano dropped his finger reluctantly. "You overestimate me. Watch out, or I might forget you have a patient waiting. And make you want to forget you have a patient waiting."

"Oh, that's right. My patient! I can't believe it. I nearly forgot about my patients. That's never happened." She was aghast.

"Then, this is a first?" he asked. There was a glint in his eye.

"A first," she confirmed and turned on her heels. But she stopped, pivoted on a bare foot, and scampered back to steal a quick kiss. Then she raced down the hall to take her shower—the warmth of his lips lingering on hers.

CHAPTER SEVENTEEN

SEBASTIANO MADE SURE to get to the second Italian class early the next evening on Wednesday. He told himself he wanted to make sure everything was in order with the classroom—that it wasn't locked, that the heat worked, things like that. All part of being conscientious, like any good teacher would do.

Who was he kidding? He wanted to see Julie before class started. True, they had exchanged emails the day before, but it wasn't the same as seeing her face to face. Her heavy patient load and his evening meeting with the Grantham Planning Board about the new hospital proposals had made that impossible.

He could handle "impossible" for one day. Two was out of the question.

So, he planted himself outside the classroom door to ambush her before entering. For fifteen minutes, he greeted the class members as they entered, exchanging pleasantries, trying to put names to faces. When only a few minutes remained before class was about to start, he glanced back inside the classroom and did a quick headcount. Just about a full contingent. His performance at the first class must not have driven people away.

Then he checked his watch. Maybe she wasn't going to come? *No, she would have called or texted,* he reassured himself.

Suddenly, he heard the sound of someone running up the stairs and the fire doors at the top banged open. Julie—all movement and energy coming his way. He couldn't help but smile.

She skittered to a stop when she saw him. The grin that split her face mimicked his. "Sorry I'm late. I had to rush home to change my clothes for the dinner later tonight at my parents." She took a deep breath then released it. "You're still on for that, right?"

He nodded, enjoying the way her cheeks were flushed from exertion.

"Anyway, you wouldn't believe it. On my way here I got caught on Main Street. The police had set up a roadblock to check for out-of-date car inspection stickers of all things."

"Yours was fine, I hope?" He could imagine a trip to the Department of Motor Vehicles was just the kind of thing she'd let slip in her busy schedule.

"Not a problem. I just take it to my dad's garage." She exhaled loudly one last time. "Finally, I got my wind back." She looked at him.

He stared at her, barely registering the movement of other students rushing to various classrooms down the hall. She might have gotten her breath back, but somehow in the process, she'd managed to take his away.

"Oh, before I forget, thank you so much for the flowers. They came right at the end of the day."

"I'm so glad you got them." He itched to move his hand toward her but held back. "I wasn't sure if you'd make it home before class, so I had them sent to your office. I hope that was all right?"

"It raised a few eyebrows, that's for sure," she answered with a smile.

"I'm sorry."

She grinned more broadly. "I'm not." She peeked over her shoulder, and when she saw the coast was clear, she furtively grabbed his hand. "They're beautiful. Tulips are my favorite. How did you know?"

"Some of your needlepoint pillows—the ones with the sateen stitch."

"Satin stitch," she corrected. "You were listening. And the card—Happy Un-Birthday—it was perfect."

"I wasn't sure."

"I am." She squeezed his hand.

They stared into each other's eyes.

"Can anyone get in on the conversation, or is this a private student-teacher conference?" Zora quipped as she leaned around Julie.

Sebastiano briefly broke eye contact and turned to Zora. "We're just talking hospital business." He said the first thing that came to his head.

"You don't say?" Zora looked down at their clasped hands. "Things must be very chummy at the hospital."

Sebastiano and Julie dropped their hands to their sides. He cleared his throat. She adjusted her shoulder bag and sniffed.

Then the buzzer sounded and Iris Phox's voice emanated from the public address system. "Classes will commence. May you all embark on the glorious journey that is education."

The words only made the situation more awkward.

Until Zora held out her arm in a gesture for Julie and Sebastiano to proceed her into the classroom. "Shall we?" she invited. "After all, even hospital matters sometimes take a backseat to learning. Besides, I wouldn't want to mess with Iris Phox."

As class broke up and people started to file outside, Zora could hear Sebastiano saying goodbye to his students. *"Alla prossima!"* he said repeatedly as he clipped his briefcase shut. For the second class, she noticed he was dressed more casually in corduroy pants and a navy-blue ribbed sweater. He seemed relaxed, happy. The class had certainly enjoyed it, judging from the fact that no one seemed ready to leave even five minutes after the bell had sounded.

Zora capped her fountain pen and slipped it into the side pocket of her knapsack before fitting her notebook into one of the center compartments. She might be living out of a suitcase while she was temporarily staying at her mother's house, but she was maniacally organized when it came to managing her knapsack and her work tools. A side pocket for every pen. A red folder for handouts, a green one for homework assignments. A zipped section for her collection of cell phones—for the U.S., Europe and Asia.

She stood up and blocked the aisle before Paul could leave. He was chatting with Julie, the two of them still seated at their desks, and she was surprised to feel a sudden pang of jealousy. She was no longer young, but Zora knew she had a certain allure for men, a trait that seemed to come instinctively.

She recalled a conversation with her mother when she'd come back to pick up Katarina in Grantham after spending a sultry trip on a colleague's sailboat in the Aegean. Zora had claimed how surprised she'd been at the offer, since she'd only met the man at a conference in Athens the week before.

"I'm not surprised he fell for you like tons of bricks," Lena had said in her embroidered English. "You have

the confidence of a hooker." The phrase had irked Zora.
Actually, *Babička* had used the Slovak word *postitútka*
for prostitute—just as insulting, perhaps more so since
it sounded so prosaic.

"Are you saying he thought of me merely as a sex
object!" she remembered sniping back. True, there had
been very little academic conservation on the boat, but
that was beside the point.

Lena, being Lena, had answered, "I think you are an
intelligent woman, one who knows her mind—maybe
too well. And that attitude attracts men like bees to
honey. You see, Zora, I tell you a secret. Men think they
want to be in charge, but, no, what they really want is
the idea—the picture—of power. What they crave is a
woman to make things happen."

Zora hated to say it, but her mother was probably
right. What did she know about why men fell—to use
another prosaic term—in love? All she knew was that
she had fallen head-over-heels in love with fellow Grantham High senior Paul Bedecker. He'd been the reason
she'd chosen to go to Cornell. Of course, she had made
him keep their relationship a secret. Did she want the
whole world—her mother, the high school teachers she
scorned and the cheerleaders she mocked—to know that
counterculture advocate Zora Zemanova was following
her "boyfriend" around like a lovesick puppy?

Once they got to college, Paul had painted his picture
of the future. "When we graduate, we'll go to Hollywood and I'll write screenplays, maybe do a little television work to pay the bills—not that I would ever do
that full-time—and we'll be so happy," he was fond of
saying.

People say lots of things when they're eighteen. Especially Paul. Especially when it came to fulfilling *his* dreams. It never occurred to him that his dreams weren't necessarily *hers*. Maybe he just assumed? Maybe he was smoking too much marijuana?

So when she'd found out she was pregnant at the end of spring term freshman year, and agonized about having an abortion or not, was it any wonder she never bothered to consult him? A baby had never figured into *his* dreams, after all. She had loved him, but he could never be a father.

She had broken up with him without so much as a by-your-leave. She never told him about the baby, and quickly transferred to Rutgers. At the time Lena had welcomed her home, naturally without pressing her for details. Though sometimes she'd sigh in the middle of a conversation. Oh, how Zora had hated that sigh! Still, she'd soldiered on, finishing school, working and raising a kid. And no matter what, she'd stuck to *her* dreams.

But when she had unexpectedly seen Paul the week before at class, she got that same old feeling she had felt thirty years earlier. Or maybe she had never lost it? Whatever. Zora wasn't one to spend a lot of time on internal soul-searching. She felt a yearning, and she aimed to act on it. If that was having the confidence of a hooker, so be it.

She watched Julie stand, towering over Paul by a good four inches. The younger woman said something and smiled. Zora felt a frisson of jealousy.

But then Julie turned to walk to the front of the class, and immediately, Zora saw the direction of her eyes… and her smiles. It was clear as daylight that Paul wasn't in the picture. Julie had eyes only for the teacher.

Satisfied, Zora rose and stepped toward Paul. "Hey there. Do you have some time to get together?"

He looked at her, his eyes narrowed. Then he nodded begrudgingly. "Sure. I've been thinking it would be a good idea."

Zora beamed. He was feeling what she was feeling, too. "Did you want to get a coffee first?" she asked. They walked side-by-side past the teacher's desk. Sebastiano waved but continued to listen while Julie talked. She glanced over and seemed relieved to see them go. Zora didn't need to guess why.

JULIE WATCHED Zora Zemanova leave with Paul Bedecker and felt a sense of relief when the last classmate didn't linger. She turned back to Sebastiano. "So are you ready to face your worst nightmare?"

"Don't joke. You have no idea the nightmares I had before walking into class. I had convinced myself that I'd find out no one had anything to say and I'd have to end the class after only ten minutes." Sebastiano took the handle of his briefcase in both hands. "How was I to know that an article on the Galileo show in Philadelphia would lead to a discussion of astrology, Philadelphia restaurants and ski trips to Cortina? Even *I* haven't been to Cortina. Do you know how expensive it is?"

Julie patted Sebastiano on the hand. "It's all right. You made it. Into overtime even. And, please, if you can afford to drive a BMW, I think you can afford to ski at Cortina."

She saw him narrow his eyes. "Don't worry. I'm just teasing. Anyway, the class loved you. In fact if that one student Irena had loved you any more, I was going to hoist myself out of my incredibly uncomfortable seat, march right up to her and tell her in my best Italian where she should *go* next."

"It's true. She's a bit much, but I don't want to dampen her enthusiasm."

"A small bucket of water right in the face would hardly be out of line."

Sebastiano ignored her comment. He rubbed his chin in thought. "I suppose it wouldn't hurt to do little grammar reviews every once in a while. Things like *piacere*. A few people seem to have a difficult time grasping its unique construction," he said, referring to the Italian verb "to please."

She would have made more fun of him, but he seemed so earnest, so utterly adorable. Besides, he had agreed to go with her to her parents. For that he deserved a medal.

"So, are we taking your car or mine?" he asked.

"Why don't we both drive. You can just follow me. That way it will be easier tomorrow morning, if you know what I mean." She left the implications hanging about him possibly staying over at her place.

"Yes, I do know what you mean. Two cars then."

He hoisted his briefcase off the desk and turned off the lights. Then he let his hand fall naturally on the small of her back. "Shall we go then?"

She smiled. "*Con piacere*—with pleasure."

"NO, A DRINK'S NOT NECESSARY," Paul said as they made their way through the high school's low-ceilinged hallway. Posters for the Science Olympiad Club and a cappella singing groups vied for attention on the wall. He held open the fire door to the staircase and waited for her to go first.

Zora frowned. She had decided to rekindle their sex life, but that didn't mean she didn't need a little loosening up. "Well, we could go to your place I suppose," she offered, brushing up against his shoulder as she passed by.

"My place would be a little awkward. I'm staying with my dad. No matter where you are in the house, you can hear the TV. Nothing like hearing a baseball game at mega decibels—all because he's too vain to admit he needs a hearing aid."

They joined the other adult students trudging down the stairs. People were chatting with friends, others on their cell phones.

"I can see where that might put a damper on the mood," Zora admitted. "I'd say we could go to my place, but I'm staying with my mom. We'd never get any privacy. She'd be too busy plying us with cake and wanting to hear your life story."

Paul stopped one foot in the air, then descended slowly. "The cake is tempting, but I'm not sure about the conversation just now. Anyway, who would have thought that at this point in our lives, we would both be living with our parents."

"Oh, I'm not here permanently. Just stopping over for a little while," Zora felt obliged to clarify.

They reached the bottom of the stairs and filed out through the old wooden door along with everyone else. While other people headed down the sidewalks to their cars, Zora made her way across the triangle of grass in the courtyard to the flagpole. In high school, students used to gather there at the end of the day. Who'd have thought at this point in her life…?

She waited for Paul to join her. "It's like time has

stood still. I remember coming here after classes and looking for you, wondering if you'd talk to me, wondering if you ever thought about kissing me."

Nighttime had long fallen, but the incandescent lights over the school's doorways and the steady glow from the streetlamps gave off enough light for Zora to notice the intense way he studied her.

"I always wanted to kiss you. I wanted to do more than that. It was just a question of getting up my nerve."

"But you always seemed so cool," Zora said in disbelief. "The editor of the newspaper. A published poet. The favorite of all the teachers. I was always on the outside, intent on doing things my own way."

"Exactly, totally sure of yourself. Totally intimidating. I still remember how one day you walked in with your head shaved, an act of protest for some cause—"

"Save The Whales. I wanted to mimic their skin." Zora recalled.

"Yeah, well, it was wild. I have never had that kind of courage. I couldn't believe my luck when I found out you were going to Cornell, too. I thought that maybe, if I played my cards right, away from Grantham's prying eyes, I could make a move."

More students exited from the building, and the swoosh sound of air-controlled door hinges could be heard in the chill of the night. Voices mingled as groups passed. The sound of cars starting up along the adjacent streets cut through the crisp evening air.

Being back in familiar surroundings, Zora felt the old feeling of testing boundaries, being outrageous for the hell of it. She put a hand on Paul's chest. There wasn't an ounce of padding beneath his black T-shirt. He was so skinny, he probably weighed the same as he did in high school. She, on the other hand, had cellulite on the backs of her thighs that hadn't been there thirty years ago. She didn't let that stop her.

"C'mere." She waved to him. "I want to show you something." She guided him around the gymnasium wing. Pine trees blocked the view to the sidewalk. The school tennis courts lay beyond.

She stopped. He glanced around, puzzled. She pushed him up against the brick wall.

"We're here. Back at high school. Now's your chance to kiss me," she said.

JULIE SHUT THE DOOR of her RAV4 and waited in her parents' driveway as Sebastiano beeped his car locked and walked toward her, buttoning his cashmere topcoat on the way.

"You look very smart," she told him, slipping her arm through his.

He raised his chin and eyed her critically. "And I couldn't help noticing that you've abandoned your customary black."

It was true. She was wearing a form-fitting aubergine knit dress that emphasized her trim figure while showing off her excellent butt, even if she said so herself.

"Trying to be festive for the occasion? Or did you want me to notice your very nice derriere?"

Julie grinned. "I cannot tell a lie. Anyway, I thought I'd let *Nonna* have the monopoly on black for the evening." She tugged on his arm, intent on leading him inside her parents' home.

He held fast. "If your family welcomes you with birthday greetings, how are you going to respond?" he asked.

The ghost of guilt showed its face briefly, but Julie willed it away. "*Con piacere!* With pleasure! You see! I don't need a lesson in class when I have my own private tutor."

ZORA TOOK PAUL'S FACE between her hands and offered up a kiss. He hesitated, but didn't refuse. He grabbed her waist, squeezing it through her Northface jacket. She slipped her tongue between his teeth and jabbed it back and forth. He slanted his head and kissed her back with a ferocity that spoke of desire and longing and something beyond the fringe. It excited and scared Zora, and that excited her even more.

She reached with her hand to unzip his jacket. She could feel heat radiating from his body. She inched the metal tab down.

But then he placed his hand on hers to stop her motion. He shifted it to her shoulders and gently pushed her away.

Zora shook her head. "What's wrong? I don't get it. You want it as much as I do. I can tell. You know, I'm not a teenager anymore."

Paul ran his hand along his shaved head. "Precisely. Neither of us is. And we never will be…again."

He stepped toward the floodlight perched on the corner of the tennis courts.

Zora joined him. She flapped her arms down hard against her sides in exasperation. "What are you trying to say? That sneaking a quickie outside the high school is a stupid idea? I'm more than happy to get a motel room on Route One if that's what you had in mind. Though I gotta say, I'm a little disappointed to find you've gotten so conventional in middle age."

Paul walked in a wide circle, coming to rest at the fence. "You just don't get it, do you? You don't get that things have changed, people have changed."

"If you mean we're older and wiser, hey, I've got the stretch marks to prove it. But who's to say we can't still have a little fun? I mean, we know what we are getting into, right?" She wasn't ready to give up yet. What had her mother said? That she knew what she wanted too well?

Paul dropped his chin to stare directly into her eyes. "Do we? I was going to write Oscar-winning screenplays and the great American novel. What happened? I became a producer of infomercials. Whatever money I made—and you'd be surprised how much money you can make on infomercials—I blew it all on ex-wives and girlfriends whose first names I can't even remember. But mostly in the form of tequila and coke, and I don't mean the kind in a can."

He looked up to the stars. In the darkened shadows, his expression was particularly grim. "So, tell me, Ms. Let's Have a Little Fun, have you ever hit rock bottom?"

There had been that moment standing in her dorm bathroom. She'd been nineteen and had just gotten a positive result on the pregnancy test.

"Don't even try," Paul answered himself. "I remember how strong you were. I was the weak one, eventually looking for courage in a white powder. You've never gotten to the point of having no reputation, let alone no self-esteem and credibility. So, in answer to the question that you never seemed to have gotten around to asking— the reason I came back to Grantham was to clean up my act and pick up the pieces. Figure out what went wrong. Start to write again, do something productive."

"But you have, right? I mean, you're taking classes?" Zora said encouragingly.

Paul emitted an abrupt laugh. "If you call taking an Adult School course classes. And you want to know why I chose Italian?"

"Of course. Tell me. I want to know."

"A long time ago when I first went out to L.A., I tried unsuccessfully for this assistant producer job. It was for a film being shot in Italy. Anyway, even though I didn't get it, the whole episode kind of lit this fire under me. I became obsessed with all things Italian—food, clothes, you name it. I even took private lessons. And then when I started raking in the money, I'd vacation in these amazing villas in Tuscany and Umbria, sometimes on Capri. It was like heaven. Can you say infinity pool? Well-stocked wine cellar? Of course, my money went and so did the vacations, but the memories remained. So now I have this dream—to go back, older and wiser, no pools and no wine. Just me, working on my book. Meaning, I've got to be content with Grantham, and I can't complain—even though I do—because the book's coming along, slowly, in large part due to joining A.A. And Italy? Well, that's still on the back burner."

"It all sounds wonderful, the way you've tackled your problems, not to mention your plans. I had no idea you had gone through such a rough time. But now you look great. Really, I mean it. And it seems to me that you've come out the other side and pulled yourself together."

"Not quite yet. I haven't sold the book, let alone se-cured an agent, just some nibbles—favors from a few old friends I didn't totally alienate," he said, not giving himself an inch.

"Still, it sounds like you have come a long way. Doesn't that mean you can make a fresh start?" Zora suggested. "Put the past in the past?"

"Does it? Isn't there something you'd like to share, too?"

AS SHE STEPPED ACROSS the threshold of her parents' home, her welcome was immediate. "*Zia Julie!* Aunt Julie!" The twins, Rosy and Amelia, her brother Dom's seven-year-old girls, tugged at her jacket.

"Where's the candy?" Rosy shouted.

Teddy, her other brother Joey's son, squirmed his way in and plunged his small hands into her pockets. "Choco, choco," the toddler Teddy chanted.

Normally the indulgent aunt, Julie squirreled away Hershey's Kisses in her pockets when she knew she was seeing her nieces and nephew, much to their delight and the horror of their parents, especially her sisters-in-law.

"I'm sorry, guys," she apologized. "I didn't expect you to be here on a school night."

"Dad said it was a special grown-up night, but that we were mature enough to come. I just learned that word—mature," Amelia said seriously. And then, taking a complete about-turn, she twirled around on the point of her Mary Janes, holding out the wide skirt of her plaid dress. "Do you like my dress?"

Julie felt a lump in her throat. "It's beautiful. Can I borrow it some time?" she asked.

Amelia giggled and pulled her twin away with her.

"Choco-choco." Teddy grabbed on her leg some more.

Julie's mother came scurrying over. "Don't bother *Zia* Julie. You know where I keep the Chex Mix in a dish on the sideboard." She gave him a friendly slap on the rump and pushed him in the right direction.

Julie slipped off her jacket and bent over to remove her black boots, silently cursing the fact that it would probably take twenty minutes to remove the skin-tight suede Cole Haans. Ah, the price she paid for vanity, and trying to impress Sebastiano. Geez, since when had she ever dressed to impress a man. Never was the answer.

"If you're trying to impress me, you've succeeded," Sebastiano whispered behind her.

She smiled, head pointed toward the floor. It had been worth it after all.

"Oh, don't bother with your shoes, Giulietta," her mother said. "We don't worry about things like that."

Julie straightened up. "Since when?"

"Since when it's a party." Her mother clucked, kissing her on both cheeks. She stepped aside to offer the same greeting to Sebastiano. "Ah, *Dottore,* we are honored you could make it. Here, Lou, take their coats."

Lou did as he was told, but before leaving he whispered in Julie's ear. "Happy birthday. But don't worry. Nobody will say anything."

She winced a smile of thanks as he squeezed her hand. Then she turned to Sebastiano. "So, once more into the breach, dear friend?" she offered, pointing the way to the center of the living room.

Easier said than done. Not only were her parents and *Nonna* there, but her brothers Dom, Frank and Joey, their wives and all the nieces and nephews—another boy of Dom's and Frank's baby—also filled the small room and overflowed into the dining room. Dom's wife, Barb, immediately grabbed Julie and started pumping her about Sebastiano. Her brothers hauled Sebastiano away and could be heard loudly predicting the outcome of the Eagles' football season. And meanwhile the kids, darting in and around everyone's feet, food stuffing their cheeks and fists, were not paying the least bit of attention when their parents' shushed them. Only when they came close to *Nonna*, did they think about stopping. She sat regally in her gold upholstered chair. A corner of one of Julie's pillows peeked out from behind her. And when the children were an arm's length away, she'd dart out her hand, slip them each a *caramella* and demand a peck on the cheek.

At one point, Julie, standing in the middle of the living room, glanced over the chaos in search of Sebastiano. She found him standing at the picture window with another sister-in-law—Mary Beth, Frank's wife. All seemed to be going well, and then Mary Beth handed him the three-month-old baby—breech, C-section, Julie cataloged in her brain.

"Oh, no," Julie said when she saw how uncomfortable he looked.

"You'd have thought he'd never held a baby before," Dom joked, coming over to Julie's side. He was holding a bottle of Sam Adams and munching on a large handful of Chex Mix, which Julie thought he could really have done without considering how the pounds were gradually creeping up on his stocky frame.

"What are you saying? Of course he has. He's a doctor, right?" Frank, the proud father, joined them. "Hey, you want me to take over?" he volunteered.

Sebastiano was gently jiggling the baby. He looked

over. "That's okay. I think I can handle it." He smiled at the baby. *"Stella, stellina,"* he softly sang the words to a traditional Italian lullaby, beginning "Star, little star." He glanced up again. "It's been a while, but it comes back, like riding a bicycle, no?"

"See, what did I tell you," Frank said. "A natural."

"Oppure, come qualcuno ch'è veramente un padre," *Nonna* announced behind them. "Like someone who is a father himself."

Julie glanced over her shoulder at her grandmother. "That's ridiculous. Sebastiano isn't even married." She watched him rock the baby and then saw that expression she knew all too well in new fathers.

Above the din of voices and squealing of children, *Nonna*'s canary could be heard warbling some off-key tune—the only pet bird that had a notoriously off-kilter musical sensibility.

Sebastiano continued to sing softly, more in key than Caruso. *"La notte si avvicina…*night is approaching."

"Wait a minute," Julie called out. "You're not married, right?"

Sebastiano stopped the lullaby and raised his head to Julie. "Technically, your grandmother's right. I am. Married. And I had a child."

CHAPTER EIGHTEEN

"I'M NOT SURE WHAT you're getting at, Paul," Zora answered.

Paul guffawed angrily. "Oh, please. Don't pretend like you don't know." He strode close to Zora and stared her down. "Katarina."

He didn't need to say any more. She glanced away. Then covered her mouth with the back of her hand, swallowed and met his gaze with a steely one of her own. "Oh, that."

"That indeed." Paul's voice rose in indignation. "Didn't it ever occur to you to tell me you were pregnant? Clearly not. You didn't even think to give me the option. Maybe I could have helped? Maybe it would have been the wake-up call I needed? Maybe it would have made me be something better than I was?"

"Don't lay your problems on me for not telling you I was pregnant," Zora countered.

"How do you think that makes me feel knowing that people think I abandoned you, abandoned her?"

Zora peered around nervously. "How about lowering your voice, would you?" She checked over her shoulder but didn't see anyone within earshot. She was angry and wanted to set him straight, once and for all. "And you can put your ego to rest. Nobody knows you're the father.

Nobody. I never even told my mother. Even Katarina doesn't know," she confessed.

"And you think that's fair?"

"Where do you get off? You think it was easy being a single mom in the eighties, still in school, practically a child myself? Don't tell me about fair. My decision to have Katarina had nothing to do with you. You were nothing more than a sperm donor. I don't know why I even contemplated sleeping with you again. I must have been out of my mind." She fumbled around for her knapsack, pawing in the dark for the side pocket where she kept her car keys. "I've had enough. I'm out of here."

"You're not the only one calling the shots now, Zora." Paul stepped even closer. "When I say it wasn't fair, I meant to Katarina, too. I'm going to talk to her. Tell her who I am. Maybe, if I'm lucky, start some kind of relationship. I'm not expecting a lot, but I think it would be good—for both of us."

Zora's head shot up. "No, you can't! I forbid it!"

"Forbid it? You don't have the right." Paul paused, looked sideways and gave himself a minute before he spoke. "Listen, I'm prepared to be reasonable about this. *You* can break the news to her first. But you've got until the end of the week—max. Then it's my turn." He waited.

She kept silent, hoping he'd just give up the argument.

"Do we have a deal?" he persisted.

Zora swung her backpack around and held it against her stomach. She frantically checked one pocket and then the next.

"Zora, are you even listening? Did you hear what I said?"

She nodded. "Yes, yes, I heard you. It's just that I don't know what's going on. I usually put my keys in one place, and I can't seem to find them. I like to keep things nice and neat just so this doesn't happen."

"Well, I'm sorry," Paul responded with little or no compassion. "But sometimes life isn't so nice and neat, is it?"

CHAPTER NINETEEN

SEBASTIANO'S ADMISSION STUNNED JULIE. But the dinner went on—for three courses.

Normally, she would have relished the meal, but tonight it tasted like dust, even her grandmother's deceptively simple yet flavorful soup *minestre con polpettini,* her mother's velvety lasagna made with homemade noodles and béchamel sauce and then veal *Saltimbocca,* that incredible combination of the thinnest of veal cutlets, prosciutto di Parma and mozzarella topped with the lightest chopped tomato sauce.

And normally, she would have embraced the bonhomie around the dining table crowded with the four generations of Antonellis. It would have been fun to play patty-cake with Rosy on one side, and on the other, listen while Mary Beth told her all about the latest food processor technology—her sister-in-law was a buyer for a high-end housewares retailer. She should have been laughing along with little Teddy while she amused him with touching the tip of her tongue to the point of her nose and then balancing a spoon on it—all her usual party tricks. And she should have been stealing glances at Sebastiano, who had been seated in a place of honor, at the far corner by the head of the table between *Nonna* and her father, catching his eye when he'd turn in her direction, smiling as she passed the bread toward that end of the table.

But she couldn't. "Technically, I'm married." What the hell did that mean anyway? Technically?

In fact, the only thing that gave her any pleasure after clearing the plates was volunteering to scrub the pans. She worked the scouring pad so hard she nearly wore the enamel off the big pot.

Then she angled her head around the open kitchen door and saw Frank had cadged Sebastiano's attention. Her brother was rotating his shoulder and pointing out the place where he was feeling some pain or other. Frank had played football in high school and still liked to think he could join pick-up games on the weekend. What a mistake. Long ago she had told him to see an orthopedist. Had he listened? Of course not. She was only his sister. What did she know?

She turned her attention back to the kitchen, searching the speckled Formica countertop for something else to clean. But there was nothing left to wash. With a sigh, she dipped her hands in the sudsy water and lifted the drain.

"*Tutti a tavola!* Everybody to the table!" her father called from the dining room. If three courses weren't enough, there was still dessert to go.

She wiped her hands on the dishtowel and, pulling back her shoulders until her spine cracked, ventured out the kitchen door, a smile affixed on her face.

"*Buon compleanno a te, boun compleanno a te.*" The whole family was singing the Italian rendition of "Happy Birthday." There was a large sheet cake in the center of the table, its tiny candles alight. Flowers of frosting rimmed the edges like a Baroque frame. The only thing lacking was the gilding.

Julie's heart sank. Just when she thought things couldn't get any worse… She stepped close, expecting all eyes to turn to her, but when she saw the letters on the cake she blinked.

The birthday being honored wasn't hers. It was *Nonna*'s.

Julie's father came over to her and put his arm around her. "I know it was your birthday yesterday, but *Nonna*'s is next week, and she is turning seventy-five. That works for you, right?" Lou asked, giving her a squeeze.

"It works for me just fine. Thanks, Dad, as always." She was worried she might start crying. She sniffed and shook her head in a quick recovery. Then she waded through the family, especially the kids, who were hanging around the table and choosing which frosting flower was theirs, and stooped next to her grandmother.

Julie kissed her on her dry cheek. For the occasion, she noticed that *Nonna* wore her best little drop-diamond earrings. The pierced holes in her ears were now more a thin line than distinct points. *"Buon compleanno, Nonna.* Happy birthday, *Nonna*."

The older woman smiled and patted her hand, then turned her full attention to the cake. She blew out her candles with the help of all the great-grandchildren. Then she herded them around her and started telling Julie's mom how to cut the cake, designating who got which piece and how big. Somehow they all got ginormous portions with flowers.

There was a loud ping on a crystal wine glass. *"At-tenzione!"* Lou tapped his wineglass again. He picked up a large envelope from the white lace tablecloth.

"Nonna," Lou began, speaking his mother's title with respect and love, "in honor of your birthday, we, the family, have decided to give you a special present." He rocked on the heels of his slippers and milked the moment. "Angela and I are taking you to Italy, back to your village in the Abruzzi. We know you haven't been back since you came to America, but we have been in touch with some of the family still there, and they are anxious to see you. And then afterward, all three of us are going on a Mediterranean cruise for ten days, along the Amalfi coast, to *Sicilia, Sardenia,* over to the French Riviera. Not bad, eh?" He gave her the envelope and a big hug.

Nonna stared blindly at the envelope, tears welling in her eyes. She pulled a white hankie from the sleeve of her black sweater and dotted her eyes. She passed the envelope back to her son, asking him to open it. "My arthritis," she complained in Italian, to mask the fact that her hands were shaking with emotion.

Lou opened the envelope, read aloud the card—it had gilt-edge flowers, Julie saw—and removed the tickets and a brochure from the cruise-ship line. He handed them to his mother, and she studied them carefully, rubbing her nose with the handkerchief.

"Scusa. Partiamo la prossima settimana? Excuse me, we leave next week?" she asked her son.

"We have to be there for your birthday," he reassured her. "The whole family in Italy has already begun cooking. And now that your heart has checked out fine, there's no excuse. Not even passports. You remember how I insisted you get one over the summer so that you would have a picture ID since you didn't have a driver's license?" Lou tapped his temple. "I was already planning, thinking ahead."

Nonna nodded, clutching the tickets. "*Che bravo figlio mio!* My terrific son!" She examined the tickets closely, then looked up. "What deck are we on the boat?" she asked in Italian. "I want a window to see out."

Everyone laughed.

"Don't worry, *Nonna*," Angela spoke up. "For you, we all got the best. A suite!" She bustled off to the kitchen to put on the coffee.

Julie leaned toward her brother Dom. "So how come nobody told me? My money's not good enough suddenly?"

Dom shrugged. "Mom and Dad didn't tell anybody but me. They probably thought you guys wouldn't be able to keep a secret from *Nonna*."

"That's true. She can read me like a book. But still, you're so good at holding your tongue? I don't think so," she teased him.

"Don't take it personally. The only reason they told me was because I could get them a good deal through the sister of the guy I work for. She owns a travel agency...."

Julie tuned out the rest. Dom was an insurance agent. He already handled her malpractice insurance, but was constantly angling for Julie to get term life insurance or an annuity or some other "financial instrument." There were times when Julie knew just where she'd like to put some of her instruments. But she was sure he'd get a good deal, come what may. She glanced over at her grandmother to smile and saw her talking to Sebastiano. For a minute there, she had almost forgotten about him.

Actually, less than half a minute, more like a quarter. Okay, ten seconds.

She peered at her watch, wondering if it was too early to leave. She could always make an excuse, claim that one of her patients was going into labor.

She made a beeline to the living room window and tried to remember when she'd last used the same lie. She looked out the rectangular panes of the bow window and saw her fragmented reflection in the glass. The image was too appropriate to be accidental. If she weren't careful, she'd start believing in superstitious powers like her grandmother.

She switched her view to the family photos lovingly displayed along the windowsill, a pictorial journey through the years of children and grandchildren—births, weddings and graduations. There used to be one of her in a U Conn basketball uniform. After the car crash, it had quietly been removed.

Julie wet her lips. Would she ever be able to get away from her past, be able to put it safely away in an emotional drawer? Last night, her conversation with Sebastiano had seemed to help. His advice had hit a chord. But what about him?

The man was full of secrets, secrets that he selectively divulged—first his alcoholism, now that he was married. In her book, there were two nonnegotiable rules when it came to relationships between consenting adults. Number One was the use of contraception, and Number Two was that both parties were single. Failure on either account was a deal breaker as far as she was concerned. She couldn't fault him on the first, but it appeared that he'd failed miserably on the second.

She sensed footsteps coming up behind her but didn't bother to look to see who it was. She knew.

How come after less than a week, she could recognize the sound of his walk, identify his subtle scent and just know? Why wasn't life as logical and rational as a medical textbook? She shook her head. It just wasn't fair.

"Do you think we can safely sneak out now?" he asked, his voice caressing the side of her head.

She swirled around, her arms crossed. "You think I have any intention of leaving with you?"

"I'm sorry. I thought from across the room that you looked tired. I was merely thinking of you, trying to help out."

She frowned.

"I've done something wrong?" Sebastiano asked. "I don't understand, especially when we have hardly talked the whole evening."

"Oh, I think you said it all when you told my grandmother that you were married." She strummed the fingers of both hands on her upper arms.

"Oh, that."

"Yeah, 'oh, that.'"

"I should have said something, I know, but it's really something out of my past, that was over a long time ago. We both wanted the divorce, very amicable, but unfortunately, according to Italian law, it still takes three years of separation for it to be legal. The whole thing should be finalized in less than a month. So you see, there's really nothing to talk about." He went to touch her arm.

She pulled back. "Why do I get the feeling there is more to this than meets the eye? You say it's just the

past, but we both know the past just doesn't go away—
even for people not as crazy as me. If it were simply a
matter of legal procedure, why wouldn't you have told
me about it already? And what about the child you mentioned? Huh? That's more than a legal procedure."

She saw him glance away. It was the first cowardly
thing she had ever seen him do. And beyond his shoulder
she noticed from the other room that *Nonna* was staring
at them. All she needed now was for Caruso to start
singing ominously, and the scene would be complete.

She steeled her resolve. "No, there's something else.
Something you're hiding. And you're going to tell me,
you are. Because, trust me, I didn't grow up in a household of three brothers without knowing how to get them
to talk."

CHAPTER TWENTY

KATARINA HUNG UP the phone on the nightstand next to her side of the bed and rolled over, snuggling close to her husband, her stomach spooning against his broad back. No matter what the temperature, Ben insisted on sleeping in the nude. She shifted the duvet over her shoulders and wrapped her arm around his waist, grateful for his furnace-like body temperature on the chilly night.

"Who was that?" Ben grumbled, half-asleep. He reached down and squeezed her hand. With a baby in the house, they had learned not to stay up late, because as sure as the sun came up the next morning, baby Rad would be up at the crack of dawn, chirping more insistently than the cardinals that had taken up residence in the Norway maples outside their bedroom window.

"It was Zora." Katarina rubbed her cheek against his shoulder.

Ben shifted his weight and turned around. "You're kidding me? Your mother? The only woman in the world who told her daughter when she was barely out of diapers to call her by her first name because 'only insipid bourgeois families insisted on such traditional paradigms.' Hell, I had to look up the meaning of 'insipid,' and I'm forty. So, tell me. What did Zora the Great want now? To let you know she was rushing out of your life yet again?"

"Oh, don't be so hard on her. She didn't have it easy raising a kid and trying to finish school and build a career."

"I'm tired of feeling sorry for her. And as far as raising a kid, it seems to me that any credit for that belongs to *Babička* and yourself."

Katarina touched him lovingly on the cheek with the pad of her thumb. "My hero. Whatever happened, it's in the past."

"Well, you know my opinion on that. Your past is never that far away—look how it still makes me such a weird misanthrope," he replied.

"You're not weird and you're not the lone wolf you pretend to be. Two children and a wife, plus regular attendance at high school orchestra concerts. Seems to me you've become a functioning member of society. And I think that makes you pretty special."

Ben frowned. "So what did she want?"

Katarina bit down on her lower lip in thought. "It was the strangest thing. She wanted to get together to talk about Matt applying to college, of all things. She never even got involved when *I* was applying."

"See, I told you she can still get to you." He rubbed his hand up and down the side of her hip, somehow managing to raise her nightgown to her waist.

Katarina smiled, keenly aware of his touch on her skin. "Whatever. I told her I'd meet her tomorrow morning at *Babička*'s. Knowing Zora, she'll probably lose interest after one sip of coffee."

He snaked his hand around to fondle her breast. "Well, as long as that's settled, about your level of interest...now?"

Katarina's breath caught in her throat as he toyed with

her nipple. "As tempting as that sounds, do you realize the baby's going to wake up in—" she stretched to read the alarm clock next to his side of the bed "—less than seven hours?"

Ben stilled his hand. "Is it that late? I've got to catch the seven-oh-five train into the city in the morning to try to interest investors in Outdoor Family Initiative. I'd like more funding to help me with new ways to reach out to multigenerational families with disabled members."

The past was never far away, Katarina realized. Ben, who had grown up an unwanted orphan, shunted from one foster home to the next, now put all his professional energies into his nonprofit organization that brought families together on outdoor adventures. She wiggled closer, her nose close to his. "Rain check, then?"

"Rain check," he concurred. "But at least, let me give you a cuddle."

She turned on her side, her back to him, and let him envelop her in his strength. Within a minute she could hear his faint snoring.

Oh, how quickly new love fades, she thought, smiling as she fell asleep.

"MOM, A LARGE Tupperware container of leftovers is a bit overkill. I think a small one will probably last me more than long enough," Julie protested as she tried to head out the door. She had not needed the patient-in-labor excuse because the party had broken up anyway— right after the children had eaten too much cake and started bouncing off the walls, cranky from their sugar highs.

Now she was just trying to extricate herself from her parents' place without having to carry her weight in lasagna. Somehow Frank and Mary Beth had managed to escape without being loaded down with food—*it helped having a sleeping baby slung over your shoulder*, Julie thought. Joey and family had slipped out the backdoor. *Totally unfair.* At least Dom had agreed to take cake for the office tomorrow.

Actually, Julie wouldn't mind gorging herself on sugary frosting right now, but somehow her mother had neglected to include that in her haul.

"Nonsense," Angela protested, handing Sebastiano an equally large container.

"You're too kind," he said, taking the food.

With cake! Julie couldn't help noticing. *There was no justice.*

"I'm sure you've seen the way she eats," Angela said to Sebastiano as if Julie weren't standing right there. "A candy bar here, a soda there. Some day it will catch up to her and she'll gain weight and lose all her teeth."

"On that happy note, thanks for the evening, Mom. And I'll stop by at the garage tomorrow and give you a check for my share of *Nonna's* birthday gift."

Angela offered up her cheek as Julie bent to kiss her. "Good. Then I can give you a copy of our itinerary. You have a key to the house, right? For when we're away."

Julie rolled her eyes. "Is the Pope Catholic?" Then she saw her mother's horrified look. "Sorry, just a figure of speech."

Angela shook her head. "Always quick with the wisecrack." She shot a knowing glance at Sebastiano.

"Why am I not surprised?" he responded with a smile.

Great, her boyfriend—no, she couldn't call him that now, and, frankly, had they ever really established that kind of a relationship?—was siding with her mother. "Mom, about the key and keeping an eye on the house while you're gone. You know my schedule. I'm always working."

"And your brothers aren't? Besides they have families to take care of, children."

Julie looked away. There was no way she could trump that double whammy.

"Anyway, it's not like you'll have a lot to do. I've already stopped the newspaper while we're gone. And I told the postman. Still, you might check that there're no packages or that no branches have fallen from the maples on the lawn. You know how your father is about the branches."

It was true, if Julie's father could have vacuumed the grass he would have. His favorite thing in the world was his gas-powered leaf blower.

"Okay, Mom, no problem. I'll make sure the lawn is clean enough to eat off. But we really have to go now. I've got to make rounds first thing in the morning."

"You always have rounds first thing in the morning," Angela pointed out.

"And Sebastiano has an early meeting," Julie added.

"Well, in that case." Angela shooed them to the door.

Sebastiano waited for her on the path, his food tucked under her arm. "I suppose you still want to talk?"

"You think you can delay this any longer?" She shot him a look. "I don't think so."

"Your place then?"

She hesitated. She didn't want to be sidetracked. Actually, tempted was more accurate. And despite her fury, she still found him oh, so tempting. "No, definitely not my place." And before he could offer the obvious, she added, "And not yours. As much as I'm curious what kind of décor a hospital CEO chooses for his abode—"

"Abode?"

She scowled. "Don't try to get cute. I think neutral territory is called for. Bean World."

"You think it'll be open at this time of night?" He glanced at his watch.

Rolex, Julie noticed with a sneer. Well, who was she to talk about name brands when she was carrying a Prada bag? She pulled back her sleeve and looked at her illuminated watch face. "No problem. It's only ten-thirty now."

"I just hope we don't run into anyone we know," he said.

"Well, my friends are new moms, and for Sarah and Katarina, late night gab sessions went out the window as soon as diapers came into the picture."

"Did you ever think that I might also have some friends?"

She fished her car keys out of her pocket and opened the back door of her car to put in the leftovers. She turned back. "So, I guess since you brought your car, too, we might as well just meet there. And frankly, I'm not so concerned about friends. It's the rest of Grantham that can be a real pain."

SEBASTIANO GOT TO the coffee shop first. *That's what happens when you don't drive the speed limit.* Julie, he knew, would make sure to go two miles under.

He stood next to the glass case containing cookies and sandwiches. In front was a small seating area that was exposed to the street. He glanced over his shoulder to survey the raised seating area at the rear of the store. There was only one guy hunched over a laptop, a woolen knit hat pulled low on his brow. The coast appeared pretty clear then. *Good.* He wanted as much discretion as possible.

A whoosh of cool nighttime air sharply invaded the cramped space. Only one person Sebastiano knew could disrupt heaven and earth so quickly. Julie. Only someone with that much force of personality could have corralled him into talking about his past. The question was, was he ready? Would he ever be ready?

Julie pulled the loose blazer tightly across her dress and her eyes met his. She strode over to him and shifted her focus, studying the baked goods on display.

"I think I'll have a brownie, two even. This moment definitely requires chocolate."

Sebastiano shrugged. Who was he to judge a woman possessed? He turned to the barista, a young woman with a pierced eyebrow and a tattoo of a dragon on her left shoulder. "We'll have two brownies for here."

"Two plates?" the barista asked, her eyebrows raised provocatively. She looked solely at Sebastiano.

Julie angled her shoulder in front. "That's one, just one."

The barista backed off. "Anything to drink?" she asked, her tone shifting to neutral.

Sebastiano turned to Julie. She was disquietingly near. "Herbal tea?"

She blinked. "Are you kidding me?"

"Of course. Foolish me. Two double-shot espressos. Also for here." He pulled out his wallet.

Julie placed a twenty and a Bean World frequent

buyer card on the counter. "Let's agree this one's on me. My gesture of goodwill."

"You really think it will be enough?" His tone was skeptical.

Julie took the plate and started to nibble. "Frankly, I hope not."

Sebastiano indicated a table in the corner all the way in the back. "Why don't you take a seat, and I'll bring over the coffees." For once she didn't argue, and Sebastiano supposed he should feel lucky. He didn't.

He was right.

"How come you've led everybody to believe you're single?" she asked, cross-examining him before he had even sat down.

He rested the tiny cups and saucers on the small round table and fished out two packets of sugar and a stir stick from his coat pocket. "I couldn't remember whether you took sugar." He pulled out his chair and sat down, resting one hand on the tabletop. The wood was sticky.

He rubbed his skin, and before she could pounce again, he answered her question. "I've never discussed my private life with anyone. What people presumed about my marital status was what they chose to believe." He drank the espresso in one gulp. The strong brew burned a hole in his already irritated stomach. He crossed his legs. It was impossible to get comfortable in the small bentwood chair.

"Why did I even assume that we could have a straightforward discussion?" She threw up her hands, then rested her elbows on the table.

"You might not want to do that," he cautioned.

She held up her hands as if to silence him.

Good. He really preferred to say nothing.

"Okay, let me start all over." She took a bite of a brownie and chewed thoughtfully. "Why didn't you tell *me* you were married?"

He recrossed his legs and sat forward. "You have things about your past. I have things about mine—things we'd all rather forget." His voice was discreetly low.

"Excuse me, less than twenty-four hours ago you were encouraging me to open up about my past, if I remember correctly."

"I remember a number of things about last night," he responded. He wasn't about to make this conversation easy on her, either.

"Yes…well…there is that." She polished off her brownie. "For the moment I'd rather forget about those other things."

"I think I'll retain the memories nonetheless."

"Yes, well, you're you, and I'm me." Julie set her jaw. "Listen, you talk about wanting to forget your past, but I find it impossible to believe that it's easy to forget you have a wife, not to mention a child."

"As for my wife, I haven't seen her for more than seven years. Besides, she's already moved on, and is living with someone else."

Julie picked up the second brownie and bit into it. She put it back on the plate. "Maybe it wasn't such a good idea to order that, as well." She still took another bite before pushing the plate away. "So let me get this straight. You claim you don't think about your wife anymore, but you'd still rather not talk about her. Does that mean that you're still not over her? I mean, I presume she left you, right?"

Sebastiano shook his head. He opened his hands,

palm sides up. "No, you don't understand." His expression was obscure. "She didn't leave me. I left her."

Julie frowned. "Now I really don't get it."

Sebastiano looked at the wall over her shoulder. There was an exhibition of artwork by students from the local Quaker school, and he found himself staring at the painting of a cat. Its head and whiskers occupied most of the picture. He noticed the card next to it, identifying the artist as an eight-year-old girl. The age Violetta would have been if she had lived.

He turned back to Julie. "Why don't we just leave it as one of those unexplained mysteries of life?"

She frowned. "I don't think so. Besides, I think you owe me."

"Why? Because we almost had sex?" He could tell immediately that his words had stung. "Sorry. That was nasty. When I feel put upon I have a bad habit of lashing out."

Julie looked like she was doing her best to put a lid on her temper. "Okay, do I need to spell out to you why I think you should tell me?"

Sebastiano swallowed. "If you're implying that we have more than a mutual physical attraction, that we appear to be laying the groundwork for something deeper, more emotionally rewarding, I'm not sure that's possible. In any case, once you hear what I have to tell you, you may not want to." He stared, not blinking into her eyes.

She wet her lips, as if digesting his words, but still held his gaze, unwilling to back down.

In a clear voice without any inflection he explained,

"Even though I was a trained physician, I willingly allowed my baby girl to die a painful death. In fact, I orchestrated it."

CHAPTER TWENTY-ONE

JULIE DIDN'T SAY ANYTHING.

Sebastiano had hoped she would have gotten up and left after what he'd said. That would have been easy.

She rested her head in her hand and waited.

Once more, life wasn't easy.

He rubbed the side of his jaw and glanced down into his empty coffee cup. The remains of the espresso coated the white china surface. He spoke, and as he stared into the murky depths, he found himself transported back to the past. He was still sitting in Bean World, but the images were as fresh as if he were experiencing them for the first time.

"I was at university, getting my medical degree. I had been married for two years. Raffaela and I had known each other since we were children. We grew up on the same street in Milano, went to school together. Our families were best friends. It had been so natural to marry."

He looked but didn't look at Julie. He was hardly aware of her nodding.

"She was studying law when we realized she was pregnant. We were happy but nervous, unsure of how we could afford a family. We were living in a studio apartment that was attached to her family's house. But she decided to quit school until the baby came, work in a law office as a clerk, make money to put away with the idea of going back to school later. We had it all planned."

He could feel his throat get tighter. "The pregnancy had been uneventful. Raffaela blossomed. I had never seen her so happy. Then the baby was born." He stopped. In his eyes, he witnessed himself holding Violetta in his arms. A shiver ran up and down his skin as he relived all the hope and pride that a new father feels.

"Then what happened?" Julie prompted quietly.

He heard her as if from far away.

"At first, everything seemed to be fine. The baby nursed well and was alert. I went to classes and was absorbed in my studies. Too absorbed. One night I came home to find Raffaela crying. She had had an appointment with the pediatrician because the baby seemed to be losing weight. Appeared listless, at times cranky.

"I said that probably she was just teething and the pediatrician was unnecessarily concerned. He was like that. I had never liked him. I thought he was too old-fashioned. He had been the choice of my mother-in-law."

Sebastiano raised his head. He seemed to see Julie for the first time. "I was wrong. We went back to the doctor. Had tests run. Violetta had a tumor in her stomach."

"Oh, no, you must have been beside yourself." Julie reached out and laid her hand atop his.

He looked down, confused to feel her touch. Then he lifted his chin to make eye contact. "No, on the contrary, I felt sure that I could cure her. When others tried to suggest that perhaps it was time to let nature take its course, I belittled them as uninformed and having no faith in the power of medicine. I sought out further specialists, put my child through numerous surgeries, rounds of chemotherapy and months of living in hospitals."

"I can't imagine," Julie said.

"Neither can I now, not really. But I was convinced that if I spent more time learning about cancer, I could cure her. Meanwhile, my wife moved into the hospital. She was essentially living there while I still went to classes. She bore the brunt of the agony, not me," he confessed.

"But you thought you were doing the right thing, everything that was in your power as a physician to help," Julie argued.

"Was I?" Sebastiano asked, the agony cracking his voice. "Oh, there were times when she rallied, when we thought she was going to pull through. I was sure I was vindicated in my obsession. What a fool! Those times turned out to be short-lived. Violetta died nine months later, never having left the hospital, with tubes and machines tied to her emaciated, shriveled body. I felt destroyed."

"As any parent would be," Julie said, empathizing.

Sebastiano blinked. He noticed she had tears streaming down her face. His own eyes were dry. He hadn't cried since the day Violetta died. "But would any parent have chosen to abandon his wife without a word, leaving no address, refusing to communicate in any way?"

JULIE RUBBED her forehead. The story Sebastiano had told was almost too much to comprehend. As an obstetrician she had seen her fair share of things go wrong, unexplained miscarriages, complicated births, stillborn babies and babies born with severe physical challenges.

But it was another to hear it voiced in such a personal and heart-rending way.

But not to reach out to his wife in such a time of distress? When as a new mother, she must have been suffering from an agony almost unheard of?

It was so easy to dismiss him as having acted cruelly. Of being selfish. But could she truly say that she would have acted differently? The only person close to her who had died had been her grandfather. After *Babbo*'s death, she remembered hiding in her closet until her mother had found her the next morning. Still, she had been a child. She played over Sebastiano's words in her mind. "How long did you run away for?"

"Forever," he said simply.

"I don't understand. I mean, I might complain about my parents and my brothers… Okay, I do complain, a lot. But bottom line, I could never imagine cutting all ties."

"Just another instance where we disagree," he replied matter-of-factly.

There was a silence between them.

"You mean, you haven't spoken to Raffaela or your parents since your daughter's death?"

He shook his head. "Not really, no. At first, I wandered, traveled to Sicily, then North Africa. I finally decided to go back to school, switched my specialty from oncology to cardiology. I couldn't deal with the first. I transferred to Rome, away from home, some place where I was anonymous. I finished my degree, but even that wasn't enough. I decided I didn't want any contact with patients. Even that was too much.

"I switched to hospital administration and went to France, getting an MBA from INSEAD, in Fontainebleau. Then I came to America, first to a job in Houston, then to Providence, Rhode Island. I did well, but I wanted to shape a hospital the way I envisioned it should run. Create something from scratch. Then came the opportunity in Grantham. I grabbed it."

"And all this time you haven't gone back to Italy?"

"Not once," he said with a single shake of his head. "It was too difficult."

She wrinkled her forehead. "Wait a minute. You must have been in touch in some way. Otherwise, how would you know about your wife? You filed for separation, even divorce?"

Sebastiano nodded wearily. "That's the problem with talking to people who actually listen. They have a way of asking questions." He sighed. "I'd like to say that after a period of recovery I took the initiative and called her. Unfortunately, it was more that my mother tracked me down. Don't ask how—Italian mothers have ways. Anyway, to make a long story short, my mother took it upon herself to visit me in France. The first thing she did was to throw her arms around me. The second thing she did after she smelled my breath, was to ask me why I'd been drinking when it was only eight in the morning?"

"So that's how you became an alcoholic?"

"I was always an alcoholic," Sebastiano corrected her. "Alcoholism isn't something that happens overnight. You're born with an addictive personality. In my case, my drinking was all part of my running away, my denial of reality. And like most alcoholics, I was convinced that I had it all under control. I reasoned that if anyone deserved a drink, it was me."

"But at the same time you hated yourself for your

dependency, and what you saw as another act of cow-ardice," Julie added, assessing the situation.

Sebastiano held up his index finger. "Are you sure your specialty wasn't psychiatry?"

Julie ignored his question. "So what did you mother do?"

"She cleaned up my apartment, cooked me enough food to last several weeks and put Raffaela's phone number on the refrigerator door. Then she put on her coat, gave me a big hug and told me to call, but only after I'd started attending Alcoholics Anonymous. My mother can be a very forceful person."

"I think I like your mother," Julie said.

Sebastiano ruminated a moment. "You two would probably get along well."

Julie took a second to study what was left of her remaining brownie. "So did you follow her advice?"

He shook his head. "Not right away. It took until I was in Houston that I was ready to confront my addiction. It's been over six years since I had a drink."

"And during that time you never spoke to your wife?"

"My mother would call every couple of months. No pressure, just chitchat—about the family, news that Raffaela had gone back to school, had moved into an apartment on her own."

"And then you finally called her?"

He breathed in slowly. "Yes, I finally swallowed my guilt and called. It was a difficult conversation, probably the most difficult one I've had—up until now."

"And what was her reaction? Did she want to see you? Get back together?" Julie couldn't imagine the myriad emotions the woman must have been feeling.

"I'm not sure. To see me? Perhaps? To get back together? I didn't think so. Not that she spelled it out in so many words. But before she could even broach the subject, I told her I thought it was time for both of us to move on, to make new lives for ourselves. I said that my mother had told me she had already gone back to school, so she seemed to be on that track anyway."

"And that was it? No argument?" Julie was astounded.

"She asked if I intended to come back to Italy, and I told her no. She didn't say anything more. I think all the feelings we had for each other had gotten used up years before."

Julie ran a fingernail against her bottom teeth. "Are you saying that you didn't love her anymore?"

Sebastiano hesitated. "It was more that I didn't have any more love to give. I still cared for her in the sense that I wanted to see her happy. And when she called me some months later to let me know she had met someone, I was genuinely glad. To move to an official separation seemed the logical step."

Julie opened her mouth as she parsed his words. "Let me get this straight. You didn't have any more love to give to *her* or to give *period?*"

Sebastiano hunched forward and steepled his hands, letting his fingertips bounce against his lips. "You must understand." He held his hands toward her. "The way I've learned to function is to lead an orderly life. No big emotional highs. And no big emotional lows. That way I keep everything in its place. And don't give me that look."

Julie tipped her chair on its back legs. "Did I say anything?"

"You didn't have to. I know what you're thinking, and however you might object, this way of living allows me to put one step ahead of the next with little drama and great care. You see, you're not the only control freak. I just manifest it differently." He started to gather up their cups, stacking the saucers on top of each other and balancing one cup within the other.

Julie pitched her weight forward, and the chair legs thumped to the ground. "Hold on a minute. You didn't think you could lay this all on me and not hear from me?"

"I suppose that was too much to ask for." He rose to put the dishes in a rubber tub by the wall.

"Just leave those dishes, would you?"

He sat.

She touched her breastbone and spoke from the heart. "I feel for you. I really do. No one should have to go through what you suffered. On the other hand, your solution to this terrible, horrible, agonizing experience? I just don't understand it."

She held out her hands, palms up, as if weighing her thoughts. "Yes, you let down people you loved and who loved you—people who were hurting just as much as you. What you did was horrible, but we all do stupid, sometimes awful things under stress. Did you go beyond the boundaries? I'm not sure. I'm certainly not one to judge."

She scrunched up her mouth. "On the other hand, I look at what you've become. I hear you talk about creating a hospital from scratch, which some might say is an act of ambition—not that all ambition is bad. But I think it's more, a part of who you are."

Julie reached across the table to Sebastiano. A sticky

surface was the last thing on her mind. "I think your professional ambition reflects your personal plan. I think it's all part of coming to America to recreate yourself, build a new you—one without a past." She squeezed his hands and let go.

But she didn't stop talking. "All I can say is, nice try. But it's a losing proposition." She held up her hand when he looked like he was going to protest. "No, let me finish. Yours is a neat and tidy solution, but as one control freak to another, life just isn't neat and tidy. Someone told me that once. The real solution, I think, is not to forget but to let go—granted, something I have yet to master. But if we could—you *and* me—we'd be able to let go of this millstone of guilt that hangs around our necks. The problem is, you *want* to be weighted down. You *want* to hold yourself to such a high standard of excellence, of control, and so you're inevitably doomed to failure, doomed to keep punishing yourself."

"Any other criticism you want to level at me? I can give you my other cheek to slap, too, if you want?" he said, turning his face.

"Sneer all you want. I admit I'm a mess, but at least I listened to what you had to say and processed it."

He raised a skeptical brow.

"Okay, semiprocessed it. And for another thing—" she jabbed her finger forward "—at least I still put my neck out there for things I believe in. My patients, their rights, my friends and family, needlepoint. No, forget needlepoint." She waved off that last item. "The thing I'm getting at, is that you may think you can isolate yourself, cut yourself off from feelings and other people as a way of protecting yourself—"

"And others," Sebastiano interrupted.

"Oh, my God, talk about guilt! Now you have the power to determine whether other people live happily? If that's the case, your problem isn't guilt, it's total, un-mitigated gall."

A shadow fell across the table.

Julie swiveled, felt a crick in her neck, right at the base. Too much stress, no exercise, falling asleep with someone else on her couch… None of those things good, it seemed.

Nor was the prospect of having to explain what was going on to Rufus, the person who had joined them. *It could be worse,* she supposed. *It could be…I don't know…her mother…Nonna…even Iris Phox.*

"Rufus, what a surprise," she exclaimed, and she really meant it. Sebastiano pushed his chair back.

"No, no, don't get up for me." Rufus stopped him with a shake of his hand. In the other, he held a take-out coffee cup. "Though I must admit, from across the room it looked like I should grab a seat, front and center, and take in the action," he joked.

Julie had the immediate compulsion to lie—otherwise her mother, *Nonna* and Iris Phox would hear what had been going on by noon the next day. Who was she kidding? By 9:00 a.m.

"Hi, Rufus. We were…ah…just hashing out this whole clinic issue again," she said, blurting out the first thing that came to mind. "You know me. Once I get the bit between my teeth, I just can't let go." *God, that sounded so lame,* she moaned internally.

"And here I thought you were just having a coffee together. I guess looks can be deceiving."

"Won't you join us?" Sebastiano offered. He reached to the side to pull over another chair.

"Thank you, but I'll have to take a rain check," Rufus said. "I just stopped by to pick up a cup of hot cocoa before heading over to the Nighttime Bar. I want to start doing an inventory, never a fun task no matter what time of day or night. But if I'm ever going to sell the place, I better find out what I've got—especially in the basement. I've got all sorts of stuff there—tools, paint cans from my father's day and I think even a gas pump that I've never quite figured out."

"You can't sell," Julie protested. "What will Grantham do without the Nighttime Bar?"

"It's like this. My new hip has given me a new lease on life, that's for sure, but it's not enough for me to keep running the place. Still, it's nice to know that while we're here, we serve the best beer in town at the best prices. Be that as it may, I still say Bean World has the best cocoa. You can keep the designer espresso drinks and chai lattes. True insiders know about the cocoa," Rufus said with a wink.

"I'll have to remember to tell people that," Sebastiano said with a nod. "It will help to change my image as a newcomer."

Rufus raised his chin. A hand-knit scarf wrapped tightly around his thin neck was neatly tucked into a dark zip jacket with the logo Grantham High School Lions on the left side. "Well, if you keep up these late night chats with one of our homegrown girls, you can't help but be accepted." He paused, his thick gray eyebrows lifting ever so slightly. "Even if it is business. Aren't I right, Julie?"

She scratched the back of her neck and looked upward to reply. "You know what they say about mixing business with pleasure?"

TRACY KELLEHER   193

Rufus carefully replaced the plastic lid on his cup and licked his fingers where the hot chocolate had spilled. "Don't tell me you believe everything people say? You know my motto? Never assume—about anything or anyone." He tipped his cap and headed toward the door.

Julie turned back to Sebastiano. "The man has real wisdom. Either that or an amazing shtick."

Sebastiano narrowed his eyes. "That's Yiddish, right? Iris was correct. I really must get a dictionary." He picked up their cups and saucers again, and stood. "So tell me, in light of all we said tonight, am I right to assume that from now on you'll simply go back to hating me?"

Julie gathered up her shoulder bag, quickly checking her phone for messages out of habit. She glanced up as she finished scrolling down and saw him waiting. "I never hated you—more like harbored an intense irritation. But then I got to know you, or, at least, I thought I did." She stopped talking and peered into his eyes.

He swallowed. "And now? Now that you *really* know me?"

"I don't know. I'm..."

"Disappointed?"

She mulled over his suggestion. "No, that's too easy an emotion. I'd say more that I'm confused, sad, even a little frustrated—at you for thinking the way you do... and for me, for maybe overreacting about... I don't know what to call it really? Possibilities? Of you and me?"

She ran her hand through her hair. Her bangs were sticking straight out from the workout she'd given them this evening. "Whatever. That's my problem, not yours. In any case, I'm too tired to think straight, and from the number of messages—" she waggled her phone in front of her "—I have another baby wanting to come into this world in a few hours. So, I'm off to the hospital to do my duty."

"You sure you're just not using that as an excuse to get away from me?" Sebastiano asked.

She laughed, though not really amused. "Never assume."

SEBASTIANO WATCHED her leave, taking whatever fresh air there was out the door with her, as well. He'd always felt that Italians, to be overly simplistic, were a pessimistic lot. After years—centuries—of living with corrupt governments and inefficient bureaucracies, most Italians, when confronted with the latest scandal or some new crisis, merely shrugged and shook their heads as if to say, "What else is new?"

And here, faced with a crisis of his own making, what had he done? Not merely thrown up his hands, but practically used them to push away the one person who had touched him physically and emotionally in longer than he cared to remember.

His phone vibrated in his pants pocket. Sebastiano smiled. An incoming text message. Maybe there was reason to go against cultural stereotypes and be optimistic? Maybe Julie had realized that there was something, albeit small, that was redeeming about him, worth believing in? As Rufus had said, never assume.

He looked down at the caller ID. And rushed out

the door—unaware that he still was holding their dirty dishes. Oh, his smile?

It was gone.

CHAPTER TWENTY-TWO

"THANKS FOR coming, Sebastiano. I figured you were the person to call," Rufus said.

"No problem." Sebastiano shook hands with Rufus as soon as he entered the Nighttime Bar.

"He hasn't actually had anything to drink, he just keeps ordering them and staring at them." He pointed toward the figure hunched over in the shadows.

"I'll take it from here then, " Sebastiano replied.

"If you need me, I'll be in the basement."

Sebastiano nodded. "Thanks. How much does he owe you?" He started to pull out his wallet.

Rufus waved him off. "Forget it. This one's on me." He stared at Sebastiano. "Good luck."

Sebastiano tipped his head. "I'll need it." He breathed in slowly and headed toward the end of the mahogany bar.

Behind it, soft lighting showcased bottles of liquor lined up neatly on glass shelves. There were the requisite photos of local sports teams sponsored by the bar. The brass handles of the beer taps gleamed from polish and years of use.

The bartender saw Sebastiano approach. He made a drinking motion with his hand as if to ask for an order. Sebastiano shook his head and silently indicated he was joining the man at the end of the bar. The communication was clear, and the bartender gave him a wide berth.

Sebastiano pulled a stool out.

Paul barely glanced over his shoulder. "If it isn't my minder," he said sarcastically. He turned back to face the bar and the line of full shotglasses arranged in a row before him. "How did you find out I was here? Did my dad call, wondering where I was?"

Sebastiano dragged over the plastic bowl of pretzels, studied them and finally popped one in his mouth. "No, Rufus gave me a ring. I'd just seen him at Bean World, so he figured I was still awake. What can I say? He found a willing sucker." He popped another pretzel in his mouth. It was too salty, but that didn't stop him from wanting more. Besides, it was something to do with his hands, other than wringing Paul's neck, which is what he really felt like doing. It had been a long day, and an even longer evening. He really hadn't needed this on top of everything else.

"You and he shooting the breeze over double-shot espressos?" Paul sneered. He seemed mesmerized by the drinks and kept his eyes firmly focused on them.

Sebastiano swallowed thoughtfully. "Actually, I was there baring my soul to Julie Antonelli. Not a relaxing endeavor, that's for sure."

"Ah, the lovely Giulietta—scary, mind you, but highly attractive. So, you and she…?" He left his words hanging.

"After tonight's discussion, I think the use of the word *and* in connection with our two names is highly unlikely. How can I put this? She asked for the truth and I didn't mince words. She probably never wants to see me again. A shame, really."

At last Paul turned to face him. "Women," he said with a disgusted shake of his head.

Sebastiano waved at the shots. "I take it that's what this is all about? Contemplating falling off the wagon?"

Paul stared at the ceiling. He exhaled noisily. "You wouldn't believe it. You know I told you about Zora Zemanova? About figuring out that she must have had my kid?"

"I think it was probably her child, too."

Paul looked at him askance. "Yeah, well, whatever. After class tonight? We leave together, and just when I think we can finally hash the whole thing out, what do you think she does?"

Sebastiano shook his head. He thought about another pretzel but decided he better not.

"She comes on to me! Can you believe it? Like she wants to have a quickie in the bushes outside the high school!"

"Whoa! I guess the lady had one thing in mind."

"The problem is that she doesn't *have* a mind. She was operating under the misguided delusion that we could just have a little fling because...because...why not?"

"And did you?"

Paul guffawed. "Please, I'm an idiot, but not that much of an idiot. I pointed out that it was no longer old times, and speaking of old times, didn't she have something she wanted to tell me. She tried to act dumb, but eventually she confessed what I'd guessed—that I was Katarina's father. And get this. She didn't even show any remorse for never telling me—and never telling her own kid, for Pete's sake. I mean, I know I had my problems—still have my problems—but what kind of woman keeps a secret like that?"

"One who's scared?" Sebastiano ventured.

"Zora? Scared? She's never been scared of anything in her whole life. Finally, when I threatened to tell Katarina myself, Zora backed down and promised she'd tell her. I gave her until the end of the week. But knowing her, I'm not holding my breath."

"So that's what drove you here? To this?" Sebastiano indicated the drinks again.

"I don't know—seeing Zora, the way she acted, probably more," Paul said sullenly. "It just all kind of hit me that maybe it wasn't worth the effort, all the work, to try to put my life back together. That maybe it's just too hard."

"So how come if it's not worth the effort, if it—whatever 'it' is—is too hard, you haven't touched the drinks?"

"I don't know. You're the man who tells the truth. You tell me."

"No, that would be too easy."

It took a couple of hours of soul-searching and hashing and rehashing the evening, Paul's dreams, his mistakes—a lot about his mistakes. In those three hours, the baseball game on the West Coast showing on the television went into extra innings and ended. The other patrons straggled home. The bartender wiped down the counter, upended the chairs on the tables and mopped the floor before cashing out and leaving. Rufus emerged from the basement, left Sebastiano an extra set of keys to lock up and saluted farewell.

Not until well past two in the morning, after Sebastiano had consumed the entire bowl of pretzels and his throat felt parched beyond belief, the truth came—not from Sebastiano but from Paul. From where it had to come.

"The thing that's too much?" he admitted, his tone full of agony. "Is that if she was going to go through with it and tell Katarina? I'd have to take responsibility and actually be there for someone else."

"The truth is never easy. But without it, we can't move on," Sebastiano admitted, as much to himself as to Paul. He got up slowly and circled the bar. One by one, he emptied the shot glasses in the sink and washed them, leaving them to dry on a cloth.

"Shall I take you home now?" he said. It wasn't really a question.

"I don't see why? I'm clean and sober as they say."

"Humor me."

Paul might have thought about arguing, but it was clear he didn't have the energy.

Carl Bedecker's house was on the same side of town as Julie's parents, just not quite as far. It faced the high school football field. A pair of magnificent holly trees flanked the portico of the Dutch colonial. An outside light shone above the entryway.

Sebastiano pulled into the driveway and, after turning off the engine, came around to guide his friend inside. They hadn't even reached the front step when the door opened.

It was Carl. Paul's father had been waiting in his bathrobe and slippers. He stepped outside and took his son by the other arm, and together with Sebastiano, they helped him inside and up the stairs into bed. Paul was asleep before Carl even closed the door.

Sebastiano let him go ahead as they went down the

stairs. He watched Carl hold the wooden handrail as he descended, needing the support to keep his balance. He was an old man having to take care of a grown son. It wasn't fair. But that was life sometimes, Sebastiano realized.

Carl stopped at the landing. "I can't thank you enough for helping out. You've been a good friend to Paul. He couldn't do it, get better, without you."

"Thanks, but it's really your support that matters most. And don't worry. Paul is stronger than he thinks. He was under a lot of strain tonight, but he didn't give in," Sebastiano said, trying to say the right thing. He was so tired, he wasn't sure he was even making sense.

"Won't you stay and have a cup of coffee before you go?" Carl asked.

"No, it's very late, and I've had more than enough coffee for one day. I think it's best if I just get going."

Carl nodded and shuffled in his scuffs to the front door. "Again, I can't thank you enough."

"Anytime. You have my number," Sebastiano said and headed to his car.

He started the engine and pulled out of the driveway. He got as far as half a block away before he pulled over and parked next to the curb. He pulled on the handbrake and leaned back in the leather bucket seat. He played out the events of the evening in his mind, from the dinner and birthday celebration at the Antonellis, to the conversation with Julie at the coffee house, and then the whole intervention with Paul. He was totally enervated. Wiped. He'd done more than pour tequila down the drain. He'd poured out his own demons tonight, too.

Yet, despite the exhaustion, he needed to do something. Otherwise sleep—what little time there was left

for it—would never come. He pulled out his cell phone,
and after staring at the keys, he placed a long overdue
long-distance call.

CHAPTER TWENTY-THREE

THE DOORBELL TO *Babička*'s house rang, its loud chime rattling the old glass panes in the front windows. Zora pushed aside her mug of English breakfast tea and slid out of the window seat behind the kitchen table. She padded in her sheepskin slippers to the front door, glancing at the grandfather clock in the narrow hallway to check the time. Katarina, she noticed, was right on time. Why wasn't she surprised?

As a child, Katarina had always been punctual, from arriving exactly on her due date at birth to getting to school in the morning. At least Zora assumed she always got to school on time. For the first day of class in each new school Zora had dutifully accompanied her to the bus stop or along the path to school, or via whatever subway was appropriate, but thereafter she had told Katarina that an accomplished woman always knows her way in life, and that it was her responsibility to fulfill her potential. Her philosophy must have worked, given the success Katarina had achieved in business—though Zora never did quite understand what her job with that large company in California had been about. In any case, Katarina certainly knew how to keep an appointment.

Today, though, as her soft-soled slippers touched the

gleaming hardwood floors, Zora wouldn't have minded a little tardiness, maybe even a last minute cancellation.

"Can you get the door?" Lena called from her bedroom. "I'm getting dressed for tennis."

Zora stopped at the foot of the steep stairway. The bedrooms of the small nineteenth-century house were all located upstairs. "I've got it. It's for me anyway," she shouted up. She took the few remaining steps to the front door and hesitated.

The bell rang again.

Resigned, Zora opened the wooden door. Katarina stood there, holding a bundled baby against her front, an umbrella hanging from her crooked elbow, poised to knock yet again.

"Oh, hi," she said, seemingly unaware of her mother's dilemma. "I wasn't sure if the doorbell worked. I know *Babička* said something a while back about having to fix it, and I didn't know if she'd got around to it." Katarina stepped over the threshold. She shifted the baby to one arm and passed Zora the umbrella. "Could you just leave this here. They claimed rain is in the forecast, but you could have fooled me."

Zora stashed the umbrella in the stand by the door and pointed her daughter toward the kitchen. "Of course she fixed the doorbell. Have you ever known her not to know how to fix something?" Zora replied. Lena had owned a hardware store and been widowed early in life. The combination made her extremely handy around the house.

Zora liked to think she could be handy when called upon. She'd just never owned a house, so…well…there hadn't been much call. But she could have been, she reassured herself and watched her daughter progress to the kitchen, the nerve center of the house.

Katarina seemed so confident, so natural as a mother. The way she strode serenely, even with the slight limp. While she'd been working in California, Katarina had been shot in a botched robbery, and afterward had returned to Grantham to recover. Zora had been in Antarctica at the time and offered to come home, but Katarina had insisted there was no reason. Rehabilitation was a solitary effort, her daughter had said over the phone. Truthfully, Zora had been relieved—but she also felt guilty.

"But I did make it back for the wedding," she muttered under her breath, still smarting from the memory of *Babička* walking Katarina down the aisle and not her. Zora passed the dining room and entered the cozy kitchen that ran the width of the narrow house.

The old cabinets were painted a cherry sunshine yellow. Café curtains, in yellow-and-white checked gingham, graced the back-door window and the bay window surrounding the window seat. The round table was covered with a Provençal patterned yellow cloth, and a handmade pottery bowl sat in the center filled with lemons. Sunlight streamed through the windows and its warm rays spilled over the patterned tablecloth. All that was needed to complete the country French tableau were some buzzing bees and a scratchy recording of Edith Piaf.

Zora scrunched up her mouth. She had always found her mother's taste prosaically Old World. She preferred clean lines, no fuss. She didn't think she even owned a tablecloth.

She stood there mute as Katarina lifted a bouncy

chair from the back of the window seat and placed it smack-dab in the middle of the table, pushing the bowl to the side.

"Here, let me." Zora moved the lemons to the counter. She turned and watched while her daughter unwrapped the receiving blanket from around Rad. She fastened the Velcro tabs to secure the baby in the seat, then tapped on the base to make the springy metal frame bounce gently.

"What a good little boy you are," Katarina cooed. "So happy." She reached for one of his little hands and kissed the fingertips.

Zora cleared her throat and sat on the window seat opposite Katarina. Rad, perched on the table like royalty in a recumbent throne, gurgled. "You're a natural mother," Zora commented.

Katarina glanced over but still held the baby's hand. "Are you kidding me? Before Rad was born, Ben and I practiced diapering this old stuffed gorilla I still had back in my old room here. I didn't know one end from the other." She smiled. "But, boy, did I learn the difference fast. And anything else…well…I just watched other moms, besides *Babička* and Amada, my housekeeper, of course. They're old pros. But then, I guess you did much the same thing."

Zora swallowed. "Not totally," she answered cryptically. In point of fact, Zora would have died before asking her mother for advice, and it was only when she was completely strapped for cash that she'd relied on her for babysitting. It had been a point of pride that she could have a baby on her own without anyone's help.

Zora turned her head when she heard a stomping coming down the stairs, followed by the sound of a bag plopped on the floor in the hallway. Her mother and her tennis gear. Thank God, she was leaving. All Zora needed was to have her here when she discussed Paul with Katarina.

Lena came bustling into the kitchen, making straight for the baby. "Is that my man?" She tickled the baby under the chin and spoke to him in a high, singsongy voice. Rad responded instantly, focusing on Lena with a rapt expression.

Lena glanced around. "Look at that. Did you see? He smiled." She bent back and squeezed a little curled foot in a polka dotted sock. "What a treat! I didn't know you were coming over this morning," she said to Katarina.

"Zora invited me over to talk about Matt's college applications," Katarina explained. She leaned toward her grandmother and patted the baby's belly.

"What's to explain?" Lena asked. "He's applied early action to Yale and he'll hear the end of November." She made kissy faces at the baby. "You know, I think he looks bigger."

"You're right. He had his three-month checkup the other day and weighed two pounds more and grew a whole half inch."

"Of course you grew." Lena winked at the baby. "You have such a good mommy who takes such good care of you."

Zora felt a sucker-punch to the stomach. She was sure *Babička*'s comments were an oblique criticism of her own parenting. *Well, not everyone is born to bill and coo,* she thought defensively. She tucked her arms at her sides and crossed her legs. "I'm glad to hear that Matt has set his goals so high and applied early…

early…" She wasn't quite familiar with the term her mother had used.

"Early action." Katarina made the effort to include her mother. "It's not the same as early decision."

Which didn't help Zora at all.

"It means you're not obliged to commit if you're accepted," Lena explained like a seasoned pro. "Not like when Katarina applied early decision to Stanford and got in."

Zora had no memory of that. "And I thought you had to go play tennis?" she asked her mother.

"Oh, I have plenty of time. We switched our reservation to later because Wanda had to take Fred to the vet for Sarah and Hunt. His annual shots. You may have noticed that she wasn't here this morning when you got up?" Wanda, Lena's housemate and Zora's old high school math teacher, was helping out with child care and doggy care for Katarina's good friends around the block.

Zora thanked heaven for small favors.

Katarina leaned over and fished a piece of paper from an outside pocket of the diaper bag. "Here's a printout of the colleges that Matt's interested in, in rank order. To tell you the truth, I try not to bug the kid too much about the whole thing because they're all under such pressure, and I figure he'll have plenty of time to fill out the other applications in case he doesn't get into Yale. It's all the common app these days."

Lena nodded in agreement.

Zora didn't have the faintest idea what they were talking about. Common app? She might be an academic, but her main focus was research and her interactions were mostly with graduate students, not undergrads.

"But if you really want to get involved..." Katarina offered.

"Why don't I look at the list later," Zora said. There was no point prolonging the inevitable—even in front of her mother.

"I didn't really want to talk to you about Matt," Zora confided. "I mean, I'm happy to talk about Matt, but that's not why I wanted to speak to you this morning."

"It's not?" Katarina looked confused.

"That's right. I want to talk about you...and me."

"Me and you?" Katarina asked. "I don't understand."

"Yes, well, there are many things I don't understand about us, but let me try to explain a few things." She took a moment to organize her thoughts. "When you were born, my life changed."

"I can imagine, having a baby at such a young age on your own couldn't have been easy," Katarina said.

"No, it wasn't, but it was my choice and I never complained."

"No, never," *Babička* confirmed. She crossed her arms and studied her daughter.

"I also decided that despite the obvious limitations that motherhood imposed I would continue my education."

"I know, you don't have to explain. I understood why you used to leave me in Grantham every summer," Katarina responded. "I mean, I can't say I didn't feel a little abandoned at times, but I had *Babička,* and we managed."

Zora sniffed. "You did better than manage. You turned out to be a fine woman who seems to have found a balance to the whole career-family conundrum far better than me. But I'd like to think that I contributed in a certain way to your success, too."

"Of course, you've always been supportive," Katarina said.

Zora shook her head. "Don't be ridiculous. I wasn't there for half the things in your life. No, I'm talking about the fact that I left you in Grantham every summer. You say you felt abandoned sometimes. Well, sometimes so did I."

"Please, don't tell me you did it as a sacrifice to your-self," Katarina said with a show of disbelief. Finally, her patience was beginning to crack. She turned her attention to her baby son, obviously trying to avoid making further accusations.

Zora waited until Katarina looked up before address-ing her. "You're right, Katarina, I was selfish—it was easier for me in terms of travel and research. But, in my own way, I was also self*less* because I realized that here in Grantham you could get something I could never give you. A sense of family."

"I know. *Babička*." Katarina looked gratefully at Lena.

"Yes, *Babička*. She was a real trouper. I admit it. You developed a relationship with her that I never had. Sometimes I think it would have helped if there weren't just the two of us, if my father hadn't died when I was young."

"It wasn't easy. For either of us," Lena admitted.

Zora focused on Katarina. "But I'm talking about more than *Babička*. Here in Grantham you became part of a larger family—the Antonelli family. I remember after that first summer, you telling me about Julie-this and Julie-that."

"Yeah, I really tagged around after her," Katarina admitted with a laugh. "She was like the gang leader, the way she was so big and confident."

"It was more than Julie. It was her whole family," Zora went on. "I'd hear about how you'd had barbecue at their house or how they took you to Six Flags or New York City. Or how her brothers were little brats."

"Especially Dom." Katarina nodded with a smile on her face. "I remember—"

"I'm sure you do," Zora interrupted. "But the point I want to make is that Julie and her mom and dad and brothers provided you with the big, noisy family life that you seemed to crave and thrive in. So, you see, leaving you here every summer was my way of giving you something that I couldn't or, let's be frank, wouldn't give you. I did it knowing that at the end of every summer when I'd come to pick you up, we'd have grown further apart."

Outside, the rain began to fall.

"Listen, I'm not asking you to feel sorry for me," Zora said. "It was my decision, and I lived with it. We all have to live with our decisions, good or bad." Zora took a deep breath. "Which brings me to the next part of this little discussion." She leaned to Katarina. "I want to talk to you about Paul Bedecker."

Katarina's confused look returned. "Paul Bedecker?" She rested her hand on the bottom of the baby seat and stopped rocking it.

"Carl Bedecker's son, who's back from Hollywood or wherever?" Lena asked. She had her mouth open as she gazed at her grown daughter. "Why would you want to talk about him? Wanda told me that he's back because he had a drug problem and lost all his money. But of course we all make mistakes and deserve a second chance," she added quickly.

How typical of her mother, Zora thought. Critical but somehow charitable. It made it difficult to resent her, yet impossible to please. "Yes, well, that's true. Paul is trying to turn things around. You know—" she paused as she inched her way to the truth "—I don't know if you know it but he was in the same class as mine at Grantham High School?" She looked at Katarina. Could her daughter intuit what she was trying to say?

"Oh, I didn't know," Katarina said without much interest. She went back to bouncing the baby chair and blowing air kisses at Rad.

"Yes, he was in my class, and I was in his."

"That's usually how it works. I think you both went off to Cornell, correct?" Lena lifted her chin and peered out the window. "That rain has started to really come down. It was in the forecast, but I was hoping we could still get our game in. I may have to call the others if this keeps up."

"Listen, I need you both to pay attention," Zora insisted.

Katarina reluctantly turned away from the baby. Lena pursed her lips.

"What I need to tell you—you both…is something important."

Her mother and daughter waited.

"The thing is, yes, we both went off to Cornell, but what you don't know is that while we were students there, we had an affair."

Lena inhaled and held her breath.

"Mom, I mean, Zora, I really don't need to hear about this. It's one thing to relive happy childhood memories with Julie and the Antonellis, but to rehash your past old affairs…" Katarina said, the awkwardness in her voice apparent.

"Oh, but in this case you do need to hear. How can I put it simply? My past sex life *is* relevant, very relevant because…because…" She took a large gulp of air yet still felt light-headed. "Paul Bedecker is your father."

CHAPTER TWENTY-FOUR

"IF YOU'LL EXCUSE ME," Sebastiano said. He crossed the room and flicked on the office lights. "That's better. I was having trouble seeing you it was so dark. You would think it was evening not the morning." The overhead spotlights and standing lamps provided a warm glow as rain lashed the windows. The windows were closed, but the vertical blinds shimmied against the glass from the force of the downpour.

"The Weather Channel forecast rain today," Rufus commented. He was seated in one of the winged chairs facing Sebastiano's desk.

"Yes, I heard that we could be expecting even worse weather in a few days—the side effects of the hurricane in the Gulf," Iris added. She rested her fingers on the folders on her lap. Her yellowing pearls gleamed in the artificial light, beacons of secure wealth.

Sebastiano settled behind his desk again. He momentarily closed his eyes, feeling the tiredness burn his dry eyes. Then he willed himself to focus and rested his forearms on his desk. "Now, where were we?"

"You know, before we go on, I just want to thank you for responding to my call so quickly last night," Rufus said. "I figured you were the one to handle the situation." He glanced around the room. "I'm being discreet here, you must understand, since it involves someone we all know."

Iris held up her hand. "No need to worry. I stopped by Bedecker's Nursery this morning to get some mums for the flower pots on the back porch, and I heard all about it from Carl, Paul's father. He couldn't stop singing Sebastiano's praises for the way he intervened to prevent a relapse. Thank goodness, Paul mentioned your name."

"There really are no secrets in Grantham, are there?" Sebastiano asked, suddenly aware that Rufus, and no doubt Iris, realized he and Paul knew each other from A.A. meetings. He wondered if that might jeopardize his plans here in Grantham.

Rufus chuckled. "You only just discovered that?"

"I know I counseled you only last week on getting more involved with the community, but I never anticipated you would go to such lengths. Truly commendable," Iris said with a nod. "You know, we may be a privileged community in many ways—"

"Others might say snobby," Rufus added.

"I don't agree, but, true, they might," Iris responded. "But that doesn't mean we aren't understanding or incapable of embracing people for whom they are—warts and all."

Sebastiano got the message and was grateful. "Thank you," he said simply. "But as for preventing any crisis, I think more credit goes to Paul himself. I was there merely to reassure him that he had the strength to remain on course." He looked down at his hands as if seeing every line and knuckle for the first time.

"Sebastiano."

Iris's lockjaw enunciation of his name brought him back to the present.

She picked up the top folder from her lap and flipped it open. "I am intrigued with the proposal that you have presented us here, though naturally I'd need to know more details," she said. "This idea for a combined health clinic/community center as a cornerstone of the hospital?"

Sebastiano cleared his throat. "Yes, I wanted to take the negative feelings in the neighborhood about the expansion of the hospital and turn them into something positive. Right now, the neighbors are concerned that tearing down houses and replacing them with a monolithic structure will rip the heart and soul out of the adjacent community. Am I right?"

"I'd say you're spot on," Rufus agreed. "Already when the hospital bought those houses and turned them into offices, people got upset. Now they see this new building campaign as further encroachment on their quality of life. As far as they can tell, the neighborhood is suffering so that other, wealthier members of Grantham benefit."

Sebastiano took it all in before responding. "Okay, here's my proposal. I say, let's expand the hospital but to such a way that it actually contributes to the betterment of the immediate neighborhood. What I'm talking about is a combined clinic/community center that would serve the local people not just medically, but in other ways to make them become healthy, active members of the town instead of marginalizing them. I'm talking about an after-school program and child care, nutrition instruction, legal counseling—things like that. It will be cost-effective in the long run, cutting down expensive emergency care in a time of crisis. But just as strongly, I believe that everyone who benefits should also be held accountable, hence the sliding payment fees, and if need be, some kind of bartering system for services." Just talking about his plans gave Sebastiano renewed energy, down to his bones.

Rufus flipped through the pages of his copy. "I like your thinking. I like the idea of the hospital as fostering good neighbors, and its neighbors, in turn, taking a greater stake in their community. I have a question, though—have you given any thought as to where the center would be located?"

There was a loud roll of thunder that prevented Sebastiano from responding immediately. He waited. Almost immediately, a clap of lightning struck. The lights flickered but remained on.

"It's a good question," he answered. "Obviously, it would have to be in the neighborhood, as close to the hospital building as possible. Right now, as the approved hospital plans stand, there isn't space for an additional structure. But let's say we *can* jump that hurdle." Sebastiano began talking animatedly with his hands. "Something else is also crucial for the project's success—the makeup of the board of directors. For once, I believe we should look beyond wealthy donors and CEOs. You'll see that I've recommended that members of the neighborhood be included."

Iris tipped up her reading glasses and studied the relevant page. "I see you've recommended putting Dr. Antonelli on the board."

"Let's just say her outburst last week provided some timely impetus for the project," Sebastiano explained. "Ideally, I think she would make a terrific head for the clinic portion, but I know she already has a lot on her plate between her private practice and her hospital visits."

"Not to mention your Italian class?" Iris added.

Sebastiano tipped his head. "What can I say? Your idea has proved very instructive for all concerned."

Iris beamed. She was not above flattery.

Rufus held the page a little farther away. "You'll have to excuse me. I forgot my reading glasses. This woman Carlotta Sanchez that you also mention? I don't think I know her?"

"She came into the E.R. the other week in great distress. Dr. Antonelli delivered her baby—"

"Ahh." Iris opened her mouth in thought. "The impetus for the doctor's outburst." Then Iris removed her glasses.

Sebastiano nodded.

"Well, as you mentioned, usually we do like to reserve board membership as an enticement for big donors," she advised.

There was another onslaught of thunder followed more closely by a flash of lightning. All three looked to the window.

"I think the weather forecast was right for once," Rufus joked.

"Given the weather conditions, I think it's advisable to wrap up this meeting as soon as possible so that you both can get home safely. But let me leave you with this thought," Sebastiano said with conviction. "We have been given the opportunity to help make an already fine community achieve greater things. Don't you want to be able to say to your children and grandchildren that when the opportunity presented itself, we did the right thing, that we didn't just think of ourselves and the usual cast of characters, but made a leap of faith and reached out to help those in need, as much for their future as for ours? Because, believe me, as someone who in his own past did not respond nobly when the opportunity presented itself, I can tell you what regret feels like."

CHAPTER TWENTY-FIVE

JULIE SAT NUMBLY staring at her coffee cup in the hospital cafeteria. It was only Tuesday, and she had already delivered three babies in less than two days, a personal record. One of the maternity nurses claimed it was due to the gigantic low-pressure region making its way up the coast.

Julie wasn't convinced. All she knew was that a healthy eight-and-a-half-pound baby boy had just entered the world kicking and screaming. Mother and baby were doing well despite the protracted delivery. The baby's father, a postdoctoral fellow in microbiology with the frame of a marathon runner and the scraggly beard of Bob Dylan, fainted dead away after Julie had given him the honor of cutting the umbilical cord. Luckily, he was suffering from nothing more severe than a bruised ego. All of life should have such complications.

Then there were her own complications, another matter completely. Here she was, feeling down in the dumps, and it didn't take a brain surgeon to figure out why. In the span of seven days, she'd suffered through her birthday blues, met a man and lost a man. She had never quite figured out what she and Sebastiano had so briefly together. On the other hand, she had no problem characterizing what they had now. Nothing.

His story had been heart-rending and infuriating all

at the same time. And while she wasn't sure she could ever forget his conduct, she felt that she had the capacity to empathize and forgive it.

Clearly, he didn't.

He had in some measure helped her come to grips with her own screwed-up past, and for that she was eternally grateful. But that didn't put her under any obligation to try to help him deal with his demons. She had tried, and what she really feared was that if she continued to try any more, not only would she fail, but she also might never recover.

Because whatever it was that they did or didn't have, Julie recognized one thing for sure—she had fallen in love. She had given her heart to Sebastiano, and now it was breaking.

She idly studied the blackening sky and watched the branches of the cherry trees in the entrance to the hospital sway violently in the wind. The rain was coming down sideways. The cars had their headlights on even though it was only midday, but the beams hardly penetrated the gloom. A woman was rushing along the sidewalk from the hospital parking garage, her umbrella pulled down close to her head like a mushroom cap. The wind whipped it inside out.

Julie recognized the frustrated expression of her friend Sarah, who abandoned any attempt to fix her umbrella and instead ran toward the revolving doors of the hospital entrance.

"Hey, look what the cat dragged in," Julie called out when Sarah finally made it into the lobby.

Sarah looked up. Her blond hair was plastered to her head, and she brushed her sopping bangs out of her eyes with the back of her hand, the same hand that still held on to her useless umbrella. Her warm-up jacket and track pants, her usual physiotherapy uniform, were soaked to a shade or two darker than their royal-blue color.

"Laugh all you want," Sarah said. "Wait till you have to make the mad dash over to your office. You won't be looking any better." She took the two steps up to the carpeted area where Julie sat. "They're saying gale-force winds are expected today, and I can believe it. The office has already cancelled patients for the rest of the day, and after I see my patients here, I tell you, I'm headed home. I already called Hunt to tell him to come home as soon as possible from New Brunswick. I don't want him getting stuck in traffic or risk having the roads closed."

Julie downed the rest of her cold coffee. "You're getting to be such a worrywart now that you're a responsible married mother. What ever happened to the wild woman gadding about town?"

Sarah unzipped her jacket and peeled it off. Her polo shirt underneath had damp splotches on the shoulders. "I was never a wild woman gadding about town, if you remember correctly. And don't try to claim that you were, either, Ms. My Patients Come First. Anyway, you might find it's the better part of valor to cancel your appointments this afternoon, too. I heard on the radio that the local schools are letting out early."

"What a bunch of wimps!" Julie replied. "I mean, really, it's only the tail end of a hurricane. It's not like we got a direct hit."

"Speaking of direct hits, did you happen to read your email this morning?"

"I was delivering a baby. What happened? Nothing to do with Sebastiano? And me?"

"What?" Sarah winced. "Sebastiano? Dr. Fonterra? No, whatever gave you that idea?"

Julie looked down.

Sarah studied her friend closely. "Maybe that's a story for another day?" She waited, but only briefly. "Right now, it's our good friend Katarina who's got problems, big problems."

Julie's head shot up. "Not the baby?"

"No, nothing like that. Lena emailed me. Katarina's mother suddenly announced to them the identity of Katarina's father, and then without wasting another breath, she declared she was going to leave Grantham immediately. I mean, talk about cowardice. She drops that bomb and then leaves everyone else to pick up the pieces."

"Maybe she's just afraid, feeling guilty about what she did in the past, and now she doesn't know how to face it?" Julie suggested. She thought of Sebastiano's reaction to his daughter's death.

Sarah wrung out her umbrella one more time. "Excuse me, but who's the one in need of our support here? Katarina, not her flaky mom."

"You're right. Of course, you're right. I'll call her right away."

A loud roar of thunder permeated the plate glass windows.

"Good luck to you. She's not answering her phone, not even for Lena, who's been trying all day. Thankfully, Katarina's got Ben to help her through this." She stepped down to the lobby. "Gotta go, then."

"Wait a minute," Julie called out.

Sarah stepped back. "Make it quick."

"Did Lena mention who the father is?" Julie whispered. She immediately thought about Zora's office visit.

Sarah leaned closer. "That's the even weirder part," she said softly. "It's Paul Bedecker."

"Paul as in Paolo in my Italian class?" Julie stood slowly. It was all beginning to make sense.

"I wouldn't know about that. From what Lena told me over the phone, he moved back to town from Hollywood after some difficult times."

A second later lightning flashed.

Julie scanned outside the window. "That was close."

"Well, if he thought he had difficult times in Hollywood, the proverbial you-know-what is already hitting the fan all around Grantham."

Another rumble of thunder started up, this time even louder.

Julie studied the torrential rain, overflowing the drains and roaring alongside the curbs. "Boy, this is getting serious. I think I *will* cancel this afternoon's appoint—"

Before she could finish another clap of lightning sounded, this time even louder. There was a crack. Close, very close. Someone's car security alarm started blaring. And then the hospital's lights went out.

There were a few screams.

Within seconds, a low level of lighting came back on.

Julie looked around. "The auxiliary generator just kicked in. That last lightning strike must have hit something nearby."

"I hope Hunt makes it home okay," Sarah said, not sounding all that convinced.

"He will. He has something to come home to," Julie

said reassuringly. "I'm just going to check in with my office and then I'm out of here."

"You're worried about your condo?"

"No, *Nonna*'s bird."

CHAPTER TWENTY-SIX

HER PARENTS' HOUSE was less than a mile away from the hospital. But it took her over forty minutes to reach it.

Power lines were down all over the eastern part of town. That meant stoplights were out. Mammoth evergreens and maple trees, the pride of Grantham, lay uprooted across roads and yards. At one house, not only had a tree taken out a corner of the roof, but it had also landed on the car parked in the driveway.

Julie gripped the steering wheel of her RAV4 and anxiously maneuvered around the back streets. She tried to approach her parents' small street from one end, but it was blocked by fallen wires. So she did a U-turn and tried to come at it from the other end, only to find her way blocked by a large maple tree that had come down, its branches forming a leafy wall.

She abandoned the car and headed off on foot. The rain was still pouring, and the grates from the storm gutters gushed torrents of swiftly moving water instead of guiding it underground.

The clogs that she wore during deliveries gulped in mouthfuls of rain with each step. Frustrated, she slipped them off and ran barefoot.

She reached her parents' house and immediately felt grateful. It appeared untouched. No trees or power lines had fallen anywhere near it. She flipped through her key ring for the front door key. Her hands were shaking. Her whole body was shaking.

"Calm down," she chastised herself and worked the key into the lock. Just as well her parents had accompanied her grandmother on her trip to Italy. "Having a panic attack is not going to save Caruso." She had visions of the bird keeling over from fright, thereby bringing down some terrible curse on the family for fifty years to come.

She pushed open the door, not bothering to wipe her feet on the mat. The house was dark. She fumbled for the brass-plated light switch by the front door. The lights didn't come on. No power at all.

Julie sprinted to the picture window and pulled the drawstring to open the lined curtains. The ominous skies blocked out most of the sunlight, but it was better than nothing.

She headed back to the stairs and up to the second story of the split-level. Her grandmother's room was at the end of the hall. The door was closed. Julie felt her way to the door, bumping into a narrow table in the darkness. A crystal bowl of potpourri fell over and scattered on the rug. The sudden inundation of rose-hip smell was almost overwhelming. She grabbed the door handle, and instinctively—uselessly—fumbled for the light switch.

She skirted her grandmother's bed and raised the shades on the windows. They looked out over the backyard and her father's vegetable garden. Julie didn't want to know what the storm had done to his plum tomatoes and pumpkin plants. She turned to the dresser and the birdcage perched on the corner. A large cloak covered the cage. Julie had once joked that it was *Nonna*'s own

Shroud of Turin, and teased her about the way she lovingly washed it by hand and had embroidered the borders. None of that had gone down well.

Julie whipped off the material and cast it on the floor. And her heart almost stopped.

There was Caruso, perched ominously still, a stiff little mass. Julie stopped breathing. *Was it possible to do mouth-to-mouth on a bird?* she wondered.

Mercifully, Caruso blinked an eye reluctantly open. He slowly rotated his head to get a full look at Julie, before opening up full throttle. It wasn't so much a joyous hello as a tormented cry. Julie could have sworn the bird was singing the aria from "Pagliacci," just like the real Caruso.

As if. She reached for the canister of bird food next to the cage and filled Caruso's bowl. She dislodged the water bin and carried it to the adjoining bathroom, where she filled it from the pink porcelain sink. Then she carefully reopened the cage door and eased it back into its proper spot.

"There you go, Caruso. And don't go telling *Nonna* I didn't think of you first during the hurricane." The bird hopped over on its perch and pecked at the seed, rejecting most of the kernels as inferior and spewing them on the newspaper on the bottom of the cage.

"What a diva!" Julie laughed. It had been ridiculous, really, her anxiety about a bird. But that kind of erratic behavior seemed to sum up her mood right now. Too much had happened. Too much was up in the air.

She left Caruso to his bird activities and collapsed in a heap on the end of the bed. At least she hadn't screwed this up. The rest of life might be in disarray, but she hadn't disappointed her family in some new, unforgivable way. She stretched out on the bed and fanned her arms out like some sad snow angel. Her fingers brushed the chenille bumps of her grandmother's bedspread. Julie turned her nose into the cotton nubs and drank in the smell of *Nonna*—baby powder, Oil of Olay and some distinctly old lady smell that was somehow comforting in a dusty sort of way.

She closed her eyes. She could feel herself ready to nod off, her heartbeat lower, her limbs relaxed. Yes, she could easily fall asleep in the quiet....

Julie shot up. It was too quiet. Houses were supposed to make noises.

Look who was the birdbrain now.

"MRS. ZEMANOVA, I'm not sure if you remember me. I'm Sebastiano Fonterra, from the hospital. I'm sorry to bother you at dinnertime." Sebastiano stood on the front stoop of Lena's house. Pots of rust-colored mums flanked the entryway and an old climbing rose curled on a trellis, the last blossoms practically inviting the person waiting to enter to lean over and take a sniff.

Or would have, if it hadn't been pouring. Even now at seven o'clock in the evening, the rain continued in a steady, uncompromising fashion, as if settling in for the long haul.

Lena held the door open wider. "Of course I remember you. I met you at the charity auction. You won the bid for my catered meal for six but then offered it to a new family in town—from Bratislava. So lovely."

Sebastiano tried to be patient, but it was not coming easily. "If you wouldn't mind?" He indicated coming in.

"Of course. The rain. I'm so sorry." Lena stepped

back. "Would you like some coffee? Cake? Please, come into the living room." She closed the door behind him and indicated the comfortable room to the side. A fire crackled in the fireplace, dispelling the gloom outside.

Sebastiano recognized a motherly instinct. He shut his umbrella and rested it by the front door. "No, no thank you. It's very generous, but I don't plan to intrude for any longer than necessary. I would have called, but your phone appears to be out."

Lena nodded. "Yes, the storm, you know? It knocked out the telephone line. Our electricity was affected, for a while, too, but, thank goodness, it came back on about an hour ago, which was good since that meant that nothing spoiled in the refrigerator. Are you sure you won't have something to eat? A little meat loaf? Stuffed cabbage?" she asked.

"No, I'm sure. To tell you the truth, I'm on a bit of a mission."

"Mission?"

"I'm looking for your daughter, Zora. She's in my Italian class at the Adult School on Wednesday evening? I have something important to discuss with her." As if that explained why he had come unannounced.

"Zora?" Lena looked puzzled. She turned her head and shouted up the stairs. "Zora! Your teacher from the Adult School is here to see you." Lena looked back at Sebastiano. "This is just like the old days. When my daughter would get in trouble in high school." She nudged closer. "I love it. But don't tell her."

Sebastiano nodded. He didn't have a lot of time. He didn't have much of a sense of humor at the moment, either. He lifted his head and watched the stairway for signs of movement.

"I'm coming, just a minute," he heard a woman's voice call from upstairs, then the sound of stockinged feet before Zora came to view at the head of the stairs.

She descended quickly, letting her hand glide down the banister as she did. "What's up? I was just on the phone to the airlines again. Nothing's flying out of Newark or Philadelphia, but I'm going to try JFK," she said. She noticed Sebastiano.

"Oh, sorry," Zora said and unconsciously patted the side of her head, slipping a lock of hair behind her ear that had sprung lose from her braid. "I wasn't expecting anyone. You see I've just been packing. Something's come up, so I'm leaving earlier than I had originally planned. In fact, I meant to email you that I won't be able to come to the rest of your classes, which I enjoyed very much by the way."

Sebastiano wet his lips and took a moment before he spoke. He knew he had only one chance—at most—and he didn't want to blow it. "That's very nice of you to say, but I didn't come here today to talk about the class."

"You didn't?" Zora asked.

"You didn't?" Lena echoed. She stared back and forth between the two.

Sebastiano focused on Zora. "I came to talk about your family."

"My family?" Zora looked puzzled. "You mean my mother? Is there something wrong she hasn't told me? I know you're a doctor."

"I'm fine," Lena reassured her.

"I have no reason not to believe that," Sebastiano confirmed. "No, I mean your other family."

CHAPTER TWENTY-SEVEN

JULIE SAT IN THE KITCHEN of her parents' home, stripped to her underwear and wrapped in a blanket. She punched in the number on her cell phone. For the past hour, she'd been lifting boxes from the floor of the basement and putting them on shelves and worktables. The lighter stuff she'd managed to hoist up the flight of stairs and put in the garage next to her parents' two cars. With the power still out, the sump pump in the cellar wasn't working. The water was rising.

At this point, it came about two and a half feet up the cinderblock walls, and she no longer felt safe wading through the water. She could hardly see where she was going, even holding a flashlight in her mouth. Potentially more dangerous, she didn't want to risk getting electrocuted. The oil burner was already submerged, as was the electric hot-water heater. The circuit breaker panel would be next.

Given that her clothes had gotten completely soaked, she'd stripped off her outer garments and after toweling off in her parents' bedroom, had decided to sit in her bra and panties rather than her mother's housecoat. The army blanket over her shoulders completed the depressing picture.

The phone picked up at the other end. "Hi, is Katarina there? It's Julie."

"Oh, Julie, it's Ben. We have company right now for dinner. Could she call you back?" Katarina's husband asked.

"Is it her father? Paul Bedecker?"

"How did you know?" Ben asked. "Oh, that's right. Lena sent you an email earlier."

Julie rubbed her eyes. "Listen, I don't want to bother you then, but please tell Katarina that if she needs me, she can call—anytime." The sweat she'd built up from dragging her parents' stuff in the basement was drying off, and she pulled the blanket more tightly around her to keep from shivering. "Anyway, give her my best, and if you get a chance, could you ask her if they have a spare generator at her office?"

"Spare generator?"

"Yeah, I'm at my parents' place and the power is out."

"Well, we're okay out here, so if you want, you can always come over," Ben offered.

"No, I'm fine. I can use a flashlight and my mom's got some candles, and if I run out, there's always my grandmother's votive candles. No, light's not a problem. Not even the fact that there's no heat—"

Ben's voice became more emphatic. "Julie, with no heat, you really should come to our place."

"It's not that cold, really. What I'm more concerned about is getting their sump pump up and running. With no electricity, their basement's flooding. I've already made calls to Home Depot and a bunch of other people, but no luck—either they're sold out, or they're using the one they've got, or they're in the same boat as me."

"Did you try your father's garage?" Ben suggested.

"That was my first try. There wasn't any answer.

I'm sure the mechanics have gone home long ago, and besides, with the roads blocked all around, I'm not sure I could even get there, let alone find what I need. But not to fear. I'll just keep trying more people, and with any luck, the power will come back on soon." Julie tried to sound optimistic.

"Okay, if you say so," Ben replied, not sounding totally convinced. "I'll make some calls from my end, too. And the number you're calling from is the best one for reaching you?"

"That's right. I'm using my cell since the landline's out. Unfortunately, my battery's running low, so I'm not sure how much longer I'll have service. I might have to hoof it to someplace nearby that's got some power—probably the shopping center. I'm sure Dunkin' Donuts will not fail me in an emergency." She laughed and switched off. Then she rested the phone on the table. She cupped her hands atop it and dropped her weary head on them. Right now, even a glazed donut didn't hold much attraction.

"I'M AFRAID YOU'RE barking up the wrong tree, Dr. Fonterra," Zora said, not bothering to mask the displeasure in her voice. "If this storm hadn't come through, I'd already be out of here. I don't know what Paul told you about his dinner with Katarina tonight, but what you might not know is that Katarina made it very clear that she didn't want me there. So if he sent you over here—"

"No, Paul doesn't know I'm here. I came because I thought it was important not to let the opportunity pass."

A phone rang in the kitchen, but nobody moved.

It rang again before Lena spoke. "That's my cell phone. I'll have to get that," she said.

Sebastiano waited for her to leave the room, then looked back at Zora. "Think of Paul," he argued.

"Excuse me. I'm supposed to think of Paul?" She pressed her hand against her fleece top. "My lasting memories of Paul are of someone who was more attached to pot and his ambitions, not exactly sterling qualifications for shouldering the responsibilities of fatherhood."

Sebastiano nodded. "Addiction is a sickness. I know. I'm an alcoholic myself. Paul's behavior was selfish and cruel. And I know he is truly sorry. But what you're doing now is just as cruel, and it doesn't help anyone."

"Ha, it helps me," Zora retorted. She paced back and forth. "I didn't come back looking to reestablish some fairy tale idea of a perfect family. Not everyone gets to be a father. Not everyone gets to *have* a father. Look at me. My father died before I ever really knew him."

"And just because you suffered, you think Paul should suffer, too?"

Zora stopped and gave Sebastiano a withering glance. "Frankly, I don't know what I'm supposed to think or feel now. I thought I had left all of this behind me."

"At least try to explain that to your daughter. Talk to her some more. Just don't run away now."

Zora harrumphed. "My daughter? Katarina? She doesn't even want to talk to me. Listen—" she held up her hand "—I'm sure you think you're doing the right thing by coming here, but it's just not going to work."

"Why? Because you're afraid?"

"No, because I know my daughter doesn't love me."

"Or maybe you've never given her a chance to love you?" Sebastiano suggested.

She glanced back toward the kitchen where her mother had just finished talking on the phone.

Sebastiano pressed his lips together. "You can believe me or not about your daughter. That's your choice. But one thing I do know—running away won't help matters. And I say that as one of the last big runners."

He stepped close to her, crowding Zora's personal space intentionally. Why should she feel secure and safe? He certainly didn't. "You can run, but you can't hide—from memories, from other people's criticisms, from the truth, but most of all from yourself."

Lena walked down the hall quickly. "That was Katarina," she announced.

Zora spun around. "Katarina? She wants to see me after all?"

Sebastiano turned his gaze to Lena. She eyed him, and then turned her focus on her daughter. "I need to say something—as one mother to another. Sometimes daughters...they don't know everything. Sometimes they are hurting. That's the time when a mother must step in, not to judge or control but to offer support."

Lena held up her hand when Zora was about to speak. "We can argue about this later—as I am sure you will. You haven't been my daughter this long for me not to know how you will react. But that will have to wait. Sometimes other people's problems take president."

"Precedence," Zora corrected.

Lena smirked at Sebastiano. "See, they never stop correcting you. But listen, I have an important message. Katarina called to say that Julie is in trouble."

"Trouble?" Sebastiano stepped toward her. "She's hurt?"

Lena raised her eyebrows. "No, she's fine. But she's at her parents' house. Apparently, they're away."

"In Italy." Sebastiano provided the details.

Lena nodded. "Of course. The thing is, their house has no power and that means the sump pump isn't working. The basement's flooded. The heat is out and there's no hot water, and now maybe the electrical wiring will short. And of course, there's all this stuff getting ruined. She desperately needs a generator. I don't have one. I have other things left over from the hardware store like tools and power saws, but no generator."

Sebastiano studied Lena then spoke determinedly. "I suppose she tried places like Home Depot and Ace Hardware?"

"So she said."

He snapped his fingers. "You know, I'm pretty sure I can get my hands on a gas-powered pump. That would work, right?"

"That sounds perfect," Lena said.

Sebastiano pulled out his cell phone but stopped before dialing. "The only problem is my car's a sedan. The pump will never fit. We need some kind of a truck."

There was a moment of silence except for the rain beating against the windows.

Lena regarded Zora critically. "So, suddenly you have nothing to say?"

Zora rolled her eyes. "All right, I have a pickup, a rental. But I *really* want to try to get out of here."

"You can't spare an hour to help out someone who's been your daughter's friend practically her whole life?"

Lena asked. "Like you really have a plane to catch in this weather?"

"Okay, okay," Zora protested. "But one hour. And then I'm gone."

Lena looked triumphant. But then she creased her brow. "The only problem is Katarina said that there're trees down in the road around Julie's parents' house."

Sebastiano smiled. "Not to worry. Didn't I just hear you say you had power saws? That wouldn't include a chain saw by any chance?"

"Not only that, I have the gasoline to power it."

"That's music to a man's ears. Now, let me just track down this pump." And he started working the phone.

CHAPTER TWENTY-EIGHT

"WHAT ARE YOU DOING HERE?" Julie stood dumbfounded in the doorway of her parents' house.

"I tried calling, but I couldn't get through," Sebastiano explained from the top step.

"I know. The battery's dead, and I was about to walk to Dunkin' Donuts to try and charge my phone."

"That makes sense. Somehow I didn't get the impression that you were preparing to entertain royalty." He gave her a quick once-over as if to prove his point.

Julie looked down at herself. She had found an old Fairleigh Dickenson sweatshirt belonging to her brother Joey, which accommodated her broad shoulders. The sleeves were hacked off somewhere around the elbows, and she'd paired the top with her mother's track pants. She wasn't exactly dressed for the ball. But she didn't much care. She was tired and sore, not to mention hungry. She stiffened her back. "My clothes got wet, and this is the best I could muster up. Besides, as far as I know, there's no dress code at Dunkin' Donuts."

"When this is over, I promise I'll take you to someplace where you do need to dress up. But for now, show me the problem."

Julie put her hands on her hips. "Wait a minute. Who told you I had a problem?"

"You need to ask in this town how he found out?" A woman's voice came from behind him.

Julie leaned to the side to get a better look at who was talking. She saw someone in a dark green anorak with the hood drawn over her face.

"You remember Katarina's mother, Zora, don't you?" Sebastiano asked. "She sits in Italian class near you?"

Zora lifted her arm and the tips of her fingers emerged from a sleeve. She waggled them hello.

"Oh, yeah, hi," Julie said, still mystified by the turn of events. "I must confess, I certainly didn't expect you here."

"You and me both," Zora said. "In my defense, I was shanghaied as a means of transportation." She pointed over her shoulder to the Toyota Tacoma.

Julie blinked. "I'm amazed that you could get that over here."

"I'd like to say it was my stupendous off-road driving ability that allowed me to navigate the way, but it's more Sebastiano's doing. Let me tell you, the sight of a man wielding a chain saw is a powerful image," Zora declared.

"I'll take your word for it." Julie glanced back at Sebastiano, and frankly, she didn't need much imagination to go there. Even after his lumberjacking act, Sebastiano looked pretty amazing. He had his jacket off and was wearing just his white dress shirt and dark trousers. Gone was the carefully knotted tie. His sleeves were rolled up and his shirt unbuttoned. Speaking of the shirt, it had turned semitransparent from the rain and was molded to his body. The muscles in his arms rippled and the tendons stood out as he stood there arms akimbo.

She realized that she'd been admiring him with her mouth open. She snapped it shut and swallowed. "So you got to play with a chain saw?" Julie asked.

"I told you I was a regular mountain man in my youth." He beamed, seemingly enjoying himself.

"Well, I'm glad I was a good excuse to make that happen again," she said.

"You're a good excuse for many things," he said, a smile tugging at the corner of his mouth.

They stared at each other.

"Listen, not to interrupt this little interlude where I'm clearly not wanted—"

Julie snapped out of it. "Don't be ridiculous," she protested.

"Please, I may have all the sensitivity of a two-by-four when it comes to dealing with people, but I am pretty confident about my abilities as a scientist to observe natural phenomenon," Zora said.

"There's nothing going on between us," Julie denied.

"I was talking about the rain," Zora clarified. "And as I understand it, you have a flood emergency. So, if we could get this thing off the truck…"

Sebastiano hopped down the steps and joined Zora. "Of course. I'm sorry to keep you here. I know how eager you are to leave Grantham."

"To tell you the truth, I was thinking of delaying my departure for a while."

"The weather?" Sebastiano asked as he undid the heavy straps that secured the bulky pump.

"That and I think that…I don't know…seeing the two of you made me think that perhaps it's time for me to grab a little dinner with...ah, close friends—family actually," Zora stuttered.

"I applaud your decision, so to speed you on your way, let me get this pump off the truck." Sebastiano clapped his hands and set to work, heaving the heavy equipment off the truck bed.

Zora bade a quick goodbye and headed back the way they'd come. Meanwhile, Julie led Sebastiano to the garage and the stairway leading to the basement. The water was still rising, with only the top two steps still visible. "I presume that pump is gas-powered?"

Sebastiano looked at her abashed. "Is the Pope Catholic?"

Even exhausted, Julie had to chuckle at his echoing of her own words. "I suppose this is when I should thank *you*," she said.

"Don't thank me yet." He peered into the murky darkness. "Have you got a flashlight?"

"Here." She passed him the one that she had left in the garage.

"Thank you," he said, taking it. Then stopped. "And I mean it, thank you."

BEN UNCORKED A bottle of wine at the dinner table, a valiant attempt to lighten the atmosphere. The fifteen minutes or so spent over appetizers of cheese and crackers and hummus and pita bread in the living room had been a less-than-successful icebreaker. The main topic of conversation had been the flowers that Paul had brought as a hostess gift for Katarina.

"They're beautiful," Katarina had exclaimed over the bouquet of mums.

"They're just from the supermarket. I'm afraid that

with the storm, all the florists were closed," Paul had replied apologetically.

"No, they're fantastic. You'd never know," Katarina had said, ignoring the plastic bag with the supermarket's logo. "And come to think of it, it's the first present I got from my father. Ben, why don't you take the baby, and I'll go put them in water."

"Why don't *you* hold Rad and I'll do it?" Ben had suggested.

"You won't know which vase," Katarina had protested.

"I think I can figure it out," Ben had answered and reassuringly patted her on the shoulder as he took the flowers to the kitchen.

And that exchange might have been the longest between Katarina and Paul, seeing as she had to keep jumping up to check on the food. Then all her movement had made the baby jittery, and the only way to calm him was a quick feed in the kitchen. Even then he refused to quiet down unless she held him.

Katarina really wasn't avoiding Paul, she really wasn't, she told herself, because after all, she *had* invited him, and she really *did* want to get to know him. But… but…she couldn't help it. She was nervous and maybe still in shock about the sudden revelation that he was her father. Not that Paul seemed any more comfortable with the idea.

But now that they were seated, things were bound to look up, or so Katarina told herself.

Ben walked around the table and stopped next to Katarina. "Wine?" he offered, holding up the bottle.

"No, I shouldn't, not with nursing the baby and all."

Paul placed his hand over the top of his wineglass.

"Water's fine for me, thanks." He reached for the pitcher and poured himself a glass.

The wooden harvest table was set with rust-colored placemats and matching cloth napkins. Winter squash from their garden and a basket of apples from the neighbor's orchard served as a centerpiece and set an autumnal mood. The light from a pair of candlesticks flickered against the rich ambers and golds. Maybe the décor would set a relaxed, homey atmosphere even without the aid of spirits? Katarina hoped.

"Well, I'm not afraid to drink alone," Ben said proudly and took his place at the head of the table. "After all, I'm not driving."

As he poured himself a glass of burgundy, there was a knock at the door.

Katarina looked at Paul.

He shook his head and shrugged.

She turned to Matt.

"No idea," he said, putting his hands up. "Maybe someone ran into trouble with the storm?" On cue, the wind lashed at the trees and branches brushed up against the windowpanes.

Katarina shifted Rad against her shoulder and rocked him gently. "Then why don't you go see who it is instead of hypothesizing?" she said to Matt. She saw Ben shoot her a glance, and she shook her head. "Sorry. I guess I'm a little on edge." Who wouldn't be, meeting her father for the first time?

"Thanks, son," Ben said, as Matt rose to get the door. "It's probably Julie. I had suggested to her to come over when she rang earlier, but she said no. She probably changed her mind."

There was the muffled sound of voices at the door.

Katarina raised her eyebrows at her husband.

"The storm's knocked out the power at her parents' place, and Julie was looking for a generator to get the electricity up and going," Ben explained.

"Then of course she should come over. I'll just put another place setting on the table." She started to rise.

"I'm happy to help," Paul said as he put his napkin on the table.

"Both of you stay and get acquainted. I can do it." Ben took a fortifying sip, pushed his chair back and headed for the kitchen.

Footsteps came from the front hallway and stopped at the doorway to the dining room.

Paul's hand stopped in midair as he went to put his napkin back on his lap. His expression remained transfixed as he stared across the table.

Katarina looked around. It was the last person she wanted to see. Zora. All the years of tamped down hostility finally came surging to the surface. "I don't remember sending you an invitation," she sneered.

Matt danced nervously next to Zora, his tall lanky frame dwarfing the small woman. "I think this might be my cue to ask if I can eat my dinner in my room while I do homework?" he ventured.

"I think it's more Zora's cue to say she's just leaving," Paul commented. His voice matched the temperature of the ice water that he drank with grim deliberation.

Katarina supposed she should have felt sympathy—felt something—for her mother standing there in a sorry sweatshirt and jeans. The bottoms of her pants were wet as was the top of her hair. But she didn't—she was fresh out of sympathy where Zora was concerned.

Katarina shifted her attention to Matt. "That's

probably a wise move. Tell you what, I'll call you down when it's dessert." She slanted her mother a critical glare. "So the coast will be clear."

Zora visibly clenched her jaw. But she stood her ground.

Matt collected his plate and hustled upstairs.

Katarina waited for him to leave before she launched into her mother. "What gives you the right to show up where you're not wanted?"

"A wise person told me not to take no for an answer," Zora said.

Katarina breathed out through her mouth. "I have half a mind to call up *Babička* now and lay into her for meddling."

"Hey, don't go jumping to conclusions. It wasn't *Babička*," Zora said. "It was Sebastiano Fonterra. He came to see me."

"Sebastiano Fonterra? The head of the hospital Sebastiano Fonterra?" It was Ben who spoke as he came walking back into the room. He stopped momentarily when he saw Zora standing there. He cleared his voice. "I guess I won't need to grab another chair. Here, why don't you take Matt's seat? It seems to be empty." He looked at Katarina.

She nodded. "I sent him upstairs. I didn't want him here if things got ugly. In any case, I wouldn't worry about the chair, let alone a place setting. Zora won't be staying." She gripped the baby possessively.

"Katarina, have a heart. You can't just send her back out into this weather. I'm not sure how passable the roads are anyway." The steady drumbeat of the heavy rain reinforced her husband's words.

Katarina rested her cheek against Rad, his little body swaddled tightly in a receiving blanket. He felt warm and comforting, and was snuffling quietly—a sure sign that he had fallen asleep. She should really put him to bed in his crib, but she didn't want to let go. She swallowed.

"All right. I suppose she can stay. But if the weather's as bad as all that, I think I'll go and call Julie," Katarina said. "She shouldn't be all alone."

"She's not," Zora said.

Her announcement brought silence to the room. The rain sounded even louder.

"Sebastiano Fonterra is there helping her. So you'll just have to face me without your faithful friend." Zora's voice didn't exactly lack an edge, either.

"Something *you* probably never had," Katarina retorted.

"That's probably true. But then single mothers with full-time jobs rarely have time for friends."

"That was your choice, as we all know," Paul interjected.

Katarina immediately felt she had an ally. She shot her mother a withering glance. "I heard enough of your sob story the other day at *Babička*'s." Katarina narrowed her eyes. "What do you mean he's helping her?"

"He rustled up a gas-powered pump to get rid of the water in the basement."

Ben cleared his throat. "Please, have a seat." He motioned Zora toward the empty chair. "Can I pour you some wine?"

Zora stepped gingerly to the table and sat down. She lifted the empty wine glass. "I could do with a little Dutch courage," she admitted.

"This Sebastiano Fonterra works quickly. First you, now Julie," Katarina observed snidely.

"Don't knock Sebastiano. He's a good guy," Paul said.

"And you shouldn't question his motives. If he went to see Zora, it's because of me."

Katarina swiveled in her chair. "You?" First he seemed to be on her side, but now? Her emotions zigzagged all over the map.

Paul nodded. "He's helped me a lot since I came back to Grantham. Been there for me when I needed him. And as for Julie? The guy's crazy about your friend. He'd do anything for her—if she'd let him."

Ben slanted his head to the side so that the candles wouldn't block his view of Katarina. "I don't know anything about his feelings for Julie, but the guy has his heart—and his thinking—in the right place when it comes to the community."

"He's been to see you, too? You never told me." Katarina was hurt. They never kept secrets from each other.

"No, we talked on the phone about my foundation, and a number of other things. I was on my way into New York to talk to those investors when he got me on my cell to chat about his ideas for the hospital and the community at large. That was when you were meeting your mother and since then…well…you've kind of had your mind on other things."

Katarina gave him a tight smile. "I'm sorry. I guess I've gotten so wrapped up in myself, I never asked you how that all went."

"Not to worry. There's plenty of time for that. Meanwhile, Zora, pass me your plate, and I'll serve you some food. You must be hungry."

Katarina's patience evaporated all over again. "Must you be so civilized? Feeding the woman who lied to me?"

"I didn't lie," Zora defended herself. She took the

plate after Ben heaped it with food, but made no move to eat.

No one else was chowing down for that matter.

"When I found out I was pregnant with you, I decided Paul was of no use, and that if I was going to go through with it, I'd have to do it on my own," Zora explained.

"Great! Now I'm an 'it.'"

Paul cleared his throat. "To be fair to Zora—on this matter at least—I wasn't exactly a prime candidate for fatherhood. I might have been a good student in college and full of heady ambitions, but that didn't mean I wasn't already self-destructing on the side. How can I put this?" He screwed up his face. "You see, for me at that time breakfast was a six-pack of Bud, and my customary appetizer before dinner was to smoke a lot of weed."

Katarina's mouth dropped open. "Did your parents know?"

"Not then. Like I said, I could still fake it. But Zora knew. I couldn't keep it from her. I never even tried to since I still thought I was in command of my life."

Katarina digested his words, then zeroed in on her mother. "Okay, let me get this straight. In the beginning you decided that Paul wasn't fit. I can understand that. But what about afterward? You didn't think to get in touch with him over the years?"

Zora wet her lips. Then she lifted her chin and focused her gaze on Katarina. "It's true, I am older, chronologically, and heaven knows, my body shows it. But emotionally, I think it's fair to say that I never really grew up. The truth—I never even considered contacting Paul because I blamed him for what had happened. I decided then and there that the world hadn't been fair to me. I wasn't going to shirk my responsibilities, but I resented him. I resented you." She said the last words barely above a whisper.

"Did you even love me?" Katarina asked. Now she was getting to the real heart of the problem—*her* problem.

"It wasn't so much that I didn't love you as I didn't love myself. I watched while other people loved you— *Babička,* Julie and her family, and it made me jealous, but there was nothing I could do. I had shut down."

Katarina stared back, unblinking, awash in emotions.

After a moment, Paul tentatively held up a hand, and the two were forced to look in his direction. "Heaven knows, I'd like to blame this whole thing on Zora. I really would. But sometimes—this time—I have to man up and accept responsibility, too. I'd sunk pretty low in my Hollywood years." Paul fingered the stem of his water glass. He seemed transfixed by the crystal. "And I like to think that if Zora had come to me then, that I would have risen to the occasion. But the truth of the matter…?" He raised his eyes to Katarina. "I can't say with any certainty that I would have done the right thing. I'm not proud to admit that, but it's something I can't change. Now, of course, I'd like to think it's another story—that I *am* worthy of being your father. I've got my book I'm working on—finally something I'm proud of." He paused and looked directly at Katarina. "And I'm in A.A. I haven't touched a drop of alcohol or used drugs in almost a year."

"Great! How lucky am I? I have a mother who's an emotional zombie and a father who's a junkie. It makes we wonder what kind of genes I am passing on to my son." Protectively, Katarina rocked her baby against her chest. Somehow Rad had managed to snore peacefully through all the upheaval.

"Katarina, nobody promised you a storybook family. But, no matter what, you now know who your parents are," Ben reminded her. "That *is* something positive at the end of the day."

"You're right. Of course, you're right." Ben, who was an orphan, would never have that luxury, Katarina realized shamefully. "I may not have model parents, but I have you and the kids. How much more lucky can I get?"

"Me, too. I feel just as lucky," Ben responded.

"And you can look at it this way," Zora suggested. "You might have inherited a few unfortunate characteristics from Paul and me, but, Katarina, you and Ben have lots of other, terrific qualities that more than balance out our lousy ones. Not that *all* our qualities are bad. I think it's fair to say that Paul and I are both intelligent and talented in our own ways. But whatever. The bottom line is that you and Ben are sensible *and* sensitive adults. You set fine examples for Rad—and Matt. And both of you will be there for your children through thick and thin. Unlike me," Zora said frankly.

"And me," Paul added.

Zora reached out. "Katarina, I can't change what's done. But can I—can we—start afresh?" She squeezed Katarina's arm before placing her hand back in her lap.

"You expect me to just forget what you did and didn't do? Forget my childhood anxieties about being unloved? My reluctance to trust anyone emotionally?" Katarina asked. Still, even she recognized that some of the steam had gone out of her anger.

"Of course not. I'm not asking you to. But with Ben

you've found a unique and wonderful support, a support based on love—real, deep love. I can't change the mistakes I've made or undo my bad decisions, but I can tell you that who you are now—your strengths *and* your weaknesses, the sum total—is shaped by your past experiences. So what I'm asking is this—that we try to work on having a future together. To get reacquainted. Can we work with what we've got? Lay the foundation for a better, more open future?" Zora ventured.

Katarina sighed, and then nodded quietly. "I suppose so. I won't promise anything, but I'll try."

Zora beamed. She sat up straight and thrust her shoulders back. She looked across the table. "Paul? What about you?"

"As the prayer says, 'grant me the serenity to accept the things I cannot change and the courage to change the things I can.' Listen, I'll always be an addict, but I'm clean and I intend to stay that way. I know it sounds pretty lame, but I think finding out about you, Katarina—that you're my daughter—has provided a piece of the puzzle that's always been missing in my life…the necessity of having to think of and do something for someone other than myself for a change. I'd like to be a part of your life, Katarina. And if you trust me, for starters, I am more than willing to offer free babysitting services. After all, isn't that what's expected of grandparents? Just start me off slowly. No diapering the first time out."

Zora seemed to study him for a minute. "You're not the same person I used to know, Paul. You've changed. The thing of it is, I came back to Grantham looking for some peace of mind that I seemed to have lost. Maybe what I really needed to look for was something I never had. And maybe, with a little luck, I'll move on from the person I've been for the past fifty years or so and become the kind of person I ought to be."

"It takes more than luck. It takes hard work," Paul responded.

Zora nodded. "You're right. But, as my mother likes to say, Zemanova women are not delicate flowers. We don't shrink from hard work." She held out her hand to Paul. "Allow me to introduce myself, my new, evolving self. I'm Zora Zemanova."

Paul snaked his arm around the centerpiece and clasped hers. "I'm pleased to meet you. I really am," he said.

Zora hesitated, and then finally pulled her hand back. She swiftly looked down at the food on her plate. "And speaking of my mother, I can tell that you're her granddaughter—Wiener schnitzel, mashed potatoes and red cabbage."

"I'm not just *Babička*'s granddaughter, I'm *your* daughter," Katarina clarified.

"You're right. And you know what? Why don't you pass me the baby so you can eat your dinner first? I may not know much about motherhood, but I do remember that by the time a mother gets to eat, the food is always cold." Zora held out her hands and Katarina passed her the baby.

Zora cuddled him in her arms and, gazing into his tiny face, smiled shyly. "Here, Radko, let me introduce myself. I'm Grandma Zora."

CHAPTER TWENTY-NINE

SEBASTIANO ENDED UP DRAGGING the pump across the rain-slicked lawn. He then attached a large ribbed hose, snaking the other end through a small basement window to reach the water.

He gassed and primed the motor, and after a few good yanks, the pump roared to life and went to work big-time. The water spilled out over the grass, down toward the street and into the storm drains.

"My God, look at it go!" Julie exclaimed. "It's like pumping out bilge water from a ship. Where did you get it anyway?" She and Sebastiano stood side by side next to the pump in the backyard. The rain had finally stopped falling, but her clothes—the ones she'd scrounged up from the house—were damp and clammy. Sebastiano's white shirt was still soaked, too, only now with more sweat than rain. Streaks of mud crisscrossed his trousers. His dark hair was randomly going in every direction, and one of his fingernails was torn and bloody.

He didn't care. In fact, he was exhilarated. "Rufus let me borrow it. Remember him telling us about the stuff he was cleaning up in the basement at his club? Anyway, sure enough, he had the pump just like he said, and he didn't need it. The power was out on his side of town, too, but he was using a backup generator to keep the sump pump and his refrigerator going." Grinning from ear to ear, Sebastiano turned to Julie. "I have to ask you, does everyone have a sump pump in Grantham?"

"Unless you're on higher elevation, just about. The soil is nothing but shale and clay, and the water table's pretty high, though I'm sure Zora could give a much better technical explanation," Julie answered.

"I think you did just fine." Julie had been tough, levelheaded—more than fine—in a difficult situation, Sebastiano thought.

She ducked down and shone the flashlight through the window. "It looks like the water's going down."

"I think you're right. Why don't we go back to the garage and take a look from there," he suggested.

"I know. We can set up some of the beach chairs and watch the water recede, kind of like the tide going out," Julie said as she walked next to him.

Laughing, he gazed down at her. "Oh, no."

"What? What is it? Are you hurt?" She immediately lifted one of his arms and started patting his ribs.

"I hate to say no if that means you'll stop."

She dropped her hand and gave him a look.

"I was concerned because I just noticed that you're barefoot."

She glanced down. "You're right. I hadn't even realized it. I was in too much of a shock, I guess."

"Then it's definitely time for you to sit down while I locate a glass of brandy."

"For once I'm inclined to agree with you. You'll find something—I'm not sure whether it'll be brandy or not—in the sideboard in the dining room. There're glasses there, too." Julie reached for a canvas-covered folding chair hanging from the wall of the garage and opened it up to get a prime view of the cellar.

Sebastiano took down another. "I'll be right back," he said.

When he returned a few minutes later, Julie was sitting under the glow of a camp light. She was bent over a sagging box. He held out a glass. "Limoncello was the closest thing I could find. I hope that will do," he said.

"It sounds heavenly," Julie said with a sigh. She sat up and glanced at a water-soaked stack of paper in her hand. "All these pictures—drawings from the grandkids that my mom was saving." She pushed to the bottom of the box. "There might even be some of mine from grade school. They're all stuck together, and I think most of them are ruined." She let them fall on her lap and looked down in dismay. "All these memories. Ruined."

"I think most of it will dry and the papers can be pressed flat. Some things might not make it, but you managed to save a lot. Think of all the things you put up on higher shelves. I'm sure they're fine."

"But the furnace, the hot water heater? Who knows if they're totally ruined? And if you hadn't come when you did, then the circuit breakers…" She stopped and swallowed. "I'm sorry. I don't mean to ramble."

"There's nothing to be sorry about. Here…" He put the glasses on the ground, removed the pictures from her lap and helped her up by the elbow. "I tell you what, why don't you go lie down for now? You look exhausted. There's nothing to be done anymore anyway. I can keep an eye on the pump, to make sure the water's still going down."

"You sure?" she asked wearily.

"Of course." He passed her the drink.

"I don't want to impose on you."

Sebastiano turned her around and pushed her gently toward the door to the kitchen. "It's no imposition."

"You're really generous, you know that?"

"It's not generosity, trust me."

Julie stopped and turned around. She looked at him, her mouth open and her eyes unblinking. "It's not?" Her voice was small, hesitant.

Sebastiano raised the flashlight to take a better look at her. Her hair was bedraggled, her expression haggard, her clothes wet and shapeless. None of that mattered. She had never looked more beautiful.

And then she changed. Suddenly, she became more alive. More defined.

Simultaneously, he and Julie lifted their heads to behold the naked bulb in the ceiling.

"The electricity? It's on?" she asked in disbelief.

Thank you, Public Service Gas and Utility, he wanted to shout and rejoice. No, he really wanted to lift her up and then carry her to the nearest bed to ravish her in ways only movie directors and adolescent boys could imagine. And then he looked closer and saw the deeply etched purple circles under her eyes and her drooping eyelids. The time for fun would have to wait. It was tough, really tough, being noble.

He compromised by brushing her forehead with a chaste kiss. *How handy not to have to lean over when kissing somebody,* he thought. *Not just somebody,* he reminded himself with a conspiratorial grin.

She staggered back. "Did you just kiss me?"

"Go to sleep," he said, pushing her through the door. "And dream of me," he murmured to her back.

JULIE WOKE UP the next morning with sunlight streaming through the windows. It took a few minutes to realize that she was sleeping in her old bedroom in her parents' house, only now it had been turned into her mother's crafts project room. She was surrounded by piles of quilting fabric, wool and scrapbook material.

She felt something affixed to her cheek and peeled off a cellophane packet of stickers. She dropped it on the bed, and then stared out the windows, squinting into the sun. "It's not raining," she announced. "And it's morning," she said. Clearly, her brain was not functioning at top speed. There was something else, she kept thinking. Something? Someone?

Sebastiano.

Julie leaped off the bed. "Sebastiano?" she called out. She raced down the hallway and stumbled down the carpeted stairs. She hopped the bottom two steps in one bound, nearly spraining an ankle in the process, and swerved into the kitchen. "Sebastiano?" she called again, reaching the door to the garage.

She didn't see him. She craned her neck around the storage cabinet that blocked her view, and holding on to the doorjamb, took a tentative step into the garage.

She heard the sound of muffled footsteps and nearly jumped. "Sebastiano?" she called out.

The footsteps stopped. She heard a box thump to the floor. Sebastiano came around. "You're awake."

"More or less." She exhaled through her mouth. "I wasn't sure if it was you."

"You were expecting someone else?" he asked, a crooked smile on his face.

But it wasn't his face she was staring at. He had taken off his shirt and was bare-chested.

She cleared her voice. "I just didn't expect you to still

be here. I'm so sorry to have collapsed like that, leaving you to do all this work." She stepped farther into the garage. He'd set up a couple of bridge tables and brought in the picnic table from the patio. Rows of glasses, old LPs out of their cardboard jackets, trays, tools and suitcases were sprawled atop. She slowly fingered a juice glass here, a punch bowl there.

He joined her. "You wouldn't believe it. I opened these wet cardboard boxes of wineglasses, and inside, each goblet was filled to the brim with water, as if someone had carefully poured each one. It was surreal. Almost as strange was the way the wine bottles had floated away from their racks and were nestled peacefully around a box of Christmas ornaments. It was as if they were sleeping."

Julie glanced up, stricken. "Oh, no, not the Christmas ornaments?"

"Don't worry. The lid was on the plastic container and everything was perfectly watertight. A miracle of modern technology."

She watched as Sebastiano turned over a row of screwdrivers to dry them on the other side. "You did so much. You must have been up all night," she said.

"There's still a lot left to do," he joked wearily. "But I must tell you. What you did before I got here, I think it prevented a real crisis—all your father's power equipment, the rest of the Christmas decorations, some tax records." He rubbed his chin. The dark shadow of his beard emphasized the sharp angle of his jaw and cheekbones.

"Probably a lot of the financial stuff should have been shredded a long time ago," she said. "I don't think my father's ever thrown out a single sheet of paper."

"I need to confess, though, I was also worried about the boiler and the hot water heater being submerged, so I shut off their circuit breakers," he went on. "Luckily, the plumber had left maintenance charts atop the boiler, so I called him. He'll be here early tomorrow morning, and then we'll find out if they made it or if they need to be repaired or replaced."

"Oh, God. I hate to think they're ruined, especially because I'm pretty sure the insurance won't cover it." Then she saw a box of photos sitting on the ground next to the picnic table. She knelt down and grabbed a few. The old Polaroid snapshots stuck to each other as if glued. "Oh, no, the pictures of the family vacationing on Long Beach Island." She dropped them back in the disintegrating cardboard box and picked up another handful. "And the time we drove across the country to the Grand Canyon and Monument Valley and Bryce Canyon. I remember that my brothers and I fought the whole time in the backseat. Dom pinched me mercilessly. The bruises lasted for weeks. But it *was* something, beyond anything I could have imagined. I never knew anything could be so big or that places looked like that outside of cowboy movies."

She dropped that pile back, too. "And now it's all gone. God, I don't know how I'm going to tell my parents."

Sebastiano crouched down next to her. "You still have all the memories even without the pictures. And as for telling your parents? There's no rush. Why worry them? What are they going to do about it in Italy? You can let them know just before they come home. Anyway, by that time, all of this will be cleaned up and the drama will be over." He squeezed her shoulders reassuringly.

She turned to him. "I understand what you're saying, but I still feel like I failed them. Things *are* broken, some gone forever."

Sebastiano brushed her cheek with his knuckles. "Don't be silly. They know that the most important thing is that you're all right. Trust me, they won't believe all that you've done for them, especially when they start hearing stories from other people. This is far from the only basement to be flooded."

"I guess so." She sniffed, not fully convinced.

He lowered his hand and lightly kissed the same spot on her cheek. "Besides, I haven't seen any of your brothers calling or rushing to help out."

"That's because they have places of their own and work and—"

"And you don't have your own place and work?"

And then it hit her. "Oh, my God, work! I've got patients scheduled this morning!" She started to stand up.

He pressed her down. "Don't worry. I've already called your office and left a message that you won't be in until the afternoon because of the storm. Your appointments can be rescheduled. And if it makes you feel any better, I've heard that many other physicians around town have done the same thing, even canceling the whole day except for emergencies."

Julie looked at him in amazement. "Is there anything you haven't done yet?"

"Hmm, in case you haven't noticed, I desperately need a shower."

Julie was aware more than ever given how close he was. "You're right. You do need a shower."

"I'm sorry." He went to pull away.

She held his arm. "No, I like it. It's real honest sweat." She rested her head on his shoulder. "Why did you do it? I mean, you've got your own place and a job and all these things that are pulling at you left, right and center. Why move heaven and earth to help me?" She lifted her head and peered at him.

He stared right back at her. "You really need to know?"

She nodded. "I really need to know." She felt her pulse quicken in anticipation of…what? What indeed?

Sebastiano took his time, speaking slowly, his accent a little more marked than usual. "You know, sometimes it takes something like a flood to clear things out. It's not all destructive. It can also be cleansing."

"Are you getting all deep and philosophical on me?"

He smiled. "No, I'm not being philosophical, merely stating a fact. Sometimes we need something big, something that turns our world upside down, to understand what really is important."

"And that something happened to you?" she asked.

"More like someone. You turned my world upside down and made me look at myself in a whole new light. Forced me to accept that I'm not completely hopeless."

Julie scrunched up her face. "Of course you're not. Didn't I tell you that?"

"Yes, but *I* needed to tell myself. And I never would have without you pushing and needling and bugging me."

"I don't bug."

"Yes, you do."

"All right, I do. I'm sorry."

"I'm not." And then he stopped speaking. He angled his head one way.

She put hers the other.

He leaned forward.

She did, too.

And their lips met in a long, slow kiss, their breathing as one.

And when the kiss ended as gently as it had begun, Sebastiano spoke, his mouth inches from hers. "I think it's time for a shower. Even if it has to be a cold one after the power outage."

Julie smiled. "Trust me. My Dad put in a seventy-seven-gallon hot water heater. There'll be more than enough hot water stored for one long and very steamy shower."

"To be shared?" he asked.

"If you've no objections."

He took her up in his arms. "And then afterward, perhaps a little nap?" he asked teasingly.

She shrugged her shoulders, and her sweatshirt raised tantalizingly to reveal bare skin. She noticed how his pupils enlarged. "A nap? I don't think so."

He breathed in quickly and kissed her again. "We may never make it to the shower at this rate," he said, resting his forehead against hers.

She clasped her hands behind his neck. "Cleanliness is highly overrated."

He laughed. "Come, before I ravage you next to your father's woodworking tools."

She laughed back and kissed him hard and swift.

It left him speechless. But only for a moment. He ran a fingertip along her hairline, gently smoothing the short strands to the side. "You know, when this is over—and by this I mean getting your parents' house back in order—"

"That I should take the time to rethink something you said earlier—about loosening the reins a little and getting a partner in my practice?" she offered.

He angled his head.

"I guess the flood has cleared out my brain a bit, too," she said.

"Remind me to talk to you about something else along that line, but not now. Definitely, not now. I have other plans."

"I know, I know, you're going to take me to dinner."

"There is that. Though I should warn you, I suppose. It will be a dinner for three."

"Three?" Julie frowned.

"Yes, I've invited my mother to Grantham, and I want you to meet her."

"Your mother? When? I mean, I want to make sure I haven't done anything crazy like put green streaks in my hair right before she comes—" She stopped babbling. "Wait a minute. You invited your mother because...?" She stared at him closely, anxiously. She could feel the pressure mounting and she wasn't sure she was ready for what she thought he might just be getting at....

"Don't worry, you have plenty of time. I invited her to come in late November."

Okay, calm down. She told herself not to get excited. That was still two months away. "Oh, I get it. Thanksgiving."

"Yes, there's that. But also because I wanted her to be here for an important occasion."

Now she was really nervous.

"I'm becoming an American citizen, and I wanted

her to be here for the swearing-in ceremony. It's very meaningful to me, and I wanted her to share it."

"Oh, my gosh, why didn't you tell me? We have to have a party. This is a big deal. And having your mother here, of course, makes total sense. You'll be able to show her how you're making positive steps in your future." She was happy for him, she really was. But she couldn't stop wondering how she could have jumped to the conclusion that he had been hinting at something to do with him *and* her? So she had fallen for him—left, right and center and any other axis on this or any other planet. That didn't mean he felt that kind of deep emotion for her. Just because he'd moved heaven and earth to help her, sacrificed a night's sleep, worked till dawn.... Or did it?

Sebastiano immediately started laughing again.

"What? What's so funny?" she asked, miffed.

"Don't ever play poker," he said. "It's impossible for you to hide your emotions. So, please…please. I'm also inviting her here because I want her to meet you."

"Me?" Where was that self-confidence when she needed it?

"Yes, *tesoro,* you. I want the most important woman from my past to meet the most important woman in my future."

"You're telling me that…that…"

"I'm telling you that I love you. You didn't think I came to your rescue only because I wanted to play with manly toys like chain saws and pumps. Though, that was really quite fun, I must say."

"Wait a minute. Forget the man toys. Did you say that you love me?"

"Yes, is that a problem?"

Julie was so overwhelmed she could feel her insides shaking. She looked at her hands. Her outsides were shaking, too. She didn't know whether to laugh, cry or jump up and down. "No, no problem. In fact, it's pretty welcome news because I also love you. Weird, no?" Even her voice shook.

"Weird, yes." He paused and narrowed his eyes in thought. "So tell me, does this mean we're even disagreeing about being in love?"

Julie scoffed. "Enough already. Can we get inside?"

He seemed momentarily distracted. "Just a minute."

Julie rolled her eyes. "You're going to kill me here."

"Always so impatient," he scolded, not seeming to mind her outburst in the least. He patted his pants, then glanced around the garage. He snapped his fingers. "My suit jacket. That's right. I left it in my suit jacket pocket, and I left the jacket in Zora's truck."

Julie started to back away. He wasn't searching for a ring, was he? They had only just established that they loved each other. But marriage? That was a huge step. Huge! Shouldn't they get to know each other better?

Sebastiano waited politely with an amused grin on his face.

"What? What are you not saying?" Julie asked suspiciously.

"Nothing. I'm just taking it all in, your little internal drama. Perhaps *little* is the wrong word? Did anyone ever tell you that you worry too much?"

"You. All the time."

"And just remember that. Meanwhile, I just wanted you to look at the handout for the next Italian class."

She narrowed her eyes. "You better pray that the Adult School is cancelled tonight because by the time I finish with you, you won't be able to make it to class."

"Is that a threat?" he asked.

"No, a promise," she answered.

And that's when he swept her up in his arms. "Whoa, you're bigger than I imagined." He staggered under the weight.

"I thought that was the line I was supposed to say to you."

They made it as far as the kitchen.

Sebastiano leaned against the counter, still carrying her in his arms. "Please tell me the bathroom is on this floor," he said.

"Sorry. It's one floor up. But it's not *that* many stairs," she protested.

He tilted his head. "You want to get there quickly, or do you want me to struggle on?"

"Since when have I ever be known for my patience?" She pushed herself out of his embrace and dashed out of the kitchen. "Catch me if you can," she taunted over her shoulder as she headed up the stairs.

He didn't need any encouragement. Taking two steps at a time, he reached her at the upstairs hallway. She was already stripping off the sweatshirt, and when she had it over her head, he grabbed her and kissed her.

She pulled back, more aroused than ever. "I thought you wanted a shower?" she asked playfully. She pulled down her track pants, and tripping over the hem of one leg, hustled to the bathroom, giving him a perfect view of her naked derriere.

"You're killing me," he called out.

She laughed and skidded into the bathroom, an ode to fifties décor—powder-pink ceramic tile and a row of frosted-white makeup lights over the vanity mirror. She bent to run the water in the matching pink tub, and he joined her—naked, as well. The warm water splashed through her fingers, and she stared at him openly. Her breath came in short spurts. She pressed the lever to switch the water to come down from the showerhead. "Are you ready?"

"You have to ask?" He swooped her up again and carried her over the side of the bathtub.

The water from the shower beat down on her shoulders and back, and she ran her hands through his hair, raking the short locks against his scalp. The steamy vapor intensified the smells—his subtle woodsy cologne, the lingering perspiration from manual labor and heat. Male Heat.

He balanced her weight on his hips, his hands moving to her shoulders, kneading and caressing. The water streamed down over their faces as he kissed the side of her mouth, then angled and kissed the other side.

She tasted his chin and tugged at an earlobe. And as she leaned back to admire the dark swirl of hair that arrowed down his chest, he braced her against the wall.

"I'll never think of pink tiles in quite the same way again," she confessed.

His eyes were hooded with desire, but he still managed a toothy grin. "Just tell me one things. Do we need to worry about protection?"

She shook her head. "I'm on the Pill."

"Thank goodness for small miracles." And then he was inside her with one stroke.

Immediately she forgot all about the tiles.

CHAPTER THIRTY

November, two months later

HER PARENTS' PLACE was packed. *Nonna* had ceded her usual golden upholstered chair to *La Signora,* as she had insisted on addressing Mrs. Fonterra, Sebastiano's mother. Sebastiano's mom, an elegant middle-aged woman who did more for a sweater set than Julie would have thought possible, encouraged everyone to call her by her first name, Fabiana. *Nonna* wasn't everyone. She had also insisted on having the head chair from the dining room placed right next to Fabiana so that they could gossip together in rapid Italian.

Julie thought it was probably a good idea that more than half the people in the room didn't speak Italian, the way the two women commented on everyone—in the nicest way possible, of course. But the few times she was in earshot and caught a word here or there, most of the conversation seemed to be centered on her and Sebastiano. Was she even surprised?

She felt hands grab her waist from behind. Then a brush of lips to her earlobe. She smiled. She turned her head in the direction of those lips. "For someone who prided himself on his reserve, you've become very demonstrative in public," she murmured. She moved a step to the side, nodding hello to Matt, Katarina and Ben's teenage son, who was headed for the food laid out on the dining room table.

It was nominally a cocktail party, but that hadn't stopped her mother and *Nonna* from producing loads of antipasto, *bruschetta* and enough garlicky dips to ward off an army of vampires.

Sebastiano reached out and entwined his fingers in hers. He brought her around to his side. "You're objecting, *tesoro*—you, who was never so restrained in public? And looking exceptionally beautiful wearing a lovely shade of blue, I might add."

"I'll have you know that I own lots of clothes that are not black," she protested. In point of fact, she had made a special trip into New York to the Babette boutique in Soho to pick up her crinkly dress in Yale blue. She told herself it was in honor of Matt's acceptance to the Ivy League college. She told herself a lot of things these days that she knew weren't totally accurate.

"And as to my reluctance regarding any public displays of affection, I just want you to know that your mother, my mother and my grandmother are watching us with eagle eyes." She also noted Iris and Rufus, sipping champagne by the picture window, smiling in their direction. "Oh, God, I might as well take out an ad in the *Grantham Courier,* declaring my love for you," she said with exasperation.

"You think everyone doesn't know already? Admit it. They all knew it before we did," he said.

Julie smiled. "You're right."

"What?" He put his hand on his chest in mock horror. "You say I'm right?"

"Probably," she qualified and planted a sloppy kiss on his mouth without the slightest regard for everyone else in the room—including Sarah and Katarina and their husbands, her parents, her brothers, their wives and their countless children.

It seemed as if her parents had invited the whole of Grantham to their party to celebrate all the good things that had happened since their return from Italy. Of course everyone came from her office, including her new partner in the practice, Olivia Blanchford. Then there was Carlotta Sanchez, the woman whose baby she had delivered in the E.R. oh, those many months ago. She was there with her husband. He was standing in the corner, proudly holding his baby daughter, Ramona, who was dressed in a sparkling-white lacey dress. Julie saw her father hone in on him and attempt to make conversation in half broken Spanish, half Italian. Soon the proud young father was beaming. Paul Bedecker was also there, drinking ginger ale and talking fly-fishing with Ben, while Lena was insisting Paul try the potato croquettes. Julie had heard she was determined to put some weight on his bones.

Even Zora had sent an email, thanking Julie's parents for the invitation but explaining that her talk at the geology conference in Bologna was scheduled the same day. Unfortunately, she wouldn't be able to attend, but she was planning to be back in time for Christmas. That would be after Paul's trip to Rome in the first part of December. Rumor had it he would be looking for an apartment, but no matter what, he had promised Julie's mom he would be back to speak at their high school reunion. Katarina had confided to Julie that life as an extended family was not always easy, but at least everyone could sit together in a room and make polite conversation without arguing for maybe forty-five minutes.

"That's a lot better than my family most of the time," Julie had replied.

But as she surveyed the house groaning under the weight of friends and family and heard the clink of glasses and murmur of conversations and the laughter and the squeals of children chasing each other, she freely admitted this was definitely one of those special moments. Was that her baby nephew really sitting under the table eating away at a stack of *crespelle,* Italian pancakes? And didn't she just hear Fabiana praise the fine handiwork of the needlepoint tray that Julie had given her as a present, while *Nonna* displayed *her* bolster pillow, which had Iris joining the conversation and speaking in her personal version of Italian, liberally flecked with dialogue from Mozart's operas? And her dad—holding and jiggling Carlotta's baby in his arms? Was there ever a man alive who loved babies more?

Julie stole a glance at Sebastiano, who had bent down to tickle one of Dom's twins, Rosy, who'd stolen a piece of salami off his plate. The little girl was beside herself with paroxysms of laughter.

Is it possible to feel happier than now? she wondered.

Then from the dining room, she heard the loud clinking of cutlery against glass. One of the wineglasses that Sebastiano had saved in the flood, she couldn't help thinking.

"Tutti a tavola per il brindisi!" her mother announced before translating for all the non-Italian speakers. "Everybody to the dining room table for the toasts!"

Dom was at the ready with champagne, making sure everybody had a filled glass, even a little for the children. "Dad," Dom said, handing a glass to his father.

Lou nodded thanks and eased his way to the head

of the table. He clutched the stem of the wineglass in his hand and dropped his head to gather his thoughts. Then he lifted his face, smiled with contentment and held out a hand to his wife, Angela, who stood proudly at his side.

"Everyone, family, friends, welcome to our house," he said warmly. "It is a wonderful occasion that we have here today—a celebration of so many things that we can be thankful for."

He held up his glass. "First, to our wonderful daughter, Giulietta, and Sebastiano—we have come to realize from tales that others have told us, that your efforts saved our house and possessions. We can't thank you enough. When you called to explain what had happened—though I think you may have left out the worst—all we could think was at least no one was hurt. Things can have meaning, but they can be replaced. People, that's another story. Giulietta, having you as our daughter has been a joy. We are, and always have been, so proud of you. So thank you for making sure we had our home to come back to, safe and sound. *Mille grazie.* Many thanks."

"Mille grazie," Angela echoed and blew her a kiss.

Julie felt a lump in her throat. She bit down on her lip and glanced at Sebastiano. "Kick me if I start crying," she whispered.

He rubbed her arm.

"Non dimentare che Caruso sia sicuro. And don't forget Caruso was safe," *Nonna* added for all to hear, a pronouncement that was greeted with laughter.

"How could anyone forget that dumb bird," Dom said none too softly. For once, Julie thought her brother was right on the mark.

"But that's not the only reason we are celebrating,"

Lou went on. He searched out the faces. "To Matt, congratulations on your acceptance to Yale. To think a Yale man in my household! Not that we won't still root for Grantham at the basketball games, of course."

Matt blushed. "I understand. Thank you."

"Also," her father went on, "we want to thank Iris Phox for matching the anonymous gifts to fully fund the new Ramona Sanchez Community Center and Clinic that will be a major part of the new Grantham Hospital. You are one of the people who makes Grantham so special."

"And I, for one, owe you, Iris, a great deal for insisting I take Italian at the Adult School," Julie added.

"It was the least I could do for the only person who has been able to teach me how to do the Turkey Work stitch in needlepoint," Iris replied.

"Hear! Hear!" Rufus raised his glass, and everyone joined in.

Iris nodded with appropriate understatement.

Julie could tell she loved it. She whispered again to Sebastiano. "So who were the anonymous donors?"

"My lips are sealed," he said softly, though she saw him give an appreciative look in the direction of Iris's son, Hunt, Sarah's husband, as well as Ben.

"Speaking of the clinic, we are very lucky to have with us Rufus Treadway and my own daughter, Dr. Giulietta Antonelli, who have agreed to be co-directors," Lou announced.

"I think I was only given the title because the Nighttime Bar is the future home of the facility," Rufus said modestly.

There was applause, more drinking.

"And we should toast little Ramona, the namesake

for the clinic here with us," he added. He held his glass in the direction of Carlotta's baby. "To the future of Grantham," he proclaimed.

"To the future of Grantham," everyone joined in. Ramona's parents beamed.

"Hey, if there're any more toasts, I'm going to have to give refills," Dom complained.

"We have plenty of champagne," Lou reminded him. Lou bent over as Angela whispered in his ear. He nodded, then looked at everyone again. "I have been told that I have hogged the stage long enough, but I can't end before giving a hearty welcome to Julie's new partner in her medical practice, Dr. Blanchard. And to Fabiana Fonterra, Sebastiano's mother, who is visiting the United States for the first time and, we hope, not the last. *Ben venuti nella nostra communità e nella nostra famiglia.*"

"Hear! Hear! *Chin, chin!*"

"*Grazie,* I am most delighted to be here, *specialmente* with my son," she said in fluent but accented English.

"And finally—"

"Thank goodness," Dom muttered.

Nonna shot him an evil look.

"Last but certainly not least, to Sebastiano, our newest American." Lou raised his glass extra high. "To those who might not know it, the Italian word for citizen is *cittadino,* which also means city dweller or member. Sebastiano, your work and spirit prove you are a true *cittadino* of Grantham—not to mention your fondness for my daughter."

There was loud, sustained clapping.

"Lou, I am proud to be considered a friend and fellow neighbor," Sebastiano said.

"Cake? Cake time?" Teddy wailed.

Everyone laughed, especially *Nonna*. "*Dalla bocca della verità.* Out of the mouths of babes!" she said. She got up from her chair and immediately started ordering Angela to get the sheet cake from the kitchen. She shooed the children away from the end of the table to give herself room.

Julie watched with amusement, wondering how many times she had witnessed similar scenes and how many more she would probably enjoy—or sometimes not really enjoy, but survive—in the future. At the same time, she realized that without Sebastiano's help none of today would have been possible. Not only did he help her get the house back together, but he also helped her get her life back together. Her memories might still be intact, but she could accept that, knowing that they would no longer control her future.

She was smiling, content, when she felt a tug on her arm.

"Come. I figure we've got about five minutes while they first serve the kids. I need to show you something," Sebastiano said. He grabbed her hand and squired her out the front door, down the steps and over to the garage. He lifted up the wide door.

"The garage? You want to show me the garage?" Julie crossed her arms, nonplussed.

"Actually, I'm taking you to the basement. I feel a certain kinship with that space."

Julie shook her head. "If you say so. Only go slow. I've got on three-inch heels, in case you haven't noticed."

Sebastiano spun around. He had to lift his chin to reach hers. "You think I haven't noticed?" He took her hand again and led her down the stairs to the basement.

He flicked on the switch. He raised his face and marveled at the bare lightbulb overhead, "Something, isn't it? I'll never take light for granted again." Then he turned around and reached into the inside pocket of his suit jacket.

Julie made a face. "Please, tell me that you're not asking me to look at next week's handout for Italian conversation class?"

Sebastiano stopped with his hand inside his coat. "I hadn't thought of that. But if you insist?"

She growled.

"All right, if you don't want to look at the handout, I guess this will have to do." He took out a small satin-covered box.

Julie stood speechless.

He flipped open the hinge to reveal an antique gold ring with a delicate rosette in the center. It was an intricate micromosaic of hand-blown colored glass and diamond chips, painstakingly assembled in a vibrant yet subtle pattern of petals.

Julie's heart started racing, big-time.

Sebastiano looked up from the ring and into her face. "Maybe if you took off your shoes and weren't so much taller at this moment, I'd feel more confident about my request." He gulped. "I'm asking you to marry me, Julie. ¿Vuoi sposarmi, Giulietta?"

Julie opened her mouth, but no words came out.

Sebastiano held up his hand. "This ring is actually from my mother. No, that's not quite right. It's my family's. Her family's, actually—a ring that's been passed down from mother to daughter through the generations."

"You asked your mother to bring the ring?" Julie

squeaked. It appeared her voice was back, but two octaves higher.

"No, she just knew to do so. She said it was the way I talked about you, my voice. So she knew to bring it. She didn't have a daughter. She had me. And now I'm giving it to you."

As if to emphasize the point, Sebastiano got down on one knee. He gazed up at her but shook his head. "No, that doesn't work. Now you're even taller."

Julie tugged at him to get up. "Please, I know the concrete is clean because I'm the one who mopped it with bleach, but that really isn't necessary."

"You may be right. The concrete *is* pretty hard."

"Then you should have thought to bring one of my pillows," she reminded him.

"I should have thought of a lot of things, but that's another matter." Sebastiano braced himself and slowly rose to slip the ring out of the cushion. "From me, a symbol of truth and beauty and fidelity, to the most important woman in my life."

Julie watched as he slid the delicate ring on her left hand. The band was a little big and the flower decoration slipped to the side. She steadied it with her other hand and held it upright and true. And then she bawled big, fat, humongous tears.

"I take it that's a yes," Sebastiano said, a note of triumph in his voice. He took her, heaving sobs and all, into his arms. "*Con amore, cara, con amore vero per sempre.* With love, dear, with a true love forever."

Julie squeezed her fingers tightly together to keep the ring from slipping off. Not that she was ever going to let that happen. "*Anch'io.* Me, too." She sniffed loudly, in very unladylike fashion. "You planned to do this a ways back, didn't you. After the flood?" she asked.

"I think I had the idea that I'd be asking you even before that. Maybe going back to when you barged into my office and into my heart. Did I ever thank you for breaking that ugly glass vase? I finally had an excuse to not display it."

"I didn't break it. How many times do I have to tell people. It's only chipped," Julie shot back.

"Yes, yes, of course, you're right. You're right about a lot of things. Especially me. I'm not perfect, I know that all too well. But now I can accept it and try to do better because I know that my heart is in the right place. With you at my side."

Julie, who thought she had cried the last of her tears, felt the floodgates about to open up again. She squeezed her eyes shut and when she thought she might just have her emotions under control, risked opening them. "I will be honored to be by your side because I know that you will always have my back."

"Provided you're not wearing six-inch heels," he amended.

"Don't go there." She pointed a warning finger in his direction. "You know, this will be the best marriage ever, provided we don't kill each other fighting."

"But think of all the make-up sex." Without waiting a beat, he kissed her senseless.

When it was over, she gasped for air. "Enough," she said, pushing away.

"Enough?" He angled his head to kiss her under the chin.

Julie could feel herself succumbing as he nibbled his way around to her earlobe, but she marshaled all her strength. "Yes, enough. Because that tap-tap-tapping that's getting louder?"

Sebastiano stopped, blinked and listened. "Yes, I hear it." He looked inquiringly at her.

"I'm pretty sure that's *Nonna* bringing us some cake."

Sebastiano took a step back and straightened his tie. "You're right. But I'm pretty sure the cake is just a pretext. What she really wants is to be the first person to see the ring."

"You think she guessed? Her spooky ESP thing?"

And that's when they heard another sound—the triumphant warbling of Caruso.

Sebastiano looked at Julie. Julie looked at Sebastiano. "Now, that's spooky," she said.

"No, that's chutzpah," he replied.

She stared at him.

"That's a Yiddish word for nerve," Sebastiano explained. "Iris taught it to me."

Julie shook her head. "I know what chutzpah means. I just didn't expect to hear it from you."

"Just think what you have to look forward to."

She squeezed her fingers together, feeling the ring press against her skin, the strange sensation seeming so right. *More than I ever imagined,* she thought. "Oh, to hell with *Nonna*," she exclaimed and threw herself at him.

* * * * *

COMING NEXT MONTH

Available August 9, 2011

You can find more information on upcoming
Harlequin® titles, free excerpts and more at
www.HarlequinInsideRomance.com.

HSRCNM0711

REQUEST YOUR FREE BOOKS!
2 FREE NOVELS PLUS 2 FREE GIFTS!

❦ Harlequin®

Super Romance®

Exciting, emotional, unexpected!

*Once bitten, twice shy. That's Gabby Wade's motto—
especially when it comes to Adamson men.
And the moment she meets Jon Adamson her theory
is confirmed. But with each encounter a little* something
*sparks between them, making her wonder if she's been
too hasty to dismiss this one!*

*Enjoy this sneak peek from ONE GOOD REASON
by Sarah Mayberry, available August 2011
from Harlequin® Superromance®.*

Gabby Wade's heartbeat thumped in her ears as she marched
to her office. She wanted to pretend it was because of her
brisk pace returning from the file room, but she wasn't that
good a liar.

Her heart was beating like a tom-tom because Jon Adamson had touched her. In a very male, very possessive way.
She could still feel the heat of his big hand burning through
the seat of her khakis as he'd steadied her on the ladder.

It had taken every ounce of self-control to tell him to
unhand her. What she'd really wanted was to grab him by
his shirt and, well, explore all those urges his touch had
instantly brought to life.

While she might not like him, she was wise enough to
understand that it wasn't always about liking the other person. Sometimes it was about pure animal attraction.

Refusing to think about it, she turned to work. When
she'd typed in the wrong figures three times, Gabby admitted she was too tired and too distracted. Time to call it a
day.

As she was leaving, she spied Jon at his workbench in
the shop. His head was propped on his hand as he studied
blueprints. It wasn't until she got closer that she saw his

eyes were shut.

He looked oddly boyish. There was something innocent and unguarded in his expression. She felt a weakening in her resistance to him.

"Jon." She put her hand on his shoulder, intending to shake him awake. Instead, it rested there like a caress.

His eyes snapped open.

"You were asleep."

"No, I was, uh, visualizing something on this design." He gestured to the blueprint in front of him then rubbed his eyes.

That gesture dealt a bigger blow to her resistance. She realized it wasn't only animal attraction pulling them together. She took a step backward as if to get away from the knowledge.

She cleared her throat. "I'm heading off now."

He gave her a smile, and she could see his exhaustion.

"Yeah, I should, too." He stood and stretched. The hem of his T-shirt rose as he arched his back and she caught a flash of hard male belly. She looked away, but it was too late. Her mind had committed the image to permanent memory.

And suddenly she knew, for good or bad, she'd never look at Jon the same way again.

Find out what happens next in ONE GOOD REASON, available August 2011 from Harlequin® Superromance®!

SPECIAL EDITION

Life, Love, Family and Top Authors!

IN AUGUST, HARLEQUIN SPECIAL EDITION FEATURES
USA TODAY BESTSELLING AUTHORS
MARIE FERRARELLA AND *ALLISON LEIGH.*

THE BABY WORE A BADGE
BY *MARIE FERRARELLA*

The second title in the **Montana Mavericks:
The Texans Are Coming!** miniseries....

Suddenly single father Jake Castro has his hands full with
the baby he never expected—and with a beautiful young
woman too wise for her years.

COURTNEY'S BABY PLAN
BY *ALLISON LEIGH*

The third title in the **Return to the Double C** miniseries....

Tired of waiting for Mr. Right, nurse Courtney Clay takes
matters into her own hands to create the family she's
always wanted— but her surly patient may just be
the Mr. Right she's been searching for all along.

**Look for these titles and others in August 2011
from Harlequin Special Edition wherever books are sold.**

BIG SKY BRIDE, BE MINE! *(Northridge Nuptials)* by *VICTORIA PADE*
THE MOMMY MIRACLE by *LILIAN DARCY*
THE MOGUL'S MAYBE MARRIAGE by *MINDY KLASKY*
LIAM'S PERFECT WOMAN by *BETH KERY*

---

www.Harlequin.com

SEUSA0811

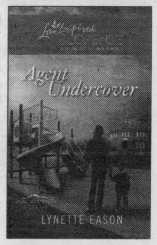

Harlequin® INTRIGUE®

USA TODAY BESTSELLING AUTHOR

B.J. DANIELS

BRINGS READERS
THE NEXT INSTALLMENT IN
THE SUSPENSEFUL MINISERIES

Chisholm Cattle Company

Alexa Cross has returned to the old Wellington Manor that her brother believes is haunted to prove to him that she is not psychic, as their mother was. Although she soon realizes that the trouble isn't with spirits but instead is all too human.

Alexa finds herself running for her life—straight into neighboring rancher Marshall Chisholm's arms. Marshall doesn't believe the old mansion is haunted. But he does believe Alexa is in serious trouble if she stays there.

Can Marshall help keep Alexa safe from a possible killer?
Find out in:

STAMPEDED

Available August 2011 from Harlequin Intrigue

3 more titles to follow...
Available wherever books are sold.